The Roswell Quest, the Prequel

The Tale of the Tarot, Book One

Melanie Simpson Mystery Series
Book One

THE MAP OF ORBIS TERRARUM

DJ SCHNEIDER

ISBN 979-8-9851453-8-0

The Theatrum Orbis Terrarum map
English translation: Theatre of the Orb of the World

And a variant of the Latin aphorism
at the bottom of the map reads:

*For what human affairs can seem important to a man,
who keeps all eternity before his eyes,
and knows the vastness of the Universe*

*This novel is dedicated to
those who share their stories
of contact, and through them,
help us achieve veritas*

Contents

When the World Stops Spinning

Awakening   1

A Different Place and Time   3

A Bit Wobbly   5

The Decision   9

Red Raines   16

Support   29

Alone in a Group   23

Pity Party   27

Four Dots   36

Getting Over Guilt   43

A New Clue   51

Destiny's Plan   61

Keeping Focused   70

Professor Lofton   79

4th of July   89

Saying Goodbyes   99

Emilee's Arrival   103

The Trials of Povolzhye   114

About Grandfather   121

Bull Again   130

Pop Tart   133

The Industrialist   140

Anniversary...kinda   145

A Proper Breakfast   151

Estranged 156

The Offer 164

The Haven 168

Mel's Plan 172

Frankie and Emilee 178

Realization 184

The Train 191

Evasive Maneuvers 198

Clandestine 205

Chase 210

Livingston 220

Pike's 225

The Call 232

Road Trip 236

Together Again 244

Psycho 247

Theatrum Orbis Terrarum 253

The Orb 258

The Music Box 267

HQ 269

On the Run 272

Fool me Twice 278

Face Off 283

Heading Home 293

The Locket 299

Hidden Truths 304

Acknowledgements

About the Author

Call to Action!

THE MAP OF ORBIS TERRARUM

Dharma is when you walk on the
path of your soul's purpose
Mrs. Crowley
The tarot card reading

When the World Stops Spinning

It's like a bad movie, playing over and over again in my head, and I can't stop it:

I walk out the door and down my driveway, fixated on the flashing lights.

Soon I break into a jog. Then a full-on run toward the dead-end of Springbrook Court.

I need to get there.

I look up at where the railroad tracks cross Lakeview to see a police car, its lights flashing, drive across the tracks toward — *toward what?*

Katch is right behind me. She tries to keep pace.

I cut up and over a small hillside trail, and through the blackberry brambles where the path gets narrow.

Thorns tear at my arms, legs, and face, but I don't care, hardly noticing as they leave bloodied scratches all over my body.

I need to get up there.

"Mel?" Katch calls after me. She is way behind now, but the word hangs like a huge question mark.

"It could be her!" I shout, not turning around. It hits me as I say it.

What if it's true? What if it is my mom?

One of the police cars has blocked off the road at an angle just past the tracks and is directing cars to turn around.

I'm up on the tracks now and running as fast as I can. I'm in flip-flops and one flies off my foot, but I keep running, the sharp rocks between the railroad ties jamming into the soft underbelly of my foot.

A policeman on the road holds his hands out to stop me.

"You can't go back there! It's a bad accident. We can't have anyone interfere."

I duck under his arms and keep running.

I come over a small rise and around a slight bend in the road.

A guardrail follows it on my left.

On the other side of the guardrail, a steep ravine descends sixty feet to Springbrook Creek below.

A large truck sits angled in the middle of the road. Its front end smashed and the radiator billowing puffy clouds of steam.

Beyond it, a fire truck appears. Just arrived. Firemen jump off and hurry in my direction.

A man stands next to the damaged truck, holding a white rag to his head, blood on it.

I see Captain Thornton talking to him, his back to me. The man looks in my direction, which causes Captain Thornton to turn.

It's me, of course, he sees ...

... running with one flip-flop on my foot, in cut-off jeans, and a bright orange psychedelic swim top. A ridiculous sight ...

... running toward a gap in the guardrail ...

... the size of a car.

A huge, open wound of pristine, beech-colored wood is exposed on a thick tree trunk surrounded by ivy. Smaller trees are snapped off or smashed over.

I lean into the ravine just as Captain Thornton grabs me.

"Melanie. Don't," he says; he pleads.

Something is down there. I see splashes of white in the creek.

Somehow it is quiet enough that I can hear the sound of water bubbling over pebbles; a simple and beautiful sound.

The undergrowth is thick, but I make out a crumpled, white wreck at the bottom of the creek bed. Through a hole in the foliage, I see a small, round window. A window found on only one type of car.

Something starts deep down inside and rumbles out of my throat. A sound I have never heard or knew I could make.

"Nooooo!"

I wrestle away from Captain Thornton.

He grabs me again as I throw myself at the ravine.

Firemen appear next to me. They set up ropes, secure them to the guardrail, and work their way down.

I hear howling: a mournful, animalistic sound from far away ...

... but I am making it.

Katch throws her arms around me.

I focus on her.

She holds me tightly, crying.

I see my flip-flop gripped in her hand; the bottom toward my face.

There is a piece of tar stuck on it,
the shape reminding me of Italy.
It is the last thing I remember.
I close my eyes
crumple to the ground
howl at life, "No, no, no ..." again, again, again
and the numbness of it all turns to darkness

Awakening

I woke up slowly, groggily, and opened my eyes to a strange ceiling. It started to spin. I closed my eyes to make it stop. The room smelled ... *hospitally*. I moaned a little and tried to sit up. Bad idea. I flopped back down.

"Now, honey, you just lay there and take your time. You've been asleep for a while."

It sounded like Mrs. Fletcher's voice. What's she doing here, and where am I? Was I hurt? I didn't feel hurt. Not bad anyway, that I could tell.

I lifted my head and opened one eye, but only a little. I could see Mrs. Fletcher sitting on a chair next to—*my bed?* She was holding my hand. Light streamed in through a window. Everything in the room looked whitish. I laid back and closed my eyes. I could hear the sound of traffic outside, like in a city.

"Where am I? What happened?"

"Oh goodness, honey. You don't remember, do you?" There was a tone to her voice, like she was unexpectedly put in a place she didn't want to be.

"No, I—"

Then suddenly I did. I shot upright. Mrs. Fletcher jumped with a start.

"Mom! Where is my mom?" I tried to get out of bed.

Mrs. Fletcher held me back. "Now, you stop that, Melanie. You lay back down."

I pushed her away and yanked a tube and some wires off my arm so I could get up.

A man and woman in hospital clothes ran into the room and forced me back onto the bed. I fought them. I wanted to get up. I wanted to find Mom. Something happened to her. I couldn't put it together, but I knew that much. She needed me. I kicked and swung my fists at these people.

"Let me up! Let me up!" *Why were they stopping me?*

"Melanie, calm down. Please try to calm down," the woman pleaded.

It just made me fight harder. I managed to get a foot under her and kicked her away. She flew into some equipment and sent it rolling across the room.

The man pushed me back onto the bed and threw his body across me, holding me down. His white doctor's coat fluttered over my face. He had one arm pinned, but with the other I pushed the coat away from my eyes and struggled to get out from under him. I reached for his head, got my hand under his chin and shoved as hard as I could. It bent his neck back at a sharp angle. I thrashed around, but he kept me pinned so I dug my fingernails deep into his flesh. The woman yanked my arm away and forced it against the bed. She held it down, her back to me. I felt a sharp prick—a needle.

"We're giving her a sedative," the man seemed to be telling someone. "She's still in acute emotional shock."

Then I heard Mrs. Fletcher's voice float across the room. "Oh, thank you, Doctor! Bless you."

A Different Place and Time

I am sitting on the floor of a room. At least, I think it's a room. Everything is in a soft white glow. There are no corners, but it isn't round either. It's endless. No furniture or fixtures, lamps or points of light. But it is well-lit, as if the illumination is coming from everywhere at once and nowhere at all. The only solid thing I'm sure of is the floor beneath, and the boy across from me.

"Hi, Melanie," he says. Like he knows me. He seems to be about nine years old.

I am looking up at him even though we are both sitting on the floor. He is bigger than me, which doesn't make sense because I am fifteen years old.

He glances down at my right hand. "How is it?" he asks.

I look at my hand and see it is tiny — the hand of a baby girl, maybe around the age of four. That's why he's so big. I am only four. I look at it again. Nothing seems wrong with it. I give him a funny look. I don't know what he's talking about. And then I ask myself, how can I be thinking like this if I am only four years old?

He takes my hand and studies it. "It was burned really bad and not healing well. They didn't like how it looked." He smiles and glances off to the side, to some movement over there I can't quite see. "So, they fixed it. Not a bad job, huh?"

I don't know what he means by 'fixed' my hand. I look up at him. He looks down at me. His green eyes shine under a tuft of dark, thick hair. He talks like he is older than nine. I wonder who he is.

"They wanted us to meet as long as you are here," he says, "because they don't know if it is me or if it is you."

I tell him I don't understand.

He gets up and pulls me to my feet and then up off the floor. I fly in the air for a moment—a feather floating in his arms—before he sets me softly back on the ground.

"You will," he says, then leans down and kisses my forehead. He smiles a big, friendly smile. I realize it's a very familiar smile for some reason. He turns around and walks away, disappearing into the white.

A Bit Wobbly

"Melanie? Do you hear me?"

I opened my eyes. It's Captain Thornton. Sitting on the edge of my bed. In street clothes, not his uniform. "Captain Thornton?"

"I'm George today, okay?"

I could hardly keep my eyes open. "Why do I feel so—weird?"

"They gave you a sedative, to calm you down. Apparently, you tried to take out half the hospital staff earlier this morning." He smiled at his little joke.

"I did?" Things were a blur. I kind of remembered something.

"Melanie, can you understand me okay?"

I looked at him. He somehow didn't seem as big and imposing in street clothes. More like a big, huggable bear. "Yeah, I think so."

"The medicine is making you a little groggy." He paused for a second; I think to make sure I understood. "Do you remember anything about yesterday?"

I tried to pull my thoughts together. My mind felt like it was wading through waist-deep syrup. A man in a white coat stood behind George. There were little red wound marks in a line along the side of his face. I remembered digging my fingernails into his jawline. I had drawn blood! *Why did I do that?*

I looked at George. "Where am I?"

"You're in a room at Physicians and Surgeons Hospital in Portland."

"I'm in a hospital? Why?"

"What do you remember?"

Some things were coming back—little flashes of scenes, like movie outtakes on a cutting room floor. "Sirens...my mom. A truck. Her car. A gap in—"

I sat up quickly. "She was in an accident. Where is she?" I frantically looked around the room as if she would be standing there.

George put his hand on my shoulder to get my attention. "She is here, in the hospital."

"What?" I focused on him. "I want to see her."

"Not just yet. You need to listen to me, okay?" He had a real solemn look to him.

"Is she dead?" I had to ask, but didn't want to know the answer.

"No. She's hurt really bad, though."

I nodded.

"She's under intensive care here at the hospital."

I tried to get up. "I need to see her."

"Slow down. You can't yet."

This wasn't making sense. "If she is the one hurt, then why am I in a hospital bed?"

"You've been here since the accident yesterday. You were in shock. You passed out, and were, well...having trouble. They gave you something to help you relax and felt it best to keep you for observation overnight. Thus, the room and the bed."

I still felt shaky, but my senses were coming back. "I want to get up now."

George looked at the doctor, who nodded. "I think she will be all right."

"Okay," George said. "Mrs. Fletcher brought you some clothes. They're in the closet. I'll wait for you outside." He left the room.

I swung my legs over the edge of the bed to get up. Now that they were out from under the sheets, I could see scratches all across my legs, and all over my arms as well. Splotches of dried blood had formed where the scratches were the deepest. The thorns on the blackberry vines. I remembered running through them, and seeing my mom's car at the bottom of the ravine. *Oh, God, my mom.*

The doctor helped me out of bed. I was a bit wobbly.

"Melanie, I'm Doctor Carlson. I'm going to wait for you here while you get ready."

I nodded, and asked, "Did I do that to you?" looking up at his face. The marks looked even worse closer up.

"Yes. You are quite strong."

"Sorry, I guess I didn't know what I was doing."

He smiled. "Don't worry, I'll heal. Are you okay to walk by yourself?"

I nodded again.

He took the clothes from the closet and handed them to me.

I carried them into the small bathroom. Once in there I looked in the mirror. There were scratches across my face as well. I sure did a job on myself. I washed up as best I could and dressed. I opened the door to see the doctor still standing by the bed.

"Melanie, I'm one of the doctors attending to your mother. If you are up to it, I would like to fill you in on her condition. Is that all right with you?"

"Yes," I replied.

"Good." He pointed to a couple of chairs in the corner of the room where we could sit. I went over and took one of them. He sat in the other.

7

He settled in and paused for a moment as he studied me. Maybe to make sure I was ready for this. "Your mother is seriously hurt. She has multiple fractures and a possible spinal injury. We spent most of last night in surgery setting the worst of the breaks and stabilizing her until we can diagnose the spinal injury better. Of greater concern—the accident resulted in a serious head injury. She is suffering from cerebral edema, which is a swelling of the brain. We had to open her cranium to release the pressure. Once the swelling subsides, we will be able to better diagnose her condition."

I sat there, dazed by what he told me—multiple fractures, spinal injury, swollen brain. I looked at him, wanting to get some sort of understanding. "Will she die?"

"We are doing everything we can to keep that from happening. But you need to understand this is a serious situation. She is still quite unstable."

I nodded, staring off into space to think.

"Melanie, do you have any relatives we can contact?"

I looked at the doctor. "No, my mom was an only child. I may have a grandmother, but I've never met her. She might have died. Mom wouldn't talk about her much. And as far as other relatives, there isn't anyone I know of. She just wasn't close to any other family. So, if there are relatives, I'm not even sure how to reach them."

"Don't worry about it. The police are pretty good at figuring those things out. They will try to locate someone. But as her closest relative, even though you are a minor, it could mean you will need to act as her power of attorney. Do you understand what that entails?"

"No."

"You will be responsible for making any decisions regarding her care here at the hospital. Are you up to doing that?"

I nodded again. I seemed to be doing a lot of that lately.

The Decision

A nurse escorted me down a hallway and onto an elevator. We went up one floor to where they had my mom. We walked to a waiting room area. Mrs. Fletcher, George, and Katch were there. When Katch saw me, she jumped up from her chair, raced over, and threw her arms around me.

She burst into tears. "Mel. Oh my God. I've been so worried about you." Her chest heaved with each gasp of breath. I grabbed her tight and cried with her. We rocked each other back and forth—one big puddle of tears in the middle of the waiting room.

Mrs. Fletcher came over and pulled me to her bosom. I put my head down on her shoulder and cried. She was the closest thing I had to my mom right then. She stroked my hair. "It's going to be all right, honey. God will take care of everything."

She walked me over to a chair and I sat down. There was a box of Kleenex on the table. I took one and dabbed at my eyes.

"Have any of you seen my mother?" I asked.

"No. Only family is allowed," George said. "But we've been here all night. We wanted to be here for both you and your mom."

"Thanks." I got up and walked over to the nurse's station. A young nurse looked up from a chart when she saw me coming.

"I'm Melanie Simpson. My mother, Gloria Simpson, is in one of your rooms. Can I see her?"

She gave me a smile; one of reassurance. They probably trained her to give that specific smile. "It's up to the doctor, dear."

"Doctor Carlson?" I asked.

"No, the attending physician is Doctor Hanson. He's our neuro trauma specialist. It would be up to him."

"Can I please see him?" I asked.

"I'll try to reach him." She smiled again, and then picked up the phone to make the call.

I walked back to the chair.

We sat in silence. I don't think anyone wanted to say anything that might bring back the memory of what happened yesterday. Yesterday afternoon. What was it, early afternoon of the next day now? Wow, I had been out of it for a while. I guess I must have gone pretty crazy. There's that word again. *Crazy.* I don't like that word.

Things were slowly coming back to me. I could remember most of what happened. I definitely recalled seeing my mom's car at the bottom of the ravine in Springbrook Creek. Now that I think about it, it was probably a good thing I blacked out. The firemen were getting ready to climb down to her. I don't think I could have handled standing there while they pried the car apart to get her out and then dragged her up the ravine strapped to a stretcher.

Over an hour had gone by before the doctor showed up. The nurse pointed me out to him.

He walked over. "Miss Simpson?"

I nodded.

"You are Melanie Simpson, Gloria Simpson's daughter, is that correct?"

I nodded again. "Can I see my mother?"

"Yes. I think that would be all right, but only for a few minutes." He sat down on a chair opposite us. "I'm sorry I took

so long to come see you. I needed to be sure of our options before I did. Your mother is stabilized, but still in a bad condition.
However, it could help to have her know you are here—to talk
to her and hold her hand."

I nodded.

"There are some things I would like you to understand first.
As I said, we have stabilized your mother as best we can. But I
believe she needs to have surgery, and soon. It is her greatest
chance for survival. As Doctor Carlson shared with you, she
suffered a rather traumatic head injury during the crash. Fragments of glass and wood are lodged in the left side of her pari-
etal lobe. We hoped the swelling would have gone down by
now, but inflammation due to the fragments is preventing that,
and if the swelling doesn't subside, we will lose her."

I couldn't follow his words. It was like living a scene from
General Hospital, my mom's favorite soap opera. It had been a
ritual last summer to pop popcorn, grab sodas, and snuggle together on the couch, waiting to see what would happen next. It
was one of the few things we did to hold our world together
when everything wanted to tear it apart. It had been a real mess
when the town got into a frenzy over our fake UFO hoax, thinking Mrs. Crowley had been abducted by aliens. And then there
was the real UFO landing near Stafford Road that freaked all of
us out. We still don't know what that was all about. But my
mom's little tirade at the town hall meeting certainly didn't
help, and ended up being what tipped her over the edge. Everyone thought she was crazy.

So, almost every day we watched the soap opera together,
and because of it, I had seen way too many moments like this
on the show, where the doctor sits someone down and has to
tell them about a life-or-death situation—only now it's real, and
it's about my mom.

"Melanie?"

It was the doctor. I had drifted. I tried to concentrate again. I looked up at him. "I'm sorry, Doctor Hanson. What were you saying?"

"I know it's hard to wrap your head around all of this." He paused for a moment, focusing on me, like trying to see this through the eyes of a fifteen-year-old girl who was possibly about to lose her only remaining parent. "I was saying, I feel her best chance is to have the fragments removed. Even under perfect conditions, this would be a touchy operation with quite a bit of risk. I wish we could wait until we reach one of your relatives, but that isn't possible. Now, I know Doctor Carlson spoke to you about being your mother's power of attorney, but this is a bit more serious and we don't have much time. According to Oregon law, and since you are not an adult, the next in line for making such a decision would be Captain Thornton and Mrs. Fletcher, as adult friends of the family."

I nodded as I looked over at them. They both seemed as confounded by this situation as I was.

"I spoke to them earlier about her condition and our options before you got here. They agreed that if I felt it necessary to proceed with the operation, then we should do so. However, we also felt it would be better to know your thoughts, even though law does not allow you to have a say in it."

I focused on a few threads coming loose in the carpet at my feet. Little strands snagged by something unexpectedly, yanked from the tucked-in comfort of their home, now dangling precariously in thin air. Alone and exposed.

I didn't really want to be involved. Funny how we teenagers feel we are so much smarter than adults, but right now I just want to be a kid and leave decisions like this to them. I finally looked up at the doctor and nodded. "Okay...I guess."

"We can't wait any longer to see if the swelling goes down on its own. I recommend we operate now to remove the pieces. I'm going to have them prepare the operating room."

I looked to Mrs. Fletcher and Captain Thornton. "Are you sure?"

Mrs. Fletcher patted me on the hand. I could see she was a big pot of emotions ready to spill over. But she was holding it together for me. "It is the right decision, as guided by God's hand, whatever the outcome."

"Melanie. We can't tell you what to think," George added. "We just believe it is the best way to go."

I turned to Katch. She grabbed a Kleenex, wiped at her eyes, and nodded. She leaned over and hugged me. I held her while I wondered if it was the right thing to do. What would Mom want?

I looked at the doctor. "You feel her best chance is the operation?"

"I'm trying to give it to you as straight as I can. She's teetering on the edge. I think it is our best chance to save her."

I stared at nothing in particular, my thoughts swishing around in my head. I nodded, mostly to myself. Only this time it wasn't just a simple motion, but one that could decide life or death. I looked at the doctor and told him, "Okay. I think we should go ahead."

He stood up. "I'll take you to her."

We walked down a long hall to an area where the walls and doors facing the nurses' station were glass. I think it was so they could see into the rooms because these patients were in such bad shape. The doctor stopped at one of the rooms. A chart sat in a holder attached to the wall. It had 'Simpson' written on it.

The doctor took the chart out and flipped through some pages. He put it back and turned to me. "I want you to be prepared for what you will see. She has quite a few bruises and broken bones from the crash, so lots of casts and splints, and she is pretty cut up. There is tubing coming out of her mouth and nose. And we have drain tubes coming from her head. The cranial opening is covered, but it is still a lot to take in." He focused on me. "Are you okay to do this?"

I nodded.

He nodded too, giving me a reassuring smile as he opened the door. "Hold her hand. Talk to her. Positive thoughts."

I walked into the room and watched the doctor close the door behind me. I turned to my mom and almost lost it when I saw her, but held it back because I knew now was not the time. She was practically in a full body cast. Her face was bruised and cut up, just like the doctor had warned me about. A row of stitches zigzagged above one eye. A thick clear tube ran into her mouth, and probably down her throat. I think it helped her breathe. I could hear a machine to the side doing something like that—breathing for her. A drape covered one side of her head, with two small tubes running out from under it. A reddish liquid gurgled in the tubes.

I sat on the edge of the bed, took her hand in mine and stroked it with my other hand. "Hi, Mom. Kind of got yourself into a pickle here, didn't you?"

She used to say this to me all the time when I was young and got into trouble. I paused for a second. Her hand felt warm and moist. A rhythmic squishing noise came from the breathing machine. Another machine on the far side of the bed beeped once in a while. I didn't know what to say to her. What *do* you say to your mother when she's in this condition and you may never see her again? I stopped. I couldn't let myself think that way.

"We're going to get you fixed up, Mom. Promise me you will fight hard. There are a lot of things we still need to do together, okay?" I raised her hand to my lips and kissed it. I held it against my chest. I wanted her to feel my heart beating,

14

because I could feel it thumping hard inside. I wanted her to know I was here, alive, and that she should come back to me.

"Remember when we lived over by Berkley Park and Dad was teaching me to pitch? What was I? About eight, I think. You got so upset. You wanted me to play with the dolls and tea set you gave me for my birthday. But I put them in my toy box, and picked up the glove and ball from Dad." I stopped for a moment, remembering a time when things were so much easier and simpler. "Well, I want you to know you never lost your little girl. I liked baseball, but it couldn't compare to being your daughter. I know I probably didn't show it enough, but I appreciated how much you loved me. It was obvious by how hard you worked to get me out of my Converse sneakers and sleeveless t-shirts, and into saddle shoes and aproned dresses. But it didn't matter what I wore. I have always been your little girl, and have always loved you, no matter how much I fought all the fluff and frills."

I kept talking to her. I reminded her about things we had done in the past—funny things and adventures together as a family. And how I looked forward to more of the same with her.

The nurse came in and quietly told me, "We are ready for her." She stepped back out.

I stood and leaned down to a spot on her cheekbone, the only place not covered in bruises, bandages, or stitches. I kissed her, letting my lips linger for a moment. I wanted to remember the feel of her skin and her warmth. A tear rolled down my cheek and into my mouth. It tasted bitter.

I kept hold of her hand, not wanting to let go. "I love you, Mom. Try your hardest to come back to me. I need you." But I had to let go. I let her fingers slowly slip from my hand, then I hurried from the room, not wanting her to hear me break down and cry. Katch stood outside the door. I fell into her arms.

Red Raines

Frankie's dad guided the boat up to the dock at Red Raines Resort and cut the power to the little outboard motor. Frankie jumped out and steadied the boat against the dock as he tied the bow line to a cleat. Beanie did the same with the stern. They were in Pacific City on the Oregon coast, and had just returned from a crabbing trip to the mouth of the Nestucca River.

Frankie's mom called to them, "Well, how did you do?"

Frankie hadn't seen her as they pulled up. He turned and waved. She stood on the deck of the rental cabin which over-looked the river. She must have been watching out the window for their return. "We limited out on crab and caught a couple of blueback trout."

"It was outta sight, Mrs. Strickland," Beanie added. "The best crabbing trip ever."

"Well, good. Let's get the pot boiling so we can have some fresh crab for dinner."

"We'll be right up, honey," Frankie's dad called to her.

Frankie climbed into the boat and handed the crab pots over to Beanie, who stacked them on the dock. They were too busy unloading to notice Mrs. Raines coming around the corner of the cabin toward them.

"Frankie?" she called out.

He looked up, wondering what she could want with him. "Yeah, Mrs. Raines?"

"You have a phone call in the house. It sounds important."

Frankie looked at his dad, who shook his head. "I have no idea. Go take the call. I'll be right up."

Who would be calling him? Mel had tried to reach him way too many times back home, but he doubted she would have the nerve to call him all the way out here. He got out of the boat and hurried up the ramp to where Mrs. Raines stood waiting.

They walked together to the Raines' house. None of the cabins had phones. That's why the call came there. Frankie's parents had been renting cabins from the Raines for more summers than he could remember. They were almost like family.

They went in the back door and through the kitchen to the living room. Mrs. Raines motioned to the phone on the table by the couch, then returned to the kitchen to give him some privacy.

Frankie sat on the couch and picked up the receiver. "Hello, this is Frankie Strickland."

"Frankie, it's Katch."

"Katch? What's going on? How did you find me?"

"You told us about the cabins when we talked about coming with you. I remembered the name, so had the operator connect me." She paused for a second, then continued. "Frankie, I need to tell you something."

The tone of her voice startled him, setting off a whole load of internal warning bells. "Is it Mel? Is she all right?"

"It's not Mel. It's her mom. She was in a bad car accident. I know you and Mel broke up, but I thought I should tell you. I'm sure she would want you to know, but her mind is somewhere else right now. I didn't want you to find out maybe when it was too late."

Too late? Frankie lowered the receiver from his ear and looked at it as if it were the source of the bad news and not Katch on the other end of the line. Was this really happening right now, when he was so far away?

"Frankie. Are you still there?"

"Yeah. I'm here." Then something hit him that scared the crap out of him. "Katch, was Mel in the car? Was she hurt too?"

"No, she wasn't in the car. But it happened up on Fairview. We heard the sirens and could see the police lights up on the road." The line was quiet for a second. "Frankie?"

"What?"

"It was like Mel knew—like she knew it was her mother even before we got there to see it. Her mom's car ended up in Springbrook Creek. It crashed down the ravine."

"Oh, my God! Did Mel see her mom in the car?"

"No, we could barely see the car at all, but she knew it was her mom. She screamed and then fainted. It was pretty bad."

"Where is Mel now? Where is her mom?"

"We are at Physicians and Surgeons Hospital. It's in downtown Portland."

"I'll be there as soon as I can. I'll get my dad to drive me."

"Frankie?" Her voice had a frantic tinge to it, like she was trying to control it.

"What, Katch? What's wrong?"

"You need to hurry. Her mom's going into surgery soon and we think she may not make it."

Support

"Dad, just pull into the turn-around and let us out," Frankie pleaded.

"I need to park. I'm sure they have a parking lot nearby. I don't want you going in alone."

"No! Just pull in. Please. It's been hours since Katch called. I can't stand it any longer. I need to find Mel."

"I'll go with him, Mr. Strickland," Beanie said. "It's okay if you let us out."

Frankie's dad sighed, and pulled into the turn-around for the hospital. "I'll be in as soon as I—"

Frankie threw the car door open even before it stopped, jumped out, and ran for the front entrance.

Beanie called out behind him, "Wait up," but he didn't. He raced inside and up to a woman working behind a reception desk.

"Where do they do surgery here?" he asked.

His sudden appearance startled the volunteer. "What is wrong, young man, is someone hurt?"

"No. No, my girlfriend's mother is in surgery. I need to find her. Please." Frankie pressed his palms against the reception counter, leaned down and closed his eyes for a moment, trying to catch his breath.

Beanie reached them. He looked at her name tag. "Mrs. Devon. Hi. Sorry about my friend. He's a little freaked out right

19

now. Can you tell us where someone would wait while a relative is in surgery?"

"Surgery takes place down on the lower level—"

Frankie bolted for the stairs, but Beanie quickly grabbed his
shirt sleeve, stopping him in his tracks, holding him in place
while he looked over at Mrs. Devon. "But?" he prompted,
knowing she hadn't finished.

Frankie looked back over his shoulder to see Mrs. Devon
staring at him, like maybe he was the one needing care. "But,"
she went on, "there isn't a waiting room down in surgery." She
pointed toward a hallway. "The waiting area is that way."

Frankie wrenched his sleeve loose from Beanie's grasp and
ran down the hall while Beanie thanked Mrs. Devon.

He turned a corner to find Mel, Katch, and Mrs. Fletcher sitting in a small waiting area. He slid to a stop as soon as he saw
Mel. The hallway was off to the side of the room, so they didn't
notice him at the entrance.

It suddenly occurred to him—maybe he shouldn't have
come. After all, Katch hadn't told him Mel wanted him here,
just that he should know what happened. But he had to come.
It wasn't even a choice. On the long drive from Pacific City to
Portland, all he could think about was the accident and how he
should have been there for her. The trip had provided plenty of
time for him to figure out how much she meant to him, and to
kill himself a thousand times over for how cruel he had been to
her during the breakup; all the time too busy wallowing in his
own grief to even think about how she felt.

So now, seeing her, he wondered if maybe this had been the
wrong idea. Maybe Mel didn't even want him here, wouldn't
want to see him. Why should she? He had treated her like crap
and ignored her attempts to make up. All he had shown was a
hard, cold shoulder right when she needed a soft, warm one. It
would probably be awkward for her. Then it came to him; he's

20

the one who would feel awkward. He started to back out of the room.

Beanie rounded the corner. He was breathing heavily. "I'm not cut out for this kind of stuff."

Everyone heard him and looked over to see them. Frankie made eye contact with Mel. She didn't move, just stared. She was obviously shocked to see him. Katch jumped up and ran to Beanie. She fell into his arms, crying. Beanie wrapped his arms around her and hugged her.

Frankie took two steps into the room. Mel slowly stood. He hesitantly moved toward her. The whole situation swiftly over-whelmed him. All he could do was shake his head in disbelief that this could even be happening, because words couldn't find their way out of him right then. Tears rolled down his face. Mel raced over the last few steps and threw her arms around him.

"Oh, God, Mel. I'm so sorry," Frankie told her, his voice breaking as he said it.

She grabbed him so tight it pushed the breath right out of his lungs. He stroked her head as she cried on his shoulder. He watched Beanie and Katch walk over to the waiting area, arms wrapped around each other as they sat down. Frankie could see Mrs. Fletcher pressing a handkerchief to her eyes. She shook her head, as if telling him it was bad. He closed his eyes and focused on the warmth of Mel against him, her soft hair woven through his fingers as he pressed her head into his shoulder. He buried his nose into her hair and breathed in deeply, needing her scent to fill his lungs, his reassurance she was in his arms again. They stayed like that for a long time. Breaking apart would mean fac-ing reality, and he didn't want that, not yet anyway. All he wanted right now was to feel her against him.

But it didn't last. A man walked around the corner with a tray full of drinks and food. He stopped when he saw them standing there.

Frankie looked up. "Captain Thornton? What are you doing here?"

Captain Thornton had a look on his face like he had just busted down the door of the wrong house. "Frankie. I, uh, was getting some drinks and snacks for everyone."

Frankie looked at Mel, trying to understand how this all worked out.

Mel let go of Frankie, but held onto his hand. "He's been here since Mom's accident. They all have." She pulled Frankie over to the chairs and they sat down. She looked at him. Her eyes were bloodshot and passive, as if all the emotion in them had finally played out. "She's been in surgery for over three hours now. We haven't heard anything about how it's going."

He nodded, not knowing what to say. He noticed the scratches on her face and arms, but knew now was not the time to ask how she got them. Frankie held her hand in his lap, and looked down at it. Her wrist was very thin and delicate. A couple of scratch lines still had little pieces of dried scab. Tiny hairs stood out on her forearm. He ran his fingers slowly along it, down the back of her hand, and along her fingers. He focused on the sensation, feeling the structure of the bones under a thin layer of warm skin. It was the distraction he needed right now. He repeated the move, over and over again. Mel leaned into him, placing her head on his shoulder.

Frankie looked up to see Captain Thornton still standing where he had stopped when he first came into the room, apparently not sure what to do. Maybe not wanting to interrupt the moment. He finally walked over and handed Mrs. Fletcher and Katch their drinks, then sat down next to Mrs. Fletcher. He put the tray with what was probably Mel's drink and a pile of snacks on the table next to him. It was the last noise Frankie heard in the room for quite a while.

Alone in a Group

I'm sitting between Frankie and Katch and can feel their focus on me, even though we are all staring straight ahead. Things had been quiet for a long time, the only sound being someone sipping at their drink once in a while, or nibbling from a bag of chips.

Frankie's dad had joined us. George took him aside when he first came in to bring him up to date. Now they were sitting next to Mrs. Fletcher. Mr. Strickland told me how sorry he was. Then it went silent again, and had been for a long while. The silence felt heavy, like a wool blanket laid over me on a cold winter night. But it wasn't cold. Or winter. And the blanket was wrapped so stiflingly tight I couldn't breathe.

I looked around the room. It was easy to see no one knew what to say. Because there wasn't anything *to* say. I'm surrounded by friends, but feel completely alone. Which was exactly what I wanted right now — to be alone.

It wasn't a new feeling. It had been my closest friend for a long time now; ever since I found the debris, and the danger that came along with it for everyone close to me.

It took a while to figure out the debris had a curse. Once uncovered, the curse clung to the person who found it. First, it was my dad, and killed him. Then it attached itself to my mother, driving her insane, and I have yet to know the final outcome there. And then *I* found it and have been in its grip ever since.

It forced me to distance myself from my boyfriend; to lie to him and my friends in order to keep them safe.

Now I am sitting here, numb. I have rolled through so many emotions over the last few months, heightened in the last few days, I can't feel a single thing inside—not even my own heartbeat. But at the same time, while I can't feel a thing, everyone around me is absorbing the terrible pain *I* should be feeling. It shouldn't be that way. None of them really want to be here. *Who would?* They are only doing it out of a sense of duty to me.

But we're just sitting here, waiting for a death certificate, right? I want to feel positive, but inside I can't. So that's all we're doing right now. Waiting on death. I thought back to Mrs. Crowley and the tarot reading. Destiny. Which card was it? The Ace of Cups, I think. I tried to remember what she said after she turned it over, *upside-down*. Something about a coming separation, and about exhausting myself in giving everything I have to family. Chills ran through my body just thinking about it. At least I was feeling a sensation. Destiny. How did she know? Or, maybe I should be asking how did the cards know?

Is that why I am so sure of the outcome right now? And if so, I need to face it alone. I have to face it alone. I stood up and turned to everyone. "Listen, I, uh, I'm sorry, but I need to ask you all to leave now."

They looked up at me in shock.

Mrs. Fletcher was the first to react. "What are you talking about, honey? We can't leave you here—alone."

"Thank you, Mrs. Fletcher. Thank all of you for being so supportive to me and my mom…but I need you to leave now. I'm sorry. Please don't ask me to explain."

Frankie looked at me like he couldn't get any sort of read on me at all—as if I were a stranger. He turned to the others, looking to see what they would do. Everyone slowly stood from their chairs.

George said, "If that's her wish, then I guess we should respect it." He looked down at the drink in his hand, not knowing what to do with it. He finally placed it on the small table to the side of his chair. He pointed to it, stumbling over his words. "Your, uh, drink is there, Melanie, if you want it." He then added, "Are you sure about this ... you really want us to leave?"

I stared at the ground, probably because I didn't want to see the confused looks on their faces when I answered. "Yes. This is what I need right now." But I knew I should face them, so I looked up. "I know none of you understand. I'm sorry."

Mrs. Fletcher and George glanced at each other, then shuffled down the hall. George disappeared out of sight, but Mrs. Fletcher stopped and turned to me. "Honey. I will be waiting for you at your home. I will not let you be alone there, and I won't take no for an answer."

I nodded.

She turned the corner and disappeared.

Katch grabbed me. "Mel. I should be here. This doesn't make any sense. You shouldn't be alone right now."

I pulled her arms from me and held her hands. "I need this, Katch."

She let go and rubbed at her nose with a Kleenex. "But, Mel?"

Beanie took her hand and gave it a little tug. She looked at him and nodded, then back to me. She let go of Beanie's hand and threw her arms around me. I hugged her back. She finally stepped away, tears flowing down her face. She shook her head. A touch of betrayal showed in her eyes because she couldn't understand this at all. I was forcing my best friend to abandon me, which meant I was abandoning her. She may never trust me again. She turned and grabbed Beanie's arm and leaned into him as they walked away.

Frankie's dad did a little hemming and hawing, then told Frankie he would be out by the reception desk.

I looked at Frankie. He was still sitting, like my request hadn't included him. But it had.

"Frankie, I meant everyone."

He looked confused. It was obvious he didn't understand. Maybe he thought it had to do with something between us.

"Mel. I'm sorry I wasn't here when this happened. I've killed myself over it, sitting here, thinking about the accident, what you saw, and that I wasn't there for you." He stood up and stepped toward me.

I reached out and took his hand. "No, Frankie. It was my fault we broke up. I wasn't being honest with you. You had every right to be mad." I pulled him toward me and kissed him gently. Just enough so he would know I meant it when I said, "I'm glad you came."

"But I need to stay. I want to stay. Why are you doing this?"

"Because I know what is going to happen, and I need to be alone when it does."

Pity Party

I looked up from my spot on the sofa to all the people in the room. I'm sitting right where Beanie was when he got shot last summer. It was something I will never forget. I could still picture the pool of blood on the floor, and Frankie pressing his hands against the leg wound, blood oozing between his fingers as he tried to stop the flow. We had shared the same thought in that moment—thinking Beanie might die. I looked down at the wooden floor. There was a little patched hole in it where the bullet had entered. I had bought some wood putty and filled it in. There was still a dark stain of blood in the hole as I pushed the putty into it. It wasn't a very good patch job.

My mother's funeral ended a little over an hour ago. We're gathered at my house for whatever people do after putting someone in the ground. Mom had bought a plot next to Dad's at River View Cemetery when we buried him nearly two years ago. Now they were side-by-side on a hill under a big maple tree with rugged, brown bark on its trunk, and branches that splayed out over their graves in a huge umbrella full of lush, green leaves. Their spot really did have a view of the Willamette River. Truth in advertising.

It turned out some distant relatives had managed to make it in time for the funeral. No one from Mom's side. If any existed, they would all live in England. These were second cousins on my dad's side, or something like that. I think Uncle Will, my dad's brother, pretty much guilted them into coming;

27

demanding some sort of family representation. Other than Uncle Will, I've never met any of them. I looked through the opening of the half-wall into the dining room to see them all huddled together in a far corner, talking.

Neighbors and other people milled about the house dressed in various forms of black. I kept getting furtive little side glances from them, apparently unable to look at me directly. I quickly grew to hate it.

Mrs. Crowley had already been here and left. She had a guilty look in her eye, probably why she didn't stay very long. I think she'd known what would happen ever since the tarot card reading.

George came in from the kitchen with a cup of tea. I slid a coaster in front of me on the coffee table. He set the cup on it and sat next to me on the sofa. He placed a spoon and small bowl of sugar cubes next to my tea. "Can I get you anything else?"

"No. I'm good. Thanks." I added a cube of sugar and stirred my tea.

He shifted his position on the couch to face me better. "Melanie, I guess there is really never a good time or a good way at a funeral to discuss things. I can't even imagine how devastating it is to have lost both your parents in such short order."

He paused, almost like he just now realized how bad that sounded when he said it out loud. "I want you to know we have worked it out for you to stay here in your house, at least for now. And we are trying to figure out a way to make it permanent. Social Services wanted to intervene, but we managed to put them off. Mrs. Fletcher will be staying here with you, but we do need to find a solution to your situation. I can't make any promises as to what that would be in the long run."

"I can stay here by myself," I told him.

He shook his head. "No, you can't. You are a minor and they won't allow it. You won't be an adult until age eighteen, and that's three years from now. So, the courts will have a say in what happens with you until then. That is, unless a relative steps up and takes you in, or someone comes forward and legally becomes your guardian."

I looked over at him. I was just in the middle of taking a sip of tea. I set the cup back on the coaster. "What are you saying?"

He leaned in closer, glanced around to make sure no one was near, and lowered his voice so as not to be overheard by the others in the room. "I told you back at Wulf's I would be here for you. I meant it then, and I mean it now. If you want, I will put through the paperwork to become your official guardian."

"What?"

He looked really nervous, like he was offering it, and would do it because he cared, but had no idea how to make it work, or if it even would.

"I know, I know," he said. "It sounds weird. But I am willing to be your guardian if you want."

"Wouldn't that mean we would have to live together?"

"Well, yes. But I don't want us to pretend I would become your dad. There is no way I would expect that kind of relationship."

I studied this massive, six-foot-three, two-hundred and fifty-plus pound man next to me, no, towering over me, and couldn't come close to imagining him as my dad.

I took a sip of tea. "Aren't you a bachelor?"

"Well, yes. I want to get married someday, but haven't met the future Mrs. Right yet."

"And how exactly do you think you would meet the future Mrs. Right if you had a teenage girl hanging around all the time, and one who isn't even your own daughter?"

"I'm not going to worry about that right now. My offer stands if you need it."

This was a big offer, but a bad one. I set down my cup and reached over to take his giant hand in mine. I shifted around to face him better. "George, I can't believe you would do this for me. It is a very kind offer, but like you said, would be very weird. And right now, you look like a fish out of water gulping at air just for making the offer. Sorry, but it's true. I know you want to do what's right, but being my legal guardian isn't the answer."

I leaned over to him and motioned for him to lower his head so I could reach it. I gave him a kiss on the cheek.

"All the same," he said. "I will be keeping an eye out for you. I know there are things going on you can't or won't share with me. Even more than what happened when we pulled the sting on that agent at your house. And my cop instincts are clanging away, warning me that whatever it is, could put you in even more danger. I've grown pretty fond of you and don't want anything to happen. So, that's what I am going to do, whether you like it or not."

I smiled at him and patted his hand. "I like the idea that you are there for me." I stood up from the couch. "I need to head in and check on Mrs. Fletcher. She and Katch have been managing everything in the kitchen, and I should probably check to see if they need help."

George stood and gave me a bear hug. "I'm sorry, Melanie. I wish things could be different."

I looked up at him. "Do you believe in destiny?"

A confused look took to his face. "Huh?"

"Destiny. As if things are meant to be. What if my father and mother's deaths were all part of some larger design?"

"I'm not following you. What do you mean?"

I couldn't even begin to appreciate the depth of her faith. "No, Mrs. Fletcher. And I'm sure God knows it as well."

She looked at Katch who answered, "Heck, no!"

"That's right. So, to answer your question in my usual, round-about way, of course not. Staying here with you is no burden at all." She gave me another quick hug. "I want you to know that if I had been lucky enough to have a daughter, I couldn't have wished for one any better than you."

"Thank you, Mrs. Fletcher. I doubt that would be true. But thanks."

"I wish you *did* have a daughter," Katch said. "It would have been great to hang out with her."

I looked over to see Frankie and Beanie by the breakfast table. They were hovering there doing everything they could to stay out of the way and avoid our conversation.

"Have they been there the whole time?" I asked quietly.

"You know how they are," Katch said. "They don't know what to say, so are doing everything they can to avoid saying anything at all. Probably not such a bad thing."

"I get it."

The boys had both been wonderful at the funeral and burial. Frankie stayed right at my side the whole time, comforting me and holding my hand. Beanie had done the same for Katch. I didn't doubt they needed a break from the whole death thing right now.

"Well," I said. "I came in to help. What can I do?"

"Nothing," Mrs. Fletcher said. "This is not a time for you to work."

Katch nodded in agreement.

"I can't just sit out there in the living room and be ignored, or even worse, hear the words 'I'm sorry,' one more time."

I had been trying to hold in my emotions all day, but couldn't handle how everyone was treating me *so* differently right now. I was beyond being able to handle it. God, what if I really did have to leave and live with a stranger? I would lose my home, my friends … and probably my mind. I didn't want to think about it. "Isn't there something I can do?" I asked Mrs. Fletcher.

She finished setting a jiggling fruit Jell-O mold on a serving dish. "Here, then." She handed it to me. "Take this out to the dining table."

I carried the dish delicately, trying not to let the mold jiggle too much. Something about the jiggling unnerved me. I walked toward the dining room with careful, light steps, turning the corner to see my relatives still grouped on the other side of the dining table, whispering. I heard my name. They didn't see me, so I stepped back and leaned against the corner of the wall, just out of sight. I wanted to know what they were saying. I peeked around the corner and listened in.

I could see an older woman with red lipstick on wrinkled lips talking. I'd forgotten her name. She was saying, "…I have no room for her." She paused and nervously licked at the red. "Barb, can't you take her in?"

"No. Ralph and I have our own issues with the kids. Our Kathy is hanging out with some of those hippy types. It's like a cult. We need to deal with that. But something has to be done. Melanie can't stay here forever."

I hated hearing those words. Why do they even have a say in what happens to me?

"We don't know this girl. Why should the burden fall to us now?" This was said by a cousin named Bob, or something like that. Maybe it was Bill. Who knows? But he was right—they don't know me and I don't know them. I only knew Uncle Will because we had spent Christmas with him and Aunt Carolyn a few times. And once we went camping together at Yellowstone Park.

Uncle Will sounded frustrated. "Carolyn and I would take her, but we are in the middle of moving to Australia. I received a grant to study at the University of Sydney, and I am to report right away. We are completely unsettled now, in-between houses and separated by an ocean."

Someone else said, "There is always foster care."

My uncle cut that off. "Are you kidding? She's fifteen! Who is going to take her in at that age? She will probably end up at some sort of orphanage." I could see he was obviously frustrated with his relatives.

"Well," Barb said, "the police are trying to get in touch with her grandmother. She is over in England somewhere. Maybe she can take her in and relieve us of this burden."

Move to England? Burden? I couldn't stand it any longer. I marched into the room and slammed the Jell-O mold down on the table right in front of them. A huge bang reverberated throughout the house as chunks flew from the mold across the table. The whole place went silent.

I stared at the group. "Stop it!" I started to cry. "Stop talking about me like that. I don't want to live with any of you. Don't you know that? It's my life. Quit making decisions about me as if I am not even here. And stop talking about me like I'm some sort of disease no one wants to catch." I ran from the room and out the front door. I couldn't stand being a part of this pity party any longer.

Four Dots

"You okay?"

I turned to see Frankie walking around the side of the picnic table. He sat down next to me.

"Just peachy." I looked out at the raft again, the place my eyes had settled when I first got down here, mesmerized by the water lapping at its sides. It had been a good way to keep any thoughts from penetrating my head. A slight breeze rocked the raft. Little dimples covered the surface of the lake from tiny raindrops. I'd been shaking from the cold, but ignoring it. Typical Oregon weather.

"Here." He put a jacket around my shoulders. "I figured you might need this."

"Yeah. I guess I didn't think my exit out very well. Short black dresses are not the best defense against a cold front and steady drizzle."

"You really bolted out of there. What gives?"

"You mean other than my mother dying and the fact that I am now parentless?"

He put his arm around me. "Yeah. Other than that."

"I just couldn't listen to them anymore."

"Your relatives?"

I looked at him. "Are they even? Seems more like strangers who got dragged off the street and into a mess they wanted nothing to do with."

"That's about the same read I got."

"I mean, what am I? A bag of kittens none of them wants, so they have to draw straws to see who ties rocks to it and tosses it into a deep lake?"

"Wow. That's quite a visual."

"It's how I feel." I turned to Frankie, threw my arms around him and gave him a big kiss.

"Wow again," he said, once I let him go. "What was that all about?"

"I need to get my kisses in while I can. Who knows how long I will be able to stay here? I might even end up moving to England; if they ever find my grandmother, and if that is what she wants."

"Isn't there another option?"

I smiled. "George offered to become my legal guardian."

Frankie looked at me in disbelief. "Who? You mean Captain Thornton? How weird, and a bit gross."

"Actually, it was pretty sweet. But I agree. He even said it would be pretty weird. There's just no way I could do that."

I leaned against him. A cool breeze hit us in the face. He put his arm around me. I snuggled into his warm body, putting my arm under his jacket and around his side. I could feel the pattern of his ribs with my fingers. I let them play in the valleys. We sat in silence and watched as the splatter of raindrops on the lake ebbed and flowed in intensity.

"What do you think she will be like?" Frankie asked. "Your grandmother, I mean."

"I don't know. I never knew her. I've been trying to get some kind of idea, but how would I know? I have nothing to go on."

"Why did your mother say she was dead?"

"I've been wondering about that, too. I don't really remember my mom ever actually saying she was dead. Maybe she let me think it by never mentioning her. Along with the fact she would quickly change the subject whenever I asked about her family. I eventually gave up asking. All I can figure is there must have been something that happened between them."

"But to let you think she was dead, instead of just telling you they weren't talking?"

"I don't have any answers to anything right now. It would really suck if I had to move to England to live with an old woman who probably needs a walker to get around." I turned to Frankie. "I don't want to leave. I'm in love with you. It would kill me to leave." I couldn't hold the tears back and they flowed down my face, a path they had come to know really well lately.

Frankie looked surprised, but not in a bad way. He turned and put his leg over the bench to straddle it and face me. He wrapped his arms around me and scooted over so I was tight against his body. "Did I hear you right?"

I laid my head on his shoulder. "I've had a lot of time to think about a bunch of things lately. And that was right up there at the top, especially when it became a possibility I might have to leave you."

He whispered in my ear, "I love you too, Mel."

I looked up at him. I wanted to see it in his eyes.

"That's all I could think about on the drive back from Pacific City, after we heard what had happened." He wiped a strand of wet hair away from my face, his touch gentle. "I spent the whole two hours worrying about you, and realizing how much I do love you. I've wanted to tell you ever since I got here, but you know ... it wasn't exactly the best time."

I could hear a sense of impending loss in his voice when he said this. Tears rolled down his cheeks. We kissed, possibly one of our last. But it was the best kiss ever—all wet with the salt of our tears and hunger of our love.

"Uh-hum." The sound of Beanie's voice came from behind us.

We broke off the kiss to see Beanie and Katch standing on the steps.

Beanie gave us a mischievous smile. "Why is it I always find the two of you down here necking? And, for some reason, it always involves tears. Kisses are still that bad, huh?"

Frankie and I quickly wiped the tears from our eyes and cheeks with our sleeves.

"Ignore Beanie," Katch said as they walked toward us. "I do most of the time, and it seems to work well in our relationship." They stopped at the end of the table. "Is it okay if a couple of other escapees join you?"

Beanie held a big paper grocery bag in his hand and lifted it to show us. I could hear clinking coming from it.

"Sure. Pity party over yet?" I asked.

"Getting close," Katch answered. "They all wisely decided it was time to leave after you freaked out."

"Glad they could take the hint."

Katch sat next to me, gave me a big smile and stroked my back with her hand. I liked the feel of reassurance it gave me. Beanie set the bag on the table, opened it and took out a stubby bottle of Olympia beer. He pulled an opener from his pocket and popped the cap off. He handed it to me. "Here, you need this." He popped the top from three more bottles, handing one each to Frankie and Katch, then stood in front of us.

"How'd you score the Olys?" Frankie asked.

"It really wasn't hard. Mrs. Fletcher was a little busy playing hostess to people as they left. I told her Katch and I were going to try and find you two. We snagged the beer from the fridge and bugged out the sliding door in back."

I tipped up the bottle and swallowed a big gulp. It only took a moment for the alcohol to hit me and it felt good. "Thanks, Beanie. I do need this."

"There's one more each in the bag. Might as well go for effect if you are going to go for it at all."

I could see Frankie peering into the side of his bottle. "What are you doing? I asked.

He glanced over to me. "Trying to check the dots on the back of the label."

"He's hoping to find that rare four-dot," Beanie told me.

"I don't get it," I said.

Beanie scoffed at me. "What, you never heard about the dots on an Oly label? It's legend."

I shook my head, feeling a little left out. "No."

"The dots are like, you know—bases. First base, second base, third, fourth. You follow?"

"Oh. Like first base is kissing, etcetera?"

"Yep. If you find a label with four dots, you get your girl-friend to sign it. Kind of like a commitment for all the way. Never heard of anyone getting that lucky though."

I looked at Frankie. "Well?"

He shook his head. "Only two."

"Well, that's worthless," Beanie said. "No one should need a two dot."

I blushed. That was certainly true. I bumped Frankie with my shoulder. "Well, don't get your hopes up. I wouldn't sign it anyway, so you might as well stop checking."

"Heck no," Beanie exclaimed. "A four dot is worth gold. There are a ton of guys out there that would pay a pretty penny for a four dot."

I smiled at him. It was nice to get out of my funeral thoughts for a moment. I'd been rolling around in them for days.

Beanie held out his beer. "To The Four Musketeers. One for all…"

We clanked the tips of our bottles to his, and responded, "…and all for one," then each took a big swallow.

Katch let out a little burp. Her eyes went wide and she quickly put her hand over her mouth. "Oops, sorry."

Beanie looked at her. "Man, that was wimpy." He let out a loud belch. We all laughed. Frankie tried to match it, but couldn't come close. We all knew from experience that Beanie held the gold-standard in this department. I gave it my best attempt, which was not quite as good as the boys. It must come naturally to them. We all laughed some more and then got quiet, settling into our own thoughts.

"It's really weird," I said.

They turned to look at me.

"I don't feel anything about my mom's death. It's like I'm immune from what a normal person feels when someone they love dies. I'm just numb."

"Who knows what normal is in these situations? Maybe you're still in some sort of shock or something," Katch offered.

"No." I shook my head. "I've thought about it and it's not that."

"It was really hard taking care of her," Frankie said. "Maybe it's just that you don't have to worry about it anymore. You know, like a sense of relief?"

"Yeah, I thought about that too. But it's something else." I stood up, suddenly feeling antsy. I needed to be on my feet. "I've been thinking a lot about what Mrs. Crowley said in the reading. About destiny."

"You really believe that?" Beanie asked. He sat on the bench where I had been, between Frankie and Katch.

I nodded and worked on the label around my beer. I peeled away at an edge as I thought about how to put it. "I'm not sure I did, before. But now, with both of my parents gone, I wonder if their deaths were all part of it somehow."

"Part of what?" Frankie asked.

"That's what I don't know. But think about it. The Orb is out there somewhere. Somehow, I have been chosen to get it. And we know my dad was on some sort of a quest or something before he died. He was looking into Earth's energy fields, like Tesla. After his death, everything shifted to me. Now it's like I'm being led down this path, but by whom or what, I haven't got a clue."

They sat in silence for a moment. The boys were focused on the stubby beer bottles in their hands. But Katch looked at me as if she were reading my thoughts, and I had the feeling she could. Maybe what her grandmother said was true and she did have the gift.

"If that is how you feel, then why have you been crying?" Katch asked. I got the feeling it was not so much a question, but more like a confirmation of what she was thinking.

"Because I may lose all of this." I gave a sweeping hand to indicate the easement. "And all of you," I answered. "And I don't want to face this alone. I don't know that I could stand it if I had to move away—because the three of you are all I have anymore."

Katch gave me a smile—one of reassurance—then stood, walked over, and threw her arms around me. A moment later I felt Frankie and Beanie do the same, all of their arms around me in a big group hug—The Four Musketeers.

"We don't want you to leave either," Katch said. "We'll just have to figure something out."

Getting Over Guilt

I walked in the front door and the place was empty. Good. I'd had more than enough of these out-of-the-woodwork in-laws. Well, not to include Uncle Will, because I liked him. He had been around all of my life.

I felt bad that no one let him know about my mom in the hospital. And I hadn't been in any condition to think about him. It had been two years since I saw him at Dad's funeral. But I would have felt so much better if he'd been there, being my dad's brother and all, like real family at the hospital to help me make the decision about the operation. In fact, if I had to move away and live with someone, I was sorry it wouldn't be him. I might have been able to survive it all that way.

Mrs. Fletcher came around the corner carrying a tray of dirty dishes. She had been cleaning up. She set it down and came over as soon as she saw me. "I was so worried about you, honey. Did Frankie and the kids find you?"

"Yes. I was down at the lake."

"And out in the rain, by the looks of it." She put her arm around my shoulder and directed me to the kitchen. "And freezing to death, too." She grabbed a towel off the rack and handed it to me. "First, dry your hair so you don't catch your-self a cold, and go change out of that wet dress. Then, I want you to eat something. I know you haven't had a bite all day. I've kept notice. And I won't take no for an answer."

I really wasn't hungry, but she said this in a way that any amount of protest wouldn't overcome her decision. "Yes, Mrs. Fletcher."

"So, we are agreed. First food, and then we will talk, because I have some news."

I looked up at her. "News?" I thought about what it could be. It must have to do with my grandmother.

"Yes. So go change."

"Okay." I hurried to my room, changed, and came back wearing a frumpy sweatshirt and some sweatpants. It felt good to be warm and dry.

"Sit." She pointed to a chair at the breakfast table. "I will fix you a plate."

I sat down and rubbed my hair with the towel while I watched her putter around the kitchen.

She came over with a plate full of food and set it in front of me. A ham and cheese sandwich, baby sweet pickles, potato salad, and a little blob of distressed fruit Jell-O mold. She had made a smiling face with sliced black olives on the potato salad. "Now you eat everything there. You may think your life is over but it isn't, and your body needs nourishment."

"I'll eat if you talk," I told her.

"We are agreed then, young lady." She waited, and when I didn't start eating, she nodded to the plate.

I picked up a triangle of sandwich and took a bite.

"Captain Thornton called while you were gone. They found your grandmother. She is living on some sort of island. Apparently, it is a place at the southeasterly end of England, so that is why it took so long to find her."

A sense of dread ran through me as she said this. "Did he talk to her? Did she say anything? What did she say? Is she going to make me go there?"

"Slow down, slow down." She sat at the table in a chair across from me. "Captain Thornton did talk with her. He says she was quite shocked to hear about your mother's death. She will need some time to figure things out. But it looks like, at least initially, she has decided to come here."

"To stay?" I asked, trying not to get my hopes up too high.

"I can't say, honey. She only now got the news. It will take some time for her to make that kind of decision."

I felt relieved. She was coming here, well, at least for now. Maybe I could talk her into living with me here, and not having to move to some island in England. It would sure help to have Frankie, Katch, and Beanie around while I dealt with figuring out a grandmother I've never met. Especially if she turned out to be a real witch. Why else would my mom have distanced herself?

"It will take a while for her to get here. Could be a week or so. Until then, you know I will stay here with you."

"Thank you, Mrs. Fletcher. I would like you to stay."

"Not that it matters at this point, but I want you to know, I would have adopted you myself if no one else stepped forward. I would have at least tried, though I doubt your relatives or the court system, would let a Negro woman adopt a young white girl. I'd have given it a shot though, anyway."

I reached out and took her hand. "I already knew that, Mrs. Fletcher, and also why it wouldn't have worked out. This world is really screwed up when someone's skin color can make that huge of a difference."

"Honey, you took the words right from the mouth of Martin Luther King, Jr." She patted my hand and I could see she was remembering something. "That's what he said when he stood on the steps before the Abraham Lincoln Monument. It was back in August of '63." She sat back, straightened her shoulders, and let a wide smile take to her face. "If you didn't know, that was when the Great March on Washington for civil rights took place."

"Yeah, I remember," I said. "I watched it on television. We lived in Portland then. It was before Dad died, so I was watching it with him. I don't remember where mom was. I was laying on the carpet in front of the TV. He said we needed to watch because it would go down in history." I took a bite of potato salad, thinking about my dad.

"I'm proud of you, child, that you remember. And of your father also, because he was right. It's something we should never forget. I never will." She leaned forward with a shine in her eyes. "I was there, you know?"

I choked down my bite. "You were?"

"That's right. Desmond had just purchased a car, so we decided to drive cross-country to attend the March. That is how much it meant to us. I don't know if you could possibly imagine what such a notion is like for Negroes in these times. A white family wouldn't give it a second thought to do such a thing, but discrimination puts a damper on such ideas for most colored folk."

She gave me a proud look. "But it was that important to us. We were lucky living here in the Northwest where white people are more accepting. I grew up in the South, so know what it is like there. But here, Desmond got himself a nice job—good enough to buy the car we rode in. The March on Washington was all about coloreds being able to get a job like his. And about everyone being able to have the same freedoms whites enjoy."

I took another bite of my sandwich, captivated by her story and the look in her eyes as she remembered the trip.

"That day we gathered on the commons by the Reflecting Pool. Well, Desmond and me, we weren't real close to the front because I heard later there was most of a quarter of a million people there. I never even imagined there could be so many.

And whites too; those that saw through to their moral soul and knew the righteousness of the event. We were somewhere in the middle of that mass of people." She had a look as if she were standing there right now. "It wasn't as hot as I expected it could be, almost like a regular day for Oregon in that month. But some seemed to think so. Or maybe their feet were sore from marching to the capitol. Shoes were off, feet dangling in the cool water of the Reflecting Pool. It was like that all up and down both sides of it. What a sight it was!" She suddenly stopped and gave me a shy smile. "Oh, my goodness, here I am just rattling on. I'm sure this doesn't interest you."

I swallowed a bite of potato salad as quickly as I could, "No, Mrs. Fletcher, please. I want to hear this."

She studied me for a moment to make sure I meant it. "Okay, then. Where was I?" She looked at the wall, as if it were a big screen where she could watch her story unfold. "Oh, yes. It was hard to even see Reverend King up at the podium, but we knew where he was because of the mass of people on the steps of the Lincoln Monument. I could see Lincoln best of all, as big as his statue was; sitting there all majestic and such, looking out through the columns of his monument. He looked proud of what he had started exactly one-hundred years before, when he issued his Emancipation Proclamation." She looked at me with a glow. "It was as if he could see his vision of freedom for all, finally unfold before him."

I sat there captivated. It wasn't merely the words she used, but how she said them. She could have been a great orator herself, had things gone that way for her.

"But even as far away as we were, I heard the Reverend King's words right clearly, as if he were standing next to me. He only spoke for a short while, but his words still ring true. I will never forget being there, listening to him with all those people of like mind, hearing those words for the first time: 'I have a dream. I have a dream that my four children will one day live in a nation where they will not be judged by the color of their skin—'"

"'But by the content of their character,'" I finished.

She turned to me. "Yes, that's right, child. I'll never forget those words, and I am glad that you haven't either." She walked over, pulled me from my chair and gave me a big hug.

"I don't think I will ever forget, Mrs. Fletcher."

She went to the window and looked out, as if trying to focus on something not quite tangible on the other side.

I sat down and waited for what she would say next, nibbling on my sandwich.

"It is our brightest hope that everyone abides by those words." She turned to me. The look she had was as if she had seen the future out that window, and that one day the world would become a better place. "Maybe someday people will accede to the moral compass deep at the center of their souls, and Reverend King's words will come true."

I took a bite of sweet pickle. When I looked up from my plate, her face had suddenly changed. She looked withdrawn.

"What's wrong, Mrs. Fletcher?"

"I stand here talking of moral compasses, when I have ignored my own." She turned to me. "I need to tell you something. It's been working up inside of me for a while. I don't know if this is the time or not, what with your mother's death, but I can't hold onto it inside any longer."

I heard an anguished tone in her voice. She was fidgeting, and obviously upset. "What is it, Mrs. Fletcher?"

She paced back and forth. "Honey, I can't get over the fact that I did you wrong. I betrayed your trust and I can't forgive myself for that."

"What are you talking about?"

"I stole that letter. I put you in terrible danger."

"But they had Desmond. They were blackmailing you."

She turned away from me, as if she couldn't face me any longer. "That shouldn't have mattered to someone of strong faith. But I failed. I spied on you, and I did it for someone that was probably working for the Devil himself."

I stood, ran over, and wrapped my arms around her from behind. "You didn't fail. You came to me and we worked out a plan. We stopped him. And it got Desmond free."

She turned around. Tears filled her eyes, and her face had a deep, painful look.

"Yes, honey. But I still betrayed you, just as Judas betrayed Christ."

I shook my head. "You can't think that way, Mrs. Fletcher. You did what you needed to do at the time."

She stood there; her eyes wide with a truth she didn't want to face.

I needed to stop her pain. "They had Desmond. They framed him, and said he could go to jail forever if you didn't help them."

She broke into long, deep sobs, pulling a handkerchief from her sleeve and holding it to her face to capture them as they uncontrollably escaped from deep within her.

"Mrs. Fletcher. You risked his life to make sure mine was safe. God can see that."

She dabbed at her eyes with the hanky as she answered. "That doesn't make it right. He watched me as I did you wrong." She wept into her handkerchief. "I also know I can't come square with God until I ask for your forgiveness."

I hugged Mrs. Fletcher again and then stood back and grabbed her hands. "It all worked out. I'm safe and Desmond is safe."

She squeezed my hands and asked, "Will you forgive me?"

I threw my arms around her and gave her the biggest hug I could manage, considering her sizable bosom getting in the way. Here, I thought I had been the one struggling with issues, when Mrs. Fletcher had it just as bad. "I forgive you, Mrs. Fletcher, if that is what you need to hear. But you did what you had to do for Desmond."

And all the while holding her, I couldn't help but wonder who could have done this to them—just to get at me and the debris. It was way too sophisticated for Major Burnham and his thugs. It must be someone else, someone powerful enough to get their man out of jail. *But who?*

A New Clue

It was early the next day. We had just parked downstairs at the Oswego Shopping Center. We rode the escalator to the upper level and headed to Wizer's Foods. Frankie got special permission from his mom to drive because she needed groceries for dinner and couldn't do it herself. She and Frankie's little sister, Suzie, were working on some sort of project for a Girl Scout meeting later in the day. He called me and said I should come along for the ride. I think he wanted to distract me from what I had been going through over the last few days.

We reached the top of the escalator and could see Mr. Wizer, as always, standing near the entrance to his store so he could greet his customers.

"Hey, Mr. Wizer," Frankie called out.

"Hello, Frankie, and my little Melanie." He walked over to me, took my hand, and patted it. "I am truly sorry about your mother. I would have been there yesterday, but I never seem to be able to get away from the store. Is there anything I can do?"

"No, Mr. Wizer. Thank you. I'm doing okay."

He held onto my hand so he could double-check to make sure I wasn't brushing him off. He must have finally decided I was telling the truth. He nodded, then let go and turned to Frankie. "Come to spend your allowance, I hope?"

"Came to spend some of my mother's allowance, and use up a stack of her double coupons." Frankie held up a grocery list with a bunch of coupons paper-clipped to it. "You know my mom. She is the double coupon queen of Lake Oswego. And today, I am the queen's designated errand boy."

"I would go broke if all of my customers were as frugal as your mother. Well, don't forget to pick out something special for yourselves since you are doing such a good deed for her ... and make sure it is expensive."

"Will do, Mr. Wizer."

Frankie grabbed a shopping cart from the rack and we headed down an aisle. Wizer's was a pretty cool store. Every aisle was spotless, and the items on the shelves were all lined up perfectly, like soldiers at attention. You could find things here you wouldn't find in regular stores, like the Safeway up 'A' street. He knew his customers as if we were all family, and made sure he carried everything we liked.

Frankie looked at the list. "A gallon of Alpenrose Dairy milk, Tillamook butter, a dozen eggs, romaine lettuce, carrots, onions, two packages of Mueller's egg noodles, two cans each of Campbell's tomato, mushroom, and cream of celery soup, and ... oh, no."

"What?" I asked.

"She wants six cans of Bumble Bee tuna fish." He looked at the coupons. "Yep. And here are the coupons for them."

I laughed.

"That's like...three tuna noodle casseroles," he said. "How am I going to survive the onslaught?"

"Probably by eating over at my place on those nights."

"Well, she's probably planning to make it tonight, so you best warn Mrs. Fletcher I will be there."

We finished shopping and took the escalator to the lower level, grocery bags in hand.

When we got to the Mustang Frankie said, "Let's put these in the trunk." He tried to shift the bags he was holding so he could get the keys out of his pocket. He almost dropped one while trying.

"Here," I said. "Give me one of them." I juggled my bag to one arm, and took one of his while he popped open the lid. We were both bent over the trunk, placing the bags in it, when a voice came from behind us. We hadn't seen anyone when we came downstairs.

"What did you do, steal that car?"

I turned quickly to see Tom Richardson standing there. "Tom?"

"Hi Melanie, Frankie."

"What are you doing here?" I asked.

"I had to come. I heard about your mother. I'm so sorry."

I ran over and threw my arms around him. I hadn't seen him since last summer when he knocked out the Russian spy and saved our lives. That was when we found out he helped my dad sneak the Orb and spaceship debris out of the Roswell site. Ever since my dad died, he has kept an eye on me and my mom.

"I couldn't come to the funeral. I have no doubt you are still being watched." He looked around as he said this. "I want to know what is next for you. Can we talk somewhere?"

Frankie nodded toward Zwicker's, which was a restaurant in the basement of the building. We loved to eat there because the food was so good. "Sure, let's get a booth."

I looked at Frankie's car. "What about the groceries? We have milk in there and other dairy products."

Frankie grabbed my hand. "It'll probably be fine. Wizer's always double-bags the stuff that needs to stay cold. And if it isn't, I'll make another run." He looked at me. "We aren't going to miss this over some spoiled milk anyway. Right?"

How could I argue with that, and food made sense. Neither of us had eaten this morning, and I could hear Frankie's stomach rumbling just thinking about what awaited us at Zwicker's. There was enough time, and it had been almost a year since we'd seen Tom.

Once inside we found a quiet booth and sat down. Rhonda came over to us, pad in hand. She was a student at LO High and would be a senior next year. "Melanie. I'm so sorry about your mom. Duke is in the kitchen slaving over the grill. When he saw you come in, he told me to extend his condolences and wants to make you his best German Pancakes ever. How's that sound?"

I was surprised. It was kind of a weird form of celebrity. I wasn't sure how to take it. "Well, okay. I guess. Are you sure?"

"Positive," Rhonda said.

Tom cut in. "I'm not sure what a German Pancake is, but I am more of an eggs, bacon, hash browns, and sourdough toast kind of guy anyway. Can we do that?"

"No problem," Rhonda said. She seemed to be giving me a look, wondering who this guy was.

"Oh, Rhonda. This is my Uncle Bob, come over for the funeral."

She nodded, as if suddenly understanding. "Oh, hi. I'm sure Duke would like to buy your meal as well."

"That would be very gracious," Tom said.

Rhonda nodded, then turned to me. "So, what's going to happen with you? Will I see you back at school next fall? It would be a bummer if I don't. I know some of the kids gave you a bad time, but most of us were on your side."

If that were true, I sure hadn't seen it. "Thanks. I really don't know. Everything is up in the air right now."

She nodded. "What do you want to drink?"

Tom ordered coffee, and we asked for a couple of glasses of milk. Rhonda headed back to the kitchen to place our orders.

Tom looked at Frankie. "So how did you end up with the spy's Mustang?"

The last time Tom saw the Russian's car was at the Hunt Club after saving us, when we grabbed the backpack with the debris out of it.

"So, after capturing the Russian agent, the Mustang was confiscated by Major Burnham," Frankie told him. "The major decided to bribe us to keep quiet about what happened, and how the spy had been running rampant in the area. Major Burnham arranged a cash reward for Mel, her mom, and Beanie. I didn't go for the money, though. Instead, I pointed out how it would be a real bummer to let such a nice car just sit in an impound yard. And he went for it."

Tom laughed. "Serves him right for all the trouble he caused you."

Rhonda came over with Tom's coffee and two glasses of milk for Frankie and me.

"Thank you," I told her as she left. I turned to Tom. "How did you know about what happened to my mom?"

"After so many years, I'm getting pretty good at keeping an eye on you. It was the last thing your dad asked me to do before he died and I'm committed to keeping my word. I even ordered a subscription to the *Lake Oswego Review*. There was an article about the accident in the paper. I came down as soon as I found out."

"Are you still up in Washington State?" Frankie asked.

"I did move after what went down last summer. I was sure Major Burnham would figure out who I am and probably where I lived. Since then, I have managed to keep ahead of him. I had to get off the grid. I'm still up north, but more toward downtown Seattle now, secreted away amongst all of the urban dwellers. I've managed to put together an alternate identity. Most know me as Ralph Morgan now."

"Ralph, really?" I questioned. "Couldn't you have come up with a better first name? Something exciting like Butch or Slate?"

"I thought Ralph would be a good, low-key name. Who's going to worry about someone named Ralph?"

"Good point," Frankie agreed.

"So, I came down a few days ago and have been trying to figure out how to make contact with you ever since. It's not like I could just show up at the funeral. This has been the first opportunity."

"Luckily my mom needed groceries," Frankie said.

I reached across the table and took Tom's hand, holding it in both of mine. "I'm so glad you did. It's kind of like having a part of my dad here."

"That's quite a compliment. Thank you." He looked reflective for a moment, then added, "So, like Rhonda said, what happens with you now?"

"Well, I guess my grandmother is coming from England. And I have no idea after that. I may need to move there unless I can convince her to live here."

"You'll have to let me know what happens when she gets here and you have time to figure everything out." He took a drink of his coffee and changed the subject. "You still have the debris and it's hidden?"

"Yes." I didn't want to say more, hoping he wouldn't ask more. But he did.

"Has anyone been after it, or you?"

I glanced toward Frankie. I couldn't lie with him here. Not about the professor at the house, anyway. But I wasn't going to tell either of them about what happened when Major Burnham kidnapped me. "Someone tried to fool me into giving him the debris. Said he was a professor with the University of

Washington, and with NICAP, but he wasn't. We caught him red-handed, though. Captain Thornton arrested him."

"Who was it? Do you know?" he asked.

"No." And I didn't. But I also didn't mention the captain had to release him, or how much power whoever it was had, to be able to do that. I hadn't told Frankie that part either. Wow, I'm really going to have to start keeping track of my lies.

"What about Major Burnham?" Tom asked.

I didn't expect him to straight-up ask about the major. I hesitated. I hated that I couldn't share what happened with either him or Frankie. I just couldn't. I shook my head. "No. Nothing."

He nodded, but with a look showing he wasn't sure he could believe me. "I'm surprised." He kept eye contact a little too long, trying to look through my words. It made me uneasy. I wasn't very convincing.

"What about the device?" Tom asked. "Have you figured out where it is?"

I was relieved he changed the subject. "The Orb? No, not a clue. We haven't really looked."

"The Orb? Why do you call it that?"

"Oh. I went through some of my dad's notes I found in a storage box. He'd been working with a professor and a couple of scientists on the earth's energy fields. I think it had something to do with the device. That's what he called it in his notes. The Orb."

"Well, that's big news." He leaned forward. "Have you talked to these men? Maybe they have the Orb, or know where it is. You need to find out what he was doing."

"No, I haven't. I never thought of it. I'm not sure I can figure out how to find them, but that's a really good idea. I'll go over his notes again. Maybe there's something in them that would help."

"Good. I remember how Roger felt about the device. The Orb. Desperate to get it out of the crash site. It must have been because of something the alien shared before I got there; in order for him to feel that way."

"You said it was like mental telepathy, right?" Frankie asked.

"Yes. The alien was dying when I arrived. I knew that as soon as I saw Roger's eyes, and the look in them. I bent over the body and the alien turned its head slightly toward me. When we made eye contact, I immediately felt the alien's presence in my mind, talking to me, but without words. I'll never forget how that felt." He studied his coffee cup as a point of focus. "I could sense the alien's concern, but not because it was dying. It wanted me to understand the importance of getting the Orb out safely.

"I could see a dust cloud kicking up in the distance and getting closer. Vehicles were coming, but I couldn't see them or tell what kind. But the alien knew they were from the military base, and if Roger was detained, they would get the Orb." Tom looked up at me from his cup. "Your dad was desperate to get the Orb out of there. It must have been because of what the alien told him about it."

Frankie cut in. "What did the alien say?"

"I don't know. It could have something to do with why they were here, or about their mission. It must have been passed along to your father. I really don't know, but that's the sense I got. He was desperate to get the Orb out safely, and he knew he couldn't do it alone. The rest of his archeology group had arrived by then. They would all be detained. That's why he gave me the satchel, pleading with me to get it out."

"And now the Orb is missing," Frankie said.

"You mean more like hidden," I corrected.

"It's important you find it," Tom said. The tone to his voice was very compelling. "I know Roger planned to get it to you when you were older. But he couldn't have anticipated your current circumstances, especially if you end up in England."

"I know," I agreed. "I've wanted to find it anyway. But I didn't have a clue about where or how to look, until now. You just gave me a great place to start." I paused for a second. An idea hit me. "Tom, how did you decide to go searching for arrowheads in that area on that weekend?"

"Funny you should ask. I had made other plans, but they fell through at the last minute. I decided to head into the desert instead, since it was a three-day weekend."

"Why did you pick that specific spot?"

"Oh, I don't know. I kind of started driving, thinking of where to go. I've been to that area before with success, so headed that way. I had never camped in the spot where I ended up." He paused for a second, wondering. "Why do you ask?"

"Oh, nothing. Just some things I've been thinking about."

Tom grabbed a napkin from the dispenser on the table, and took a pen from his jacket pocket. "Melanie, with your mom gone, I want you to be able to reach me. I'm going to give you my phone number." He wrote it down on the napkin and pushed it over. "Memorize it and then destroy the napkin. Best not to have my number written on anything, to keep it from falling into the wrong hands."

"This is crazy," Frankie said. "It feels like we are in a spy movie or something."

I looked over at him, "I know, doesn't it?" I studied the napkin, folded it and put it in my pocket. I looked up at Tom. "I'll get rid of it as soon as I get home."

Rhonda arrived with our food. Two big German Pancakes appeared before Frankie and me. The smell was heaven as she set them down.

Tom's eyes went wide. I guess he had never seen one before. "Those are really impressive."

"And they taste as good as they look," I said.

The pancakes were shaped kind of like a bowl, and took up the whole plate. Their sides rose over four inches all around. Powdered sugar had been liberally sprinkled across the inside, and a huge scoop of butter melted away in the center. Rhonda set Tom's plate in front of him and a bowl of lemon wedges on the table.

I spread the butter around the pancake and squeezed the juice from a couple of the wedges over it.

Tom grabbed the Heinz catsup bottle and removed the cap. "I want you to call me any time you need to," he said, as he poured catsup next to his hash browns. "No matter what the reason, okay?"

"I will. I promise."

He took a forkful of hash browns and dipped it in his catsup, pausing before he took the bite. "Just be sure you don't call from home. As long as you have that debris, these men will still be after it and watching you. We know that probably includes tapping your phone."

He was right about that; in a lot of ways.

Destiny's Plan

Mrs. Fletcher had left for the store. Frankie, Beanie, Katch and I were all in my bedroom. It wasn't like I wanted her to be gone while we talked. I wasn't worried about her being a spy anymore. It just made things much easier if I didn't have to worry about her overhearing us and wondering what we were up to.

She'd already asked a bunch of questions two days ago, when she saw me pulling down twenty-plus boxes of my dad's stuff from the rafters and spreading them around the garage floor. I told her I was trying to sort through things because we needed to get rid of most of the stuff. And as I said this, I realized it was true. Both in having to get rid of most of it, and in it now being my responsibility. There was no one else to do it but me.

I searched for anything as far back as his days at Texas Tech, and right up through his research on Tesla's ideas. The men he worked with could have been friends he met from earlier projects, or school.

Mom was in a pretty bad state when she packed up the boxes, so there really was no rhyme or reason to any of them. It took me a couple of days to get things organized. I didn't want to miss anything that could help. When finished, I managed to get everything worth looking at into four boxes. I secreted them away in the garage until we could meet. Now they were sitting against the wall of my room.

Frankie was laying on my bed, propped up against the headboard.

Katch was sitting in the chair at my vanity looking around my room. "Mel, I tell you, every time I come in here, I still can't believe it."

Beanie stood next to her, leaning against the wall. "I know. You'd think she was a princess or something."

My face turned a shade of pink, which was completely offset by the absolute white of my room—everything from the four-poster bed, with canopy on top, to the vanity and chair Katch sat in. My mom went all out trying to turn me into something I'm not. Regardless of her efforts, I still wore my sleeveless t-shirts, jeans, and Converse high-tops. Even Katch's efforts to improve my wardrobe hadn't taken hold the way she hoped.

"It's really a bit embarrassing," I told them.

"Yeah, I get it," Beanie said. "I have mom issues myself." We all chuckled. Then he nodded to the boxes on the floor. "So, that's everything, right?"

"Well, what I could find here at the house, anyway. Who knows what Dad has stashed away with the Orb, wherever that could be? This is everything related to Roswell, his school, or research."

They all looked at the boxes as if an answer was hidden inside one of them, and it was just a matter of uncovering it. Hopefully there was.

I took one of the boxes, put it on the bed, and opened the lid. The two articles about the 1947 UFO crash from the Roswell Daily Record were on top. They were old and yellowed. I picked them up and handed them to Katch. "I told you about these back at your house. I wanted you to see them."

"Hey, I remember those," Beanie said. "They started this whole thing, right? Wow, it seems like ages ago since we last saw them."

I pointed to the first article Katch held. It was the one on July 8th with the title: "RAAF Captures Flying Saucer on Ranch in Roswell Region." I remembered back. "Something got us interested in UFOs—"

"It was the movie we saw," Frankie cut in. "What was it called?"

"'War of the Worlds,'" Beanie answered. "At the Lake Theater last summer."

"Oh, yeah. And I got the books on Exeter and the Hills too," Frankie added.

"Mel showed me the one about the Hills," Katch said.

"Yeah. 'Interrupted Journey'," Frankie remembered.

I went on, "Anyway, I remembered my dad had some stuff about Roswell in his garage, and he was studying it when I was little. I found these articles. Basically, the Air Force covered up the crash there and said it was all a big mistake."

"But we know different, don't we?" Frankie pointed out.

"Yeah," Beanie said, "it's a little hard denying something exists when you've held pieces of the spaceship in your own two hands."

"I still so want to see that stuff," Katch said. "I never got the chance after what happened to your mom."

I looked over at her. "I can't make any promises. I don't want to take the chance of bringing it out of hiding. Not unless there's a reason, anyway."

"Okay," she said, half-heartedly.

I pointed to the first article again. "In this first one, the Air Force admits they found a UFO, which we know is true. But the next day," I pointed to the other article, dated the 9th with the title: 'Gen. Ramsey Empties Roswell Saucer,' "they are in complete denial about the truth, and pulled their hoax saying it was only an old weather balloon. Well, that's what led us to talking about UFOs and coming up with our own little hoax. If we hadn't done that, we may never have known about my dad getting the Orb and some of the spaceship debris out of the crash site."

"Oh, I doubt it," Beanie rebutted. "Once they knew your dad had some of the debris, they never would have let it rest. Remember, you said they trashed your house in Portland looking for this stuff. That was *after* he died and before you even had a clue as to all of this. I'm sure they would have figured out a way to screw with you and your mom to get this stuff, even if you didn't know it existed or where it was hidden."

He was probably right. It made me think about how this has destroyed my family. But I still couldn't help but think, if I hadn't pursued the hidden debris, maybe my mom would still be alive today. I sat down on the bed. I felt like everyone in the room could see the guilt on my face.

I looked up at Frankie. "Why do you think she was driving so crazy when she crashed?"

"Huh? Your mom?" I could tell he was confused by what I just asked, it being out of the blue and all.

"The article in the paper said she was driving erratically all the way from downtown Oswego. It must have been true. No one else owns a white T-bird in this town, so it wasn't exactly hard to identify her. Witnesses said she almost hit two other cars, and was going nearly eighty-miles-an-hour on Iron Mountain Boulevard. Why would she do that?"

"Maybe someone was chasing her?" Katch suggested.

"No. People would have seen the other car too and reported it." I looked from Katch to Frankie and then to Beanie. "I've been thinking about it. Someone must have scared her somehow."

"You mean someone got to her?" Beanie asked.

"It's the only thing that makes sense. She went to the liquor store. Something must have happened then to make her go nuts."

"Maybe someone did get to her," Beanie said.

Then it came to me. There really could be only one thing to cause my mother to react the way she did, and that would be some sort of threat against me. Whether it was Major Burnham or this mystery group of guys, she must have been racing home to find out if I was safe.

Frankie scooted over and put his arm around me. He must have seen the look on my face. "Hey, let's forget about this and get to work looking through the boxes."

He was right. It wouldn't do any good to wallow in my own guilt. I decided to refocus on finding clues about the men Dad worked with.

I got up, picked up a box from the floor and set it in Frankie's lap. "Here, you and Beanie go through this one. Show me anything of interest. Katch and I will do this other one. When done, we'll each take another box."

Frankie stood and went to set his box on the floor in a space where he and Beanie could work through it together. They opened the lid and took out documents, sorting them out on the floor.

Katch came over and peered into the box on the bed which held the Roswell clippings. I knew it also held the notebook my dad used during his research, so I wanted this one for myself. I took out the notebook and carefully flipped through the pages, searching for names.

I looked over at Katch. "I'm thinking if he mentioned their names, they would be in here. This is where he wrote all of his notes while doing his research. This is where I found out about Tesla."

"Tesla?" Katch said. "You mentioned him before, at the easement right after the funeral. Who is he?"

"Oh. I forgot. That was before I met you. Tesla was a scientist back around 1900. He was looking into earth's energy. I read some things about him, and it looks like he was trying to figure out how to use free energy to run things like cars, trains, and airplanes, to light our homes and things like that."

"Really? Is such a thing possible?"

"He thought so. And it looks like he was figuring it out. But he couldn't get anyone to back him, so he never finished. Somehow my dad learned about his research and was looking into the same thing." I kept flipping through the pages, studying each one. "He was working with another archeologist and some scientists. I'm hoping he wrote something about them in here."

"Why would an archeologist be researching earth's energy?"

"Exactly," I agreed. "That's the great mystery. It must have been something to do with the Orb. And if we can find even one name in these boxes and how to contact him —"

"We may be one step closer to solving this mystery," Katch finished.

"Hey, Mel. Did you see this?" Frankie asked.

I looked over at him. He and Beanie were sitting on the floor with the box between them. He held up an old, stained file folder. I couldn't tell what it said on the tab. There were a bunch of folders in the boxes. I tossed anything in I thought might be of interest.

"It's a folder for a research expedition your dad was on while at school," he said. "Did you see the date on it?" He got up and walked over to me, setting it on the bed. "It's dated June, 1947."

"What? That's the month just before the UFO crash."

I took the folder, knowing my dad had held it. Touching it felt like I was connecting with him again. I opened it. A quarter-inch of paperwork sat inside. The papers were old. Some were yellowed. I took half of the stack and handed it to Frankie. "You and Beanie look through these. Katch and I will do the rest."

Frankie and Beanie moved to the other side of the bed, facing us. They spread the paperwork out so they could go over what was there.

"Dad went to Texas Technological College," I told Katch. "He got his degree in archeology there. I knew he came onto the crash site while on an expedition searching for Indian artifacts nearby. I had no idea we would find anything in these boxes about it."

"Where is the college?" Katch asked.

"It's in Lubbock, which is in the northwestern part of Texas, and maybe a couple hundred miles east of Roswell."

"How old was your dad then?" Frankie asked.

I needed to think about it. "I don't know. Twenty-three or four, maybe? He graduated the next year in '48. His degree from the college was in one of the boxes."

"Mel, look at this." Frankie handed a paper across the bed to me.

"What is it?"

"I think it's the proposal for the archeological expedition. Look at the recommended expedition date."

I scanned the document and found what he was referring to. The expedition was planned to include the three-day weekend of July 4th.

"Mel?" Frankie said. "It looks like your dad was planning it. This is his report to the head of the department recommending where the expedition should go."

The report was two pages long. I read it, and a tingling sensation worked its way through my body as I realized what it meant. I felt tiny pinpricks on the surface of my skin, moving across my whole body.

Katch could see the look on my face. She took the paper from my hand. "It looks like the head of the department was Professor H. R. Holden. I think Frankie is right. From this report, it looks like your dad was the professor's main assistant. He was tasked with researching the expedition site."

"This is freakin' weird," Beanie said. "This means your dad decided where they would go."

"It seems so." I looked at Katch and took the paper from her. "Do you know what Indians would have lived in the area, north of Roswell?"

"That's way east of where my people now live. But the whole area had all sorts of tribes over thousands of years. Just within the Puebloans, my ancestors, there were the Hopi, Zuni, Acoma, and Laguna, with dozens of sub-tribes. And then there were the Navajo, Comanche, and Apache. In that specific area, I think maybe it was the Apache. Probably the Mescalero Apache. They were a wandering tribe in the Pecos River Valley. My grandmother told me a little about them and other tribes as part of our oral history."

I studied the report again. I wanted to see if there was anything specific about why he chose that particular spot. But there wasn't, at least not in this paperwork. "Could he have gone somewhere else to find Indian sites?"

"Yeah," Katch nodded. "Like I said, there were lots of tribes all throughout the area, and hundreds of ancient settlements where he could have set up an expedition."

"But out of thousands of square miles to choose from, my dad picked that specific place, on that specific weekend, and only about a mile from where the spaceship would crash."

Frankie looked at me, realizing where I was going with this. "You mean you think he was somehow directed to choose that site?"

"I wouldn't say it that way. Not like he received some sort of message or something. But, how could it possibly just be coincidence?"

"Are you on your destiny thing again?" Beanie asked, giving me a bit of a look.

I glanced over at him. He was saying it in a wisecracker sort-of-way, maybe to try to relieve my tension, but he was probably right. "Call it whatever you like. I think Dad was meant to be there, that weekend, in that location."

"So, he could be the first one to the crash site," Katch suggested.

"And get to the alien before anyone else," Frankie said.

"Before the alien died so it could tell him something, just like Tom said," Beanie added.

I put the paper down on the bed and looked at everyone as I thought about the significance of what we discovered. "And be the anointed one to receive the Orb."

Frankie's face took on a startled expression. "But, Mel. It's not him anymore, it's you!"

Keeping Focused

Frankie peeked out his bedroom door for the third time in the last ten minutes. "Where are they?" He was getting ticked off that Katch and Beanie hadn't shown up yet.

"On Beanie time, no doubt," Mel answered, plopping down on his bed.

He looked out one more time, then left the bedroom door slightly ajar so he could see when they arrived, and wandered over to Mel. She lay on his bed, her face to the radio on his nightstand, playing with the tuning knob in search of a good song. Frankie watched her as she twisted the dial, bits and pieces of radio stations sounding from the speaker as she whirled through them in her search.

He was dying to know if she learned anything else about her dad, or the people he was working with. He asked her when she first came in, but she wouldn't say a thing until everyone was here. He could tell how frustrated she must feel. Now that her mother had died, she seemed to have this need to find the Orb. Maybe refocusing on her dad and finding it was how she coped with her mother's death. It wasn't just about the debris anymore, though that was still a huge problem. He knew one thing though—if there was any way possible to help her figure this all out, he would be there by her side, doing exactly that.

She was still tuning through the radio channels, and it brought him out of his thoughts. "No sense doing that," he told her. "You know Beanie will take over when he gets here."

"Yeah. But how long will that be? Maybe there's a new song out or something. It would be fun to get the upper hand on him for once."

"I doubt you'll be able to, at least when it comes to music."

They heard the sound of the sliding glass door opening. "Knock, knock?"

It was Katch.

Frankie called out, "Enter at your own risk." He went to the bedroom door to let them in.

Beanie and Katch walked in, and Frankie closed the door behind them.

"Oh my God, what *is* that you have on the radio?" Beanie pleaded.

Mel looked up from her focus on the radio dial toward him. *"What?"*

She had somehow ended up on a station playing a Frank Sinatra song just as he walked in.

Frankie watched Beanie quickly walk to the bed and hover over Mel and the radio. "'Fly me to the Moon'? *Frank Sinatra?* This is serious, Mel."

He bent down as if leaning over a ticking time bomb, trying to figure out which wire to cut to keep it from exploding as time was running out. Lyrics flowed from the radio: *'Fly me to the moon, let me play among the stars, let me see what spring is like on Jupiter or Mars...'*

"Slowly release your hold on the knob," he told Mel, his voice intense.

Frankie walked to the side so he could get a better view of the action. After all, these Beanie moments were always good, and he could tell this would be one of them. He looked over at Beanie to see little beads of sweat forming on his forehead.

Beanie nervously put his hands out to direct Mel, as if one wrong move would be the end of them all. "Careful, now," he motioned with his fingers, "not too quickly."

Mel looked up at him like he was totally crazy, which at this point, he was. She took her fingers off the knob.

Beanie let out a deep sigh of relief. "Never do that again, okay? Please leave the radio to the experts. Frank Sinatra—really? What, you're desperate to find out what spring is like on Jupiter or Mars?" He reached for the tuning knob and quickly and skillfully adjusted it to his favorite KGW station. The song, *White Rabbit*, by the Jefferson Airplane played through the speaker.

"Now, that's more like it," Beanie said. "It might take a little while to clear all of the negative energy from the room, but if anyone can do it, Grace Slick and her hypnotic lyrics certainly can."

Mel sat up on the bed and looked over to Katch. "How do you deal with him? I mean, he is our friend and all, but it must really be tough being his girlfriend."

"I've been checking out a lot of books on child psychology from the library lately," Katch answered. "It seems to be working, but he still has a long way to go."

They all laughed. Even Beanie.

"Well," Beanie said, "as long as we all understand I march to the beat of a different drummer, so to speak, we are good."

"Different drummer," Frankie said. "That's a good one, Beanie."

"Well, when I say different drummer, I'm thinking Ginger Baker and his five-minute drum solo on *Fresh Cream*. That guy can really swing the sticks."

"How is it you always manage to tie everything to music?" Mel asked.

"It's a gift," Beanie replied, "just like how you are tied to the stars and the Orb."

"I'm not sure that's a gift," Mel muttered.

"So, Mel, why did you call a meeting of the Musketeers, anyway?" Katch asked, looking over at her. "Did you figure out who was working with your dad?"

It had been a few days since they were at Mel's and discovered her father had been the one in charge of the expedition. Once they had figured that out, they spent the rest of the time talking about whether it was just coincidence or destiny, like Mel seemed to be so set on. Before they knew it, Mrs. Fletcher came back from the store and needed help fixing lunch. After that, they didn't have time to keep looking.

"I've been going through his stuff when I can, but there is so much, and I don't want to miss anything," Mel said, sitting up on the bed. "It's taking me a while, but I did find the names of at least some of the people he was working with. There were three men—one named Pendleton, and another named Sweringen. I'm guessing they were both scientists, and a guy named Professor Lofton. But I haven't found anything on who they are, how to contact them, or where they might work or live. I still have a lot of stuff to look at. There's so much information in my dad's files and notes. I doubt he would just write their contact info on a big, blank piece of paper in black marker. As careful as he's been, he would probably hide it in some way, like he hid the clue for how to find the debris. I'm afraid if I go too fast, I will miss something."

"Then, I don't get it. I thought you would have big news for us. Why are we here?" Beanie asked.

Frankie frowned. "Hey, I'm sure she has a good reason." He looked over to Mel. "Right?"

She sat there for a minute, quiet-like and thinking. Frankie studied her. She looked like she was trying to decide whether to tell them something. She slowly shook her head, probably not even realizing she was doing it. Frankie didn't like it, or the look on her face. She was still hiding something.

"What is it, Mel?" he asked.

She was kind of startled out of her thoughts. "Oh, sorry. It's just that I've been thinking—what with my mom dying and what happened to my dad, maybe I shouldn't pursue this anymore?"

"What do you mean?" Frankie asked, a bit thrown off by her comment.

She stood, walked over to Frankie's desk, leaned against it and continued. "Well, it doesn't matter anyway, because that thought didn't last long. As soon as I considered it, I realized it just isn't in me to stop. I guess I wanted to share what I was thinking with all of you." She paused for a second. "I know Dad was pursuing something important. It was important enough that he died while protecting the debris and the Orb. He was willing to endure torture rather than give it up or the quest. I can't just drop what he was doing."

"Maybe they got the Orb," Katch said, sitting down on the bed where Mel had been. "I mean, we don't know where it is. Maybe they did get it out of him."

It sounded like she had a tinge of guilt to her voice as she said this, like she didn't want Mel to think badly of her for suggesting it.

"No," Mel replied. "I've already thought about that. If he had given up the Orb's location, he would have also given up where he hid the debris, and we know that wasn't the case."

"So ...?" Frankie said.

"So, I know he said that someday I would be finishing his quest, whatever it is."

Beanie sat down next to Katch. "Remember, Mel? We were thinking when you are older, maybe sometime after college."

Mel nodded. "But that's a long time from now. I can't sit back and wait for *someday*. Just like Tom said. I need to do something now. Especially if my grandmother decides to take me to England. How am I going to get the Orb then, when it's most likely somewhere here in the States? I don't know how my dad has it planned to get me the Orb, but what if that doesn't happen if I move? Maybe it would never be able to find me if I'm stuck in some God-forsaken place in England on the other side of the planet."

Frankie sat down in the desk chair next to Mel and swiveled it so he could look up at her. "What's the game plan then? Do you even have one?"

"No," Mel answered, putting extra emphasis on the word. "I don't. But there is just too much going on in the world with the cover-up. People are not only being misled about UFOs; they're also being manipulated by our government. And all the while if they would come clean and countries would communicate about it with each other, we would be safe."

"I don't get it. What do you mean, safe?" Beanie asked.

Mel swept some things out of the way on the desk, and then hopped up so she was sitting on it with her legs dangling over the edge. "Do any of you remember the Cuban missile crisis that happened a few years ago?"

Frankie shook his head, and saw Katch and Beanie do the same.

"I didn't either. After all, it happened in 1962, so we were only about nine or ten at the time. But it came up in my newsletters from NICAP. Russia was putting nuclear missiles in Cuba. If they succeeded and a war broke out, they could take out our east-coast cities and the government in Washington before we even knew what hit us. President Kennedy decided to do a naval blockade of Cuba so no more missiles could get through. And he demanded they remove the ones already being built there. We came really close to a full-fledged nuclear war before the Russians finally backed down."

"Hey, remember the duck and cover drills we did in grade school?" Beanie asked. "Everyone was really worried about an atomic bomb attack back then."

"And still should be," Mel said.

"I'm not getting why this was in your newsletter," Katch said. "What does it have to do with UFOs?"

"Because we are in a big cold war with the Soviet Union right now. The two governments don't trust each other at all. They are both on high alert, watching the skies in case the other launches a nuclear missile strike."

Frankie wondered where this was going. "And?" he said, like as in 'get to the point.'

"And ..." she mimicked him, giving him a look, "NICAP has inside info that there is real concern by our government that we, or the Russians, could mistake a flight of UFOs for an incoming missile strike and launch their own nuclear missiles in retaliation."

"Wow!" Beanie said. "It could wipe out the whole world, and it would have been all a big screw up."

"That's the point. And it could easily be prevented if the leaders of the world would admit UFOs exist and work together instead."

"A united front, so to speak," Frankie said.

"Exactly. I don't know which is scarier—their lack in admitting UFOs exist, or lack of understanding the consequences if they don't."

A knock came at the bedroom door. Frankie got up and opened it to find his little sister, Suzie, standing there. She was still in her Girl Scout uniform. Frankie remembered she had a meeting earlier in the day. She wore a crisp white shirt, a khaki vest with all sorts of diamond-shaped emblems on it, and equally pressed khaki shorts. It was all topped off with a little khaki beanie sitting on her head at just the right angle. Sometimes Frankie felt she wore her uniform like she was part of a Hitler Youth movement.

She gave Frankie a fake little smile. "Mom wants to know if your fellow cult members are staying for dinner."

Frankie looked over to them.

"What's for dinner?" Beanie asked. "Tuna-noodle casserole?"

"Naw," Suzie answered, peeking around her brother to see Beanie, "she's going to cook some sort of barbequed pork-ribby thing or something."

"I'm in," Beanie said. "I could go carnivore. Ripping meat from a bone sounds like fun."

"That's just gross," Katch said. "But sure, why not."

Mel nodded.

"Okay. Let Mom know it's a go," Frankie told her.

"Great. I'll start hanging the plastic sheets to catch all the splatter. I've seen Beanie eat and it isn't—"

Frankie slammed the door shut to cut her off. Suzie had to be taken in measured quantities and if they were going to eat with her later, there was no sense in putting up with her nonsense now.

He turned back to Mel. "You were saying?"

She took his cue. "That's why it is so important to continue the cause. Maybe we need to release the debris. I know it would be a big media sensation, and probably screw up the rest of our lives because of it, but what else is there to do?"

Frankie shook his head. "Let's not do anything until we figure out who these men are your dad worked with, and if there is any way to contact them. They may be able to help."

Mel looked like she was thinking about it. "Okay. I'll keep going through the boxes, but if I can't find out how to get in

touch with them, then we will need to figure out a plan to release the debris to the public."

"Well, we had better do one or the other, and soon," Beanie
said, "before the whole world gets blown up."

Professor Lofton

I'm sitting in the middle of my bed with paperwork spread out all around me. I've been working on the boxes for hours, ever since I got home from dinner at Frankie's. I think I finally found something. A phone number. It had to be for Professor Lofton because the notes had something to do with the work they were doing together. I almost missed it because the notation was a bit cryptic, like I thought it might be. I was glad I had taken my time. The phone number was buried in a series of numbers which looked like an arithmetic mean formula of some sort.

It reminded me of Elementary Algebra formulas we studied in school this year. My dad must have done it this way on purpose—to hide it. I only caught it because the number 206 stood out. It was the same area code for the phone number Tom gave me, so I recognized it. Then I noticed the next seven numbers were separated between plus signs in quotation marks. It all blended into the rest of the formula, but stood out at the same time. If it was a phone number, it would be for somewhere in Washington State, which was a good thing, since it wouldn't be so far away that I couldn't get there if I needed to.

I wanted to call right away and see if it really was a phone number for Professor Lofton, but then remembered Tom's advice not to make any calls from home. The clock on my nightstand showed it was well past eleven o'clock. Wow, I didn't know it was so late. Way too late to be calling, anyway. I would have to do it in the morning.

Frankie would be excited to know I might have found Professor Lofton's phone number. But before I got too far with that thought, I just as quickly decided I needed to call Professor Lofton first on my own. I needed to make sure it was his number. I didn't want to get Frankie's hopes up, and then have them dashed if it turned out I was wrong.

I decided I would ride my bike to Remsen's in the morning and call from the phone booth there. I wondered if I would be followed again. I was sure now that whoever tried blackmailing Mrs. Fletcher and Desmond, were also the ones who followed me when I tried to call Major Keyhoe at NICAP. Then I wondered if they might have tapped the phone booth as well. I needed to be careful, but decided they probably hadn't. How would they even know I would be using this phone again?

I wrote the professor's number on a piece of paper and tucked it into my coin purse, also checking to make sure I would have enough coins for the call this time. It would be much less expensive than when I tried calling Major Keyhoe at NICAP all the way across the country. Luckily, the professor was a lot closer.

I woke up early the next morning. The clock next to my bed said it was a little after eight o'clock. I wanted to get up, but knew I shouldn't. All sorts of alarms would go off in Mrs. Fletcher's head at a teenager getting up so early. She would know immediately something was going on, so I tried to sleep some more, but it was a worthless effort. All I could think about was being able to talk to someone who worked with my dad.

I had a lot of questions. What were they working on together? Did he see the Orb? And if so, does he have it or know where it is? Was he aware of what happened to my dad? Did he have any idea *he* could be also in danger? Too many questions to figure out.

I stared at the ceiling as all of these thoughts swirled in my head. I finally got up and grabbed the latest issue of the *UFO Investigator*, NICAP's newsletter, and settled back into bed, propped against my pillows and the headboard.

It was the same newsletter I showed Frankie when we talked about the UFO encounter at the Air Force base in Montana. There was an article in it I wanted to read, but never got around to. I found it on page eight. The title read, '1947 Sighting Wave Report.' I thought it would be good to finally read since the twentieth anniversary of the Roswell crash was only a couple of days away. The article said a guy named Ted Bloecher, a member of NICAP, was compiling a list of UFO sightings from June and July of 1947. Up until now, only a few sightings from then were well known, like the one by Kenneth Arnold near Mount Rainier in Washington State.

This Bloecher guy had traveled around the country over the last five years, and reviewed over one-hundred different newspapers from major cities covering the time period. He found out there was a big UFO wave back then, discovering over seven-hundred sightings. The sightings peaked right around July 4th through the 7th—right when the Roswell crash happened.

The article finished up by saying, that if a similar search could be made of all the local daily and weekly papers throughout the country, the number of sightings would more than double.

It made me even more concerned about the chance of a mistaken nuclear war. Seven-hundred sightings in just a couple of months. Maybe double the amount! Now that we have enough nuclear weapons to wipe out the world three times over, no wonder our government was worried.

I looked at the clock. It was only nine, but I couldn't stand it anymore. I got up, went to the bathroom, and then dressed.

Mrs. Fletcher heard the commotion. "Is that you, honey? You're up a bit early."

Just as I thought. I headed down the hall toward the kitchen. "I know. I couldn't sleep anymore. I was thinking about something." I realized my mistake before I could catch it.

She stuck her head around the corner and watched me walk toward her. "Thinking about what?"

Now I needed to come up with an answer. I went to the breakfast table and sat down, giving myself time to think. Mrs. Fletcher was drying a dish in the kitchen.

"I want to get a gift for Frankie. He has been so supportive of me. Maybe I'll ride my bike up to Remsen's this morning to see if I can find anything there." I quickly looked out the window as soon as I said this, worried it could be raining, but it wasn't. Good, because it would have been an issue to ride my bike there in the rain. Mrs. Fletcher would have insisted on driving me.

She came over and gave me a big hug. "Now, isn't that just like you? Thinking of others."

I felt a twinge of guilt in my white lie to her. But what else could I do?

"I'm going to fix you a big breakfast before you go."

Remsen's was up ahead. I kept an eye out for anything unusual during the ride there, like maybe a black sedan following me slowly down the street. The bad guys were either really good at following, or no one was there since nothing appeared out of place. I rode my bike up the small driveway to the store parking lot and leaned it against the phone booth. I waited for a few minutes, in case a car did follow me, but no cars entered the parking lot so I opened the phone booth door, went inside and closed it.

I dialed '0' for the local telephone operator. When she answered I asked to be connected with long-distance.

"Long-Distance, can I help you?"

"Yes. I would like to place a person-to-person call to a Professor Lofton." I gave her the number. I learned from last time to place the call person-to-person so if they weren't there, I wouldn't be charged.

"One moment, please."

I waited, hearing a series of clicks over the receiver. I looked around the parking lot one more time to make sure no one was lurking around in a dark suit and sunglasses.

A man's voice came across the line. "Hello."

"This is the long-distance operator. I have a call for a Professor Lofton. Is he available?"

"That would be me."

My heart skipped a beat. I guess I hadn't expected it to work.

The operator said, "Your connection is complete." She told me how much it would be for the first five minutes. I deposited the coins. "And it will be thirty-five cents for each additional five minutes, as needed." She left the line.

I suddenly didn't know if this was a good thing. His voice sounded younger than I expected. I worried he might be the same professor who came to my house? I seemed to have forgotten for a moment that his number came from my dad's notes. How *can* you tell someone's age over a phone, anyway? I decided I must be getting gun-shy. "Professor Lofton?"

"Yes, who is this?"

"Can you hang on for a second, I need to deposit some more money." I put in a whole dollar's worth of coins. I didn't want to take the chance of losing the connection. "Hi, my name is Melanie Simpson. Did you know my father, Roger Simpson?"

"Roger. Yes, of course. We worked together for the better part of a year, and then he up and disappeared on me. I haven't heard from him since. I eventually decided to move on to other projects." Then his voice changed. "Why would his daughter be calling me?"

"He died, almost two years ago. I found your number in his notes. He was working with you on some sort of research?"

"Died. How? Last time we talked, he was worried he might have been discovered."

"It's a long story and I can't take the time to tell you right now. What were you working on?"

"Before we go there, I need to ask a few more questions of you. Especially now that I know he is dead. He was pretty secretive about our research. He needed to be, but obviously that wasn't good enough. First, how did he die?"

"A Russian agent tried to get the material from him. My dad wouldn't give it up, so was killed."

"Oh. I'm so sorry."

He didn't know the half of it. "Look, Professor Lofton, I don't have much change left. Is it okay if we keep going? What else do you want to know?"

"Yes, yes. I understand. Your father told me you used to play a game together. What was it?"

"We'd play catch. He taught me how to pitch."

"Good. And he said he made something for you to keep your gloves and ball in."

I was surprised my dad would tell the professor about the toy box. Maybe for this very reason. And then I wondered if this was how he came up with the idea of where to hide the backpack.

"He made a wooden toy box for me. We buried it under the back deck of our house and kept our gloves in it."

84

There was a short pause and then he said, "Excellent. No one else would have that information. So, tell me what you know so far, Melanie."

"I know about the debris and the Orb. Do you understand what I am talking about?"

"Yes. I've seen both."

I couldn't believe what I just heard. "You've seen the Orb?"

"Your father was very protective of it. It took him a while to even divulge it to me, and how it came to him. I think he finally did so only because we couldn't continue our research without letting me know how he came upon his theory. Which, of course, was via the Orb."

"What theory?" I asked.

"About the Ley Lines and relational positioning to the earth's energy field. It is a rather amazing theory, but it seems to have a ring of truth. The problem is, we never were able to continue. He disappeared, and was so secretive I didn't have a clue on how to contact him. He'd always been the one to seek me out. Very mysterious in that regard. Other than the information he shared about you, I knew nothing else in regards to him *or* your family."

I needed a moment to think. Where do I go next with this? I knew I was running out of time, so I jumped right to the biggest question of all. "Do you have the Orb?"

"No, of course not. He would never let it out of his sight. But what an amazing device. I still can't figure out how it worked, or how it projected the hologram."

"The what?"

"Oh, of course. I suppose you haven't seen it. Let me explain. A hologram is a three-dimensional image, unlike a photograph, which is two-dimensional. However, the Orb projected this hologram into the space above it. Think of it like a movie projector projecting an image onto a movie screen, but here the image is projected into thin air and in three dimensions. Have you ever heard of Theatrum Orbis Terrarum?"

"No."

"It's Latin for 'Theatre of the Orb of the World', and it is literally a map of the world made back in 1570 by Abraham Ortelius. Really, it was a compilation of maps put together by him to make up the first full cartographic map of the entire earth…well, what they knew of it at the time, anyway."

I couldn't follow where he was going. "What does this have to do with the Orb?"

"That is how he named the device. The Orb. The Orb of Orbis Terrarum."

"What do you mean?"

"It's quite amazing, actually. When your father first activated the Orb, an image of the map appeared before us—the map of Theatrum Orbis Terrarum. But projected in three dimensions, so you can see elevations of the terrain. And the ships and sea monsters depicted on the map are also three-dimensional and animated. I guess whoever made this hologram liked to have a little fun as well. It is really quite something to see."

This was just crazy stuff. "Why would that image come up?"

"We wondered the same thing. But we soon discovered it was only an initial image, which opened and acted like a … how to describe it? A control panel, I guess. You could touch locations on the map and interact with them. We think it has multiple layers, and this is only the first one. We found out the locations on the map are relational to the concept of ley lines on earth, which most academia believe to be pseudo-science."

This was all very amazing, but he was getting way too much into specifics. I worried about getting disconnected, and I didn't have any more quarters.

"I'm going to run out of phone time. How can I find out more about the Orb?"

"I can show you."

"But you said you don't have it."

"I don't. I have a picture of it. Actually, I have film footage also, and of your father holding it. The new Super 8 cameras just came out back then. They were easy to load and use, so we decided to document our trips and research."

I leaned against the phone booth to prop myself up. I couldn't catch my breath. He had a film of my father. And of the Orb. I tried to focus. "I need to see the film. Can I come and see you? Is that okay?"

"Yes, of course. Your dad was an amazing individual. I'm really sorry to hear he's gone. It would be wonderful though, to meet his daughter and wife."

I couldn't tell him what was going on here. I didn't want to scare him, and I needed to see the film footage of my dad. "Okay, that would be great. How soon can we come up?"

"It is actually a good thing you called today. I'm leaving tomorrow to visit a colleague and continue some exploratory research we are conducting at his lab. I'll be gone for a couple of weeks."

Two whole weeks! I was disappointed. Then I realized it probably worked out anyway. It would give time for my grandmother to arrive, and for me to assess that whole situation. "Okay, I guess we will have to wait until then. What's your address?"

We worked out a date and the details. I told him I would call the day before I left to make sure he was back and things were still a go. I thanked him and hung up the phone. A few coins fell into the return slot. I didn't use up all the minutes, but came close. I took out a dime and a nickel.

I grabbed my bike and headed home. Frankie, Katch, and Beanie will freak out at this news. They would definitely want to go with me, and we can all go up in Frankie's car. But a thought hit me so hard, I pulled to the side of the road to stop for a second. I realized I probably shouldn't tell them. It would be too dangerous. I couldn't worry about them getting hurt or worse. And even if that didn't happen, they would all still be in a bunch of trouble.

As it is, when I leave, everyone will think I ran away. It wouldn't be good to have Frankie, Katch, and Beanie's parents think they did, too. I couldn't put them or their parents in that position. Me? I didn't have any parents anymore to worry about. I needed to go. I had no choice. But I do have a choice with my friends. I decided I couldn't even tell them about this because they would insist on going, or even worse, try to talk me out of it. And I wouldn't let them do that. I had to see the professor and that film.

I needed to think about this some more. What was the right decision? Having them along would be a big help. Going alone would be really scary. What if Major Burnham or the other bad guys found out what I was up to?

I checked the oncoming traffic, kicked onto my bike and headed home again. This was too big of a decision to make right now, especially if bad guys got involved. There was a lot to do and a lot to think about. I would definitely need a plan, and I would need Tom's help.

4th of July

We parked up on Palisades Heights and walked down a dirt road to the water tower. We carried a pile of blankets, a cooler full of food and drinks, and a bag of snacks. Frankie and Beanie knew about this place. Katch and I had never been here before. Frankie thought it would be the perfect place to spend the 4th watching fireworks. He said only a few kids from high school knew about it, so we hoped to have it to ourselves.

We planned this out a few days ago when Frankie told me his parents would be going out of town for the 4th, and Suzie would be spending the night at a girlfriend's house. That meant we would be able to use his Mustang.

Mrs. Fletcher went up to Desmond's in Seattle for a family barbeque and to watch the big fireworks display up there. She will be back tomorrow. She had been worried about leaving, but I told her I would be fine. Still, she didn't want to be gone more than overnight.

I liked the idea that Frankie wanted to do this, rather than take advantage of one of the empty houses. Just one more reason to be so into him. Beanie and Katch were all about the idea of coming up here as soon as we told them about it.

We walked through a last thicket of trees and came out into a clearing with a sweeping view from south to west, and all of the valley below.

"All right! We have it to ourselves." Beanie dropped his bag and ran onto a huge, round metal shape covering the ground in front of us.

"What is that?" I asked.

He jumped and smashed his feet on the surface. We heard a big reverberating sound, like a giant drum. "This is the water tower."

I guess I imagined a regular water tower, on legs and sitting high in the sky. But the top of this water tower was level with the ground where we stood. I walked between two big rocks stationed in front of it, maybe there to keep someone from driving onto the thing. I heard little echoes of my footsteps. Once I got to the far edge, I understood.

The tower was built into a steep hillside. Level with the ground at the top of the hill, while the other side was exposed where the hill abruptly dropped off. I peered over the side to see a distance of about thirty feet to the ground below. The hill sat higher than any of the other hills for quite a distance, so it had an amazing view.

"Pretty awesome, huh?" Frankie said.

"Yeah, pretty awesome," I agreed. It was around eight-thirty in the evening and the sun hovered above the horizon on our right, getting ready to set. We would have a perfect view. The sky was clear of any clouds, and the temperature hit the mid-eighties earlier, so now it was cooling down to be a perfect evening. A slight breeze helped keep us cool.

Frankie pointed to a cluster of buildings off in the distance. "That's Tualatin over there, and Durham."

I squinted to see where he was pointing. It was right into the sun.

He continued, "I think they will have some sort of display. We may see something from Wilsonville way to the south," he pointed. "Nothing major, though. That all happens north of us in Portland, and we won't be able to see those shows. But there should be a ton of fireworks shot off all over the place. And those can get pretty big."

"Yeah," Beanie added. "And some illegal ones too, which should look really bitchin'."

We spread the blankets out and sat down.

Beanie pulled his transistor radio out of his bag. He tuned it to KGW, and we heard the DJ talking about the fireworks displays in the area. "… and we will try to keep to an Independence Day theme as we spin the vinyl for you tonight. Here is Paul Revere and the Raiders hit, *Just Like Me*."

"This is pretty amazing." I took in the view. It felt so good sitting here with friends and being able to forget everything else for a while.

I laid out some food I brought from home. There was salami, cheese and crackers, sliced apples, grapes, along with some Lays potato chips and other snack items.

Katch put her hands out to stop us before anyone could dig in. "Hey, before we go on a fooder, we'd better get a buzz on."

I looked at her, not understanding, "Fooder?"

She nodded at my question. "This seems like the perfect time for a joint," then reached into her purse, pulled out a little white stick and held it out for me to see. "Fourth of July, sunset, and a bunch of munchies waiting to be scarfed down. What better time?"

"I've never gotten high," I told her. I knew it was the 'in thing' to do, but should I? Would I like how it made me feel? I heard it can make you pretty goofy. I had been dying to tell them all about Professor Lofton and the Orb, but just couldn't. Maybe this would help me forget about it and relax.

"Well, now is as good a time as any, especially with all this great food to drool over afterward," Beanie said.

I looked over at Frankie. He smiled. "Why not?"

Katch took out a zippo lighter and lit the joint. She coughed a little and then held it out to me. I studied it for a second, hesitant to take it.

"Here, let me demonstrate." Beanie took the joint. "Inhale and then hold it in like this." He took a big puff and made a show of holding his breath.

He handed it to me. I took a puff and immediately coughed it out. It burned my throat.

Beanie exhaled. "Oh, should have warned you about that. It's a little rough taking it in. Try again, but inhale slower."

I tried again and was able to keep it in this time, but just barely. I handed it to Frankie and held my breath as long as I could before letting it out. I didn't feel anything. "I don't think it's working."

"Give it time," Katch said. "It will. This is good stuff."

We passed the joint around. When it got short and hard to hold, Katch took out what she called an alligator clip. It had a little chain of porcelain beads with two colored feathers dangling from the end.

I must have given her a strange look because she said, "No, this is not part of my Hopi medicine kit. It's simply a roach clip."

She put the joint on it so it could be smoked right down to the end. I stopped after one more puff, a little wary of what it would do. Everyone else kept at it until it was gone.

I wondered what it would feel like when I suddenly started laughing—at absolutely nothing. I couldn't stop. Everyone else joined in and before you knew it, we were all rolling around on the blankets, doubled over in laughter. It lasted long enough that my sides hurt. Eventually we wound down to where we could catch our breath and get control of ourselves.

I looked around at the scene. The light from the setting sun made everyone glow in warm tones of amber. "So, this is what it feels like." I studied my fingers in the light, as if I had never really seen them before. The low angle of the sun caught the wavy ridges of my fingerprints, all parallel and even, like the lines of a recently plowed golden field. Everything seemed new and fresh to me.

I looked over at Frankie. "I need to tell you something." It came out before I could stop myself. For a moment there, I wanted to tell him what happened with the professor and my plan.

He saw my expression. "What? You sure are serious all of a sudden."

I didn't know what to do. *Why did I say that?* I had to get out of it. "Oh, uh, I was just thinking that we're going to have to try some of this when we are alone together sometime."

He gave me an odd look, like he knew that wasn't what I had planned to say. He must have decided to drop it because he slowly nodded, then said, "Sounds like a plan to me."

Beanie cut in. "You know that was an oxymoron, don't you?"

I looked at him. "What?"

"Alone together. Opposites. How can you be alone and together at the same time? That's what an oxymoron is."

"You're seriously joking, right? I know what an oxymoron is," I told him.

"See, you did it again."

"Oh, I did, didn't I?" I giggled. "I'm clearly confused." Obviously, the pot was having its effect.

They all laughed.

"What?" I asked. They stared at me, goofy smiles on their faces.

Frankie said, "You did it again."

"Yep. Come on," Beanie challenged, "you're on a roll. Shoot us another one."

I had to think.

"Jumbo shrimp," Katch cried out. She broke into a big smile. "Sorry. It just came to me. I love them, and always wondered how they could be both big and small at the same time."

"Right on, girlfriend. That's a good one," Beanie told her.

"You mean stuff like deafening silence?" Frankie asked. "I never quite got that one."

"Yeah, or dull roar," I added.

"Don't forget silent scream," Beanie threw in.

"Or loud whisper," Katch said, in a loud whisper.

"Oh, that was awful good," I told her. We were all laughing, and could hardly contain ourselves at this point.

"Who comes up with these things anyway?" Frankie asked, trying to serious up.

"Oh, my God," Beanie howled, falling back on the blanket. "My mind is going into freezer burn."

This was getting way out of hand, and my cheeks were hurting from smiling so much. "Okay, stop already!" I shouted, trying to catch my breath. "We need to stop."

Katch looked at me, then blurted, "I give you even odds we don't." She rolled over in hysterics, looking up at me. "Sorry, I couldn't help myself."

"Oh, man. It's getting pretty ugly," Frankie added, doubling over with that one.

"Stop, Stop," I told them. "You guys are killing me from laughing so much. Stop!"

We had worn ourselves out, and it took a little while to settle down. Everyone gathered themselves together and we eventually caught our breath again.

Finally, Beanie said, "You know, the funny thing about it?"

We all turned to him as he sat up. We waited.

"What?" I finally asked.

He smiled at us. "Oxymorons seem weirdly normal."

We all moaned. Katch hit him in the shoulder, and Frankie pushed him back down.

We sat in silence for a while. I looked out at the valley below us. Everything seemed so surreal. The sun was just setting—a giant orange ball dropping imperceptibly below the hills to the west. And I don't remember ever seeing such a deep, deep blue to the sky above. A couple of stars had appeared. Or maybe they were Jupiter and Mars. Ode to you, Frank Sinatra.

A few fireworks sounded in the valley. Mostly firecrackers and M-80s. Once in a while a bottle rocket shot upwards, trailing little sparks before making its perceptible pop.

Frankie snuggled up next to me. I leaned into him. He felt so good. I really did love this guy.

"Hey, guess what I brought?" He looked at me with a mischievous smile.

"What?"

He pulled out a bota bag. I saw him bring it, but never thought to wonder what was inside.

"This, everyone, is Henry's famous Rhubarb Wine. I managed to score it yesterday once I knew we could pull this off. Believe me, it wasn't easy."

"What, Gallo isn't good enough for you?" Katch asked, obviously giving him a dig because it was her last name.

"Hey, beggars can't be choosers. It was hard enough getting this. His wine is very popular considering he doesn't ask for ID when you buy it from him."

He passed me the bag. I popped off the top and sprayed a stream into my mouth. It was very sweet, but tasted really good. No wonder it was so popular. We passed the bag around.

It was right about then the munchies hit. We all dove into the goodies I brought. I can't remember when a slice of salami and cheese on a Ritz cracker tasted so good.

The sun, now gone, left behind darkness and shadows. I looked up. More stars appeared above. "Where do you think they come from?" I asked.

Everyone looked at me, not quite understanding.

"The aliens. You all do realize this is the twentieth anniversary of the crash at Roswell?"

"Wow," Frankie said. "I have been so focused on it being the 4th for the fireworks and such, I never realized it was also the day your dad got the debris."

"And the Orb," Beanie added.

"Grandmother thinks from Orion," Katch said.

I looked at her. "What do you mean?"

"It was the constellation she pointed to the night she called them your Sky People."

I looked up at the sky, now bright with stars. I'd thought about what her grandmother said a bunch, and still couldn't even come close to figuring out what she meant. "I still don't understand. I mean, how can they be my Sky People?"

"Maybe we'll find out one day," Beanie said. "I'm sure if that is the case, then the next time they take a vacation to earth, they will want to drop by to visit their relative."

I gave him a look. "Sure, Beanie. I'll give you a call when it happens so you can come help carry their luggage into the house for the stayover."

Katch looked up at the darkening sky. "There must be lots of them out there. It can't just be one species of alien."

"I've read a bunch of eyewitness reports in my NICAP newsletters," I told her. "And the descriptions of the aliens encountered are different enough to confirm there are multiple species.

Think of it. How many stars there are in our galaxy alone, and then how many galaxies there must be. And the millions, if not billions of planets out there. And no doubt a whole bunch that sustain life. We are kidding ourselves to think we are the only planet with intelligent life forms."

"And myopic," Beanie added. "Which is a good example of why we should be careful in using the word 'intelligence' when applied to the human race. In fact, there is my final example of an oxymoron for you tonight—human intelligence."

Frankie chuckled. "Beanie, for someone way out there himself, you sometimes say some pretty down-to-earth stuff."

"Right you are, Kemosabe."

I looked up at the stars again as more appeared, and wondered why everyone felt I had such a connection to them. I guess I didn't want to admit it, but somehow I knew they were right.

It was totally dark now and the fireworks were underway. Some were right in the neighborhood below and exploded not far from us. Others were spread out all across the valley. A regular commercial display began over in Tualatin like Frankie thought might happen. And way off in the distance, another one in Wilsonville. Plumes of color all across the valley as far as I could see; the hint of spent gunpowder drifting to us on the breeze.

Frankie put his arm around me. I leaned into him and gave him a kiss. I could see the reflection of the fireworks in his eyes. Little flickers of color dancing about his pupils—which were very dilated, by the way. I laughed. He looked at me and smiled, then leaned down for a kiss. I loved the softness of his lips. I let them linger there for a moment.

We separated when a big firework happened right in front of us. We weren't in danger, but it was close enough to make us all jump. I watched the celebration as trails of sparks flew from the darkened valley floor and exploded in giant balls of color. I could barely make out any details in the valley now, other than streetlights that marked the roads, and the occasional house light not blocked by Oregon's abundance of trees. Off in the distance to the west, I could see the I-5 freeway marked by headlights and taillights of those who apparently needed to get somewhere important at this special hour.

I leaned into Frankie again. He put his arm around me. We were all silent, watching the display and listening to Beanie's transistor radio, which played a rolling orchestral arrangement they said was matched to some far-off fireworks display.

And it made me wonder—what fireworks were still ahead in my future?

Saying Goodbyes

"But, Mrs. Fletcher. Do you really have to go?"

"Now, honey, your grandmother will be here in a few hours. Captain Thornton called last night and said he would be picking her up today, and expected to get here sometime before noon. The two of you will have a lot going on. My presence would only get in the way. I think it best if I am gone when she arrives."

She was packing her suitcases in the spare bedroom where she had been staying. I sat on the edge of the bed watching. She was very particular in how she folded and packed her clothes, but I wouldn't expect otherwise. I dreaded her leaving, just as much as I dreaded the arrival of the unknown.

"Now you need to understand something, Melanie. I know this is a big deal to you, but it is also as big a deal to your grandmother. You're not the only one who has had the rug pulled out from under them. Your grandmother disrupted her life in offering to come all this way, just so you can stay in the safety of your own home."

"We don't know if that is for sure."

"It will be, at least until the two of you can figure things out. Better than having you whisked away to England right off the bat."

I nodded in agreement. "You got that right."

"So be respectful when she gets here. I know how you teenagers can get all moody over things. Don't be doing that to her."

"I won't," I promised, which kind of thwarted how I wanted to be.

She closed the suitcase, set it on the floor, put another on the bed, then took the rest of her clothes out of the dresser and continued packing.

"You're not leaving because of your color, are you?"

Mrs. Fletcher stopped packing for a moment and gave me an inquisitive look. "Now, why would you say that, child?"

"I don't know. Maybe she could be prejudiced?"

"And why would that matter anyway? No, I think I would get in the way is all, when the two of you should be focused on each other. Does that make sense to you?"

"I guess so, but what if I don't like her?"

"Well, then you had better look inside yourself as to why that would be," Mrs. Fletcher said.

"What if she turns out to be an old witch or something? You know, all mean and a face full of warts."

"Then I guess you would have good reason, but making up such things is not. You might be surprised by her." She nodded toward the closet. "Get me the rest of those clothes, won't you, honey?"

I grabbed the last bunch of blouses and laid them on the bed. "I hope I like her. It would be a big help if I'm going to get stuck with her for the rest of my life."

She took a blouse off its hanger, folded it, and put it in the suitcase. "No one ever has to get stuck with anyone. You will be eighteen in a few years, and you can make your own decisions then, if you don't like her."

"I guess so. And if I don't, I hope those years go by fast."

Mrs. Fletcher finished packing the blouses and looked around the room. "Enough of that. And just as well. It looks like I am finished and the morning is getting on, anyway." She closed the suitcase, set it on the floor and smoothed out the bed cover with her hand.

She stood there for a moment, staring down at the bed. She must have been thinking of something. She turned to me. There was a touch of sorrow in her eyes for a moment, and then she shrugged it off. "Here. Help me carry these suitcases to my car."

She picked one up and I grabbed the other. I followed her down the hall to the front door. She set the suitcase down and turned to me. "Melanie, honey, I want you to know you mean a whole lot more to me than you may ever know. God did a great thing bringing you into my life, though the method by which such things happen is the mystery of His wisdom. I guess He can always find a silver lining for a dark cloud." She took the suitcase from my hand and set it down. She held my shoulders and said, "I know you have the soul of an angel. There is no doubt to that. And it is because you are an angel, you have forgiven me my sins. Thank you." She pulled me into her and gave me a big hug.

I threw my arms around her and hugged as tight as I could. "I'm not sure I deserve to be compared to an angel, Mrs. Fletcher, but I do know one thing. I couldn't have survived all of this if you hadn't been here. So, maybe you're the angel. And what you said about God, well, that seems pretty right on to me." I didn't want her to leave. It was as if I were turning to a new chapter in a book with no idea of where it was going, but couldn't stop reading. I closed my eyes and cried.

She pulled me from her shoulder so she could look into my eyes. Seeing the tears, she took a handkerchief from her sleeve and dabbed at them. "Don't you think you are rid of me. I won't let that happen. I raised three sons, but never had a daughter. Well, God seemed to notice that, too. It has been a blessing having you fill such a void. So, I'm not about to let you go. We will work it out to see each other, understand?"

I nodded.

"I'm not far away in Portland, so expect we can figure out a way for you and your friends to get there, even if I have to come collect you myself."

"I would really like that, Mrs. Fletcher."

She picked up a suitcase. "Come on, I hate drawn-out good-byes." I grabbed the other one and we took them to her car. She put them in the trunk, gave me a quick hug, got into the car, closed the door, and rolled down the window.

Spots of morning sunlight filtered through the trees and landed on her face in warm, dancing tones. It made her eyes shine.

"Goodbye Mrs. Fletcher. I'm really going to miss you."

"And I you, honey." She got really serious all of a sudden. "Now, you be careful. It seems the whole world is exploding around you for some reason, so you need to do everything you can to remain safe. You understand?"

I nodded. "Thank you, Mrs. Fletcher. I will."

She backed the car out and drove away, and by doing so, took with her any sense I had of stability.

Emilee's Arrival

I tucked the sheet end under the mattress and folded down the bedspread. Katch did the same on the other side. I hadn't touched Mom's room since she died, and I think Mrs. Fletcher knew it was off limits, so she had left it alone.

But we had to get it ready now for my grandmother. So, this morning we dusted, cleaned, put on fresh sheets, and cleared out Mom's clothes from the dresser and closet, boxing them up and storing them in the spare bedroom now that Mrs. Fletcher was gone. I left everything else alone. Since her death, I haven't been able to get myself to go through her jewelry box or any other personal things.

"What do you think she will be like?" Katch asked.

"I have no idea. Probably old and wrinkled and only able to move around with the help of a cane."

We were done in the bedroom, so headed down the hall to the kitchen and the boys.

"I doubt she's that bad," Katch said. "How old is she anyway? She would have to be a hundred to be as bad as you think."

"I don't know. I'm not sure how old she was when she had my mom. Maybe she was sixty."

Katch laughed. "No one has kids when they're sixty.

We walked into the kitchen to see the boys hanging out at the breakfast table. I went to the fridge and took out a can of Dr.

Pepper. "You want something?" I asked her. I could see the boys had already helped themselves.

"Sure. Have you got an RC?"

I pulled one out and handed it to her. She popped it open and took a sip. We joined the boys at the table.

"Hey, you guys, thanks for hanging in here for me and being my backup. I really appreciate it." I'm not sure how I would have been able to handle this if they weren't here.

"You know we wouldn't let you face this alone. Right?" Katch said.

Beanie gave me a wide grin. "I'm just cooling it here so I can see the big reveal when she walks through that door."

The big reveal—I didn't like that thought, because I still didn't have a clue what she would be like.

He must have noticed, so quickly followed it up. "Anyway, I know you're capable of handling whatever that is—um, I mean, she is."

"Everything will be fine, Mel," Frankie reassured me. "Nothing to worry about."

I so wanted to believe him, but I was leaning more toward Beanie's perspective. I needed a distraction. "Maybe I should get the appetizers out. What do you think, Katch?"

Mrs. Fletcher had made up a bunch of stuff early this morning before I even got up. She said it would be good to have something for them to eat when George and my grandmother arrived.

Katch looked at the boys, who suddenly lit up at the suggestion. "Yeah, I guess so, as long as Beanie and Frankie don't eat everything before they get here."

"I doubt that could be possible. Mrs. Fletcher doesn't do anything in moderation when it comes to food. There will be plenty."

I walked into the kitchen and took out three trays wrapped in Saran Wrap. Katch followed me in. I handed her two of the trays and carried one myself, along with some small plates and napkins. We set them on the table. As usual, Mrs. Fletcher had outdone herself. Katch sat down again and I removed the wrap from one of the trays.

"Are you nervous?" Frankie asked.

I looked up from what I was doing. "Of course. Wouldn't you be when meeting a grandmother you've never even seen before?"

"Dumb question, ditwad," Beanie told Frankie.

I could see Frankie felt he needed to explain himself. "I guess I'm just curious as to why your mom kept it such a secret, that she was alive and living in England."

"Well," Katch said, "she'll find out the reason soon enough."

"It's not the first thing I am going to bring up," I told them as I took the wrap off the last tray. "I think that kind of thing should wait. I want to get a feel for her first." I wadded the wrap into a ball, walked into the kitchen and tossed it into the trash can. Then the doorbell rang.

We all looked at each other. I froze into a statue. I couldn't move. Katch saw this and got up. She went through the archway to the living room and answered the door.

"Hello, Katch," I heard George say.

Frankie and Beanie jumped from their seats, practically knocking each other down on their way to get a look.

"Boys, will you help Mrs. Harris by getting her trunks out of the boot?" George asked.

I heard Beanie question him. "Trunks? Boot?"

"Yes, trunks. Mrs. Harris informed me that's what chests are called in England. And the boot is the trunk of the car."

"Okay, so get the trunks out of the trunk," Beanie said, chuckling.

I heard the commotion of them going out the door and soon returning, then the sound of heavy thumping on the living room floor, intermixed with a little grunting. This happened a couple of times. *How much did she bring?*

I still couldn't move. I felt weak and was having a hard time breathing. I took slow, deep breaths, trying to get a rhythm to them. I knew I would have to face her, but geez, this was going to be hard.

"Where is Melanie?" George asked.

"In the kitchen," Katch answered.

"Well, I guess I will need to go in there and introduce myself," a voice said. "I'm sure she has all sorts of ideas about me. I certainly can't blame her for hiding." It had to be my grandmother, but it didn't sound like a grandmother's voice. It sounded too young. Too full of vigor. Too positive.

I stepped into the archway so she could see me. And I would be able to see her.

She looked more like my mother's older sister than a grandmother, and very cosmopolitan. Kind of like the models in the fashion magazines Katch and I went through at the library when she was working on my look.

She reminded me of Audrey Hepburn, from *Breakfast at Tiffany's,* just older. She wore a white, wide-brimmed hat with black accent netting that flowed over the edge and partially covered her eyes. A matching silk ribbon surrounded the hat, with a big bow tie at the front. Multiple strings of cream pearls were wrapped delicately about her neck, and accented the black and white fitted dress she wore. Her arms were covered in long-sleeve white gloves. The strap of a small black and white handbag rested in the crook of her delicate elbow. She was tall and somewhat thin, different from my mother who had more curves. But I could tell. She was definitely my grandmother.

Maybe the thing that bothered me about my mental comparison to Holly Golightly in *Breakfast at Tiffany's*, was that although Holly looked like she was well-put-together, she was actually very flighty and didn't have her act together at all. I hoped this would not be the case with my grandmother.

I glanced over to Katch, who stood by the front door, her eyes as wide as could be, no doubt as shocked as I was by her appearance.

George saw me in the archway. "Melanie, this is Emilee Harris, your grandmother."

Emilee pulled off her gloves as she walked toward me. "Oh my, you are a grown woman, aren't you?" She leaned in and kissed me on the cheek. The netting tickled my nose. She stood back and studied me. "Look at you. I am completely gobsmacked at how beautiful you have turned out to be."

I heard Beanie and Frankie snicker a little at that. But I couldn't take my eyes off her. I couldn't help but stare. She noticed and did a quick spin.

"Do you like it?" she asked. "I had to make a proper entrance. I couldn't just appear in some old rags now, could I?"

"No, I guess not," I answered.

"When I arrived late last night, I knew I would be absolutely knackered, so arranged for accommodations at the Benson Hotel in Portland. A quite marvelous place, really. I wanted to be all fresh and pretty for you. I don't suppose I am what you expected, at least by the look on your face."

I smiled. "No, not really. Maybe someone more...matronly."

"Right so. Well, I haven't exactly had the practice of being a grandmother now, have I?"

"No, I guess you haven't."

"Nor you a granddaughter, so we will just have to figure these things as we go. And we can start by having you call me Emilee. I feel much too young to be called grandmother." She turned around and looked at Frankie, Beanie, and Katch. "And these must be your chums. Very American and hip, I see."

George jumped in. "Let's get these trunks to her room." He looked at me.

"Oh, take them back to my mother's old room." I looked at my grandmother. "I hope that's okay, for you to stay in her room." I never thought about whether she would want to stay in there or not.

"It will be perfect," she reassured.

It was then I saw her luggage actually did consist of real trunks. Two big ones. She also had two more standard size suitcases and a tote bag.

She noticed where I was looking. "It is all I could manage to bring. We will see how things go. Perhaps a trip shopping down the road."

George and the boys lugged the trunks through the hall and into the bedroom.

"Can I get you something to drink?" I asked.

"Have you any tea?"

I hadn't remembered that tea was a big deal to the English. I drank some once in a while, but it was Lipton, and most of the time over ice. I doubted it was up to the level of English tea. I didn't want to disappoint her, but had no options. "I have some Lipton tea, if that will do?"

"Lipton." She seemed to be searching her memory. "Yes, it has been years. Lipton will be just fine. With a little milk if you have any."

"Sure." I went into the kitchen to put the tea kettle on the stove.

Emilee followed me in through the archway. "Oh, my. Did you make all of these hors d'oeuvres yourself? Oh, look at those little tea sandwiches. How marvelous."

"No. Actually, Mrs. Fletcher made those. She was looking after me until you got here."

"And, where is she?"

"She left this morning. She didn't want to intrude."

"A shame. I would have liked to thank her. She was gracious in attending to you."

She set her purse and gloves on the kitchen counter, and took off her hat. She had sunny blonde hair, tied up in a bunch. It reminded me of Tippi Hedren's hair in the Alfred Hitchcock movie, *The Birds*, where she meets Rod Taylor in Davidson's Pet Shop. Now, with her hat off, she let it down and it fell across her shoulders in wavy curls. She fluffed it and straightened it with her fingers. I couldn't help but notice how similar it looked to my own.

"Well, I must try a tea sandwich in honor of your Mrs. Fletcher. I really am quite famished." She studied one of the trays and then selected a sandwich and took a bite. "Excellent."

The boys came in and sat down at the table, both grabbing a plate from the stack and filling it with food from the trays.

George stood in the archway. "I best be getting back to the station. It's been a real pleasure meeting you, Mrs. Harris."

"George. You don't need to leave," I told him. "I want you to stay and have some food."

"I'd love to Melanie, but work calls. We are a little short-handed today. I'd better get back."

I walked over to him and gave him a big hug. "Thank you for picking up Emilee."

"I'm around whenever you need me. You know that."

Emilee walked over to George. "Captain Thornton, thank you for your kind help. I can see my Melanie has been in good hands."

"Well, you two have a lot of catching up to do. I'll leave you to it." He nodded to Emilee and left.

She rejoined the kids at the table while I went in and checked on the kettle. I waited for it to boil and thought about how she was nothing like I expected. Then I had to wonder, how could she ever be comfortable living here? There was no way she would want to stay in this house. Not the way she looks and talks. She probably lives in a castle back in England. I tried to put these thoughts out of my mind. I needed to give it a chance. I needed to stay positive.

The kettle whistled. I grabbed a cup and saucer from the cup-board, filled the cup with hot water, set the tea bag next to it on the saucer, and took them to the table along with a small con-tainer of milk. Emilee was sitting down and had a plate in front of her with a few appetizers on it. She was telling Frankie, Beanie and Katch something, and they were all hanging on her words. "…well, it's not really a castle, just a bunch of ruins now. I'm afraid a number of battles over history, along with Father Time himself, did some fairly serious damage to it."

Katch saw me enter. "Did you know your family owned a castle?" she asked excitedly.

Oh, my God. She did live in a castle. "No. Of course I didn't!" I realized I had said this with more than a touch of hostility in my voice.

"Umm. Sorry," Katch apologized. "I forgot you haven't been in touch." Her eyes brightened again. "But it's true."

I looked over to Emilee, who nodded. "Owned is the key word there. Long ago. It is now held in public trust. As I was telling your chums, we Harrises have a lengthy history in Eng-land. In fact, we are descendants of James Harris, Second Earl of Malmesbury, and once Governor of the Isle of Wight in the eighteen-hundreds. That happens to be where I have my home now."

"Do you really live on an island?" Frankie asked.

"Yes. It isn't a big island. I've lived there, off and on, since I was a child. I have a place there that has been in the family for generations." She took a small bite from a strawberry. "It is now a bed and breakfast."

"What is that?" Katch asked.

"The home is a bit bigger than I need. And, being in the south of England, and on the Channel, the island draws quite a few holiday-goers. So, I rent out rooms to visitors. We call it a bed and breakfast, because we serve a nice morning meal to our guests as a good start to their day."

"You can really make a living doing that?" Beanie asked.

"Oh, I seem to get by," Emilee answered.

"Obviously," Katch had to add.

"Well, it wasn't what I set out to do. I suppose, when we are all young, like you are now, we have certain ideals—plans to change the world. Just as you young ones are protesting the Vietnam War and demanding civil rights today, I was as vocal and my morals as pure back then."

I perked up at this. "What do you mean?"

"When I was young, after university, I decided I needed to do my part to make the world a better place." She set a pose. "I haven't looked like this all my life."

"How did you do that?" Frankie asked.

"Where else do you change the world, but in the places that need it the most. I think I was about twenty-one. I had just graduated from the LSE: the London School of Economics and Political Science. I went there for that very reason. I thought the best way to make change would be through those very things. Or so it seemed to me.

"It turned out to be rather scandalous though. Our family had attended either Oxford or Cambridge for generations, so I immediately became the black sheep." She rolled her eyes at this. "As far as for my family, I felt change would be good for them as well. Why must we do everything the same?"

And now she was doing exactly that, changing even before my eyes, her layers unfolding, and exposing someone I didn't see when she first walked in.

"In my second year at LSE, the school adopted its Latin motto: *reum cognoscere causus*. In English it means, 'knowing the causes of things.' I took that motto to heart right away because it speaks to truth. It is by knowing the cause of things, that we are then able to right many wrongs."

I sat there, a little in shock. I can't remember ever hearing Latin in my life before, and now I have heard it twice in only a matter of days. With both quotes having meaning to what I'm going through. First, the 'Orb of the World,' which seems to be set to open up a whole new world for me. And now, 'knowing the cause of things,' so true to what I am feeling, because I could understand so much more if I were to understand this path I am traveling, and whatever was driving my destiny.

She continued. "Well, I am diverging. The point is when I graduated, I needed to do something. While working toward graduation, I became involved in an organization called 'Save the Children.' It is a rather large organization today."

"I think I've heard of it," Katch said.

"Well, young lady, I was actually at Lady Catherine Cortney's Chenye Walk house in Chelsea in 1919 when the organization was first formed by Eglantyne Jebb and her sister Dorothy. I learned about the meeting while in Trafalgar Square a few days earlier, which is only a short walk from the University. It was as if I were meant to be there, because it was the same day Eglantyne stood in the square handing out flyers showing a starving German child."

I felt a little jolt run through me when she said she was meant to be there. *Is this destiny again?*

"She was protesting the British naval blockade of Germany, which had continued even after World War One ended. The blockade prevented needed food from getting to the German children. Those poor little ones were dying by the hundreds daily. It wasn't right, and she felt it her charge to show the state what was happening and demand we stop the blockade. They arrested her. But doing so only brought more publicity to her cause. I even skived off a class to go to the trial. That is how I met her and Dorothy. She was fined five pounds, but the media attention was tremendous. It is what drove them to form 'Save the Children.' But my studies didn't allow for me to become more involved at that time. However, once I graduated in 1921, all that changed. It was time for me to do something, so I went to Russia."

"Russia? Why Russia?" I asked.

"Well. That is a long story, probably better left to another time. I am eight hours ahead of you." She looked at the wall clock. "It is just noontime here, but it is eight o'clock in the evening in England. I would like to get my things in order and rest for a while."

Everyone looked a little disappointed. She could see that. "How about this," Emilee offered "what if you all come back for dinner tonight and we can talk some more? Then I will tell you all about what I did during the Russian revolution, and about the Povolzhye Famine of 1921." She looked at me, "And how I met your grandfather there."

The Trials of Povolzhye

"Hey, George, it's Melanie." I leaned against the wall, twirling the phone cord around my finger.

"You sure managed to track me down."

"I called the station. They said you were off work and at home. Have you made plans for dinner tonight?"

"I'm staring at a can of SpaghettiOs, why?"

"I'd like to invite you to dinner. I feel bad you didn't get to stay after helping Emilee this morning. Can you come?"

I heard a laugh on his end of the line. "Did I mention the can of SpaghettiOs? Sure, that would be great."

"Oh, good." I thought for a second. "Maybe we could get some chicken from Specks?"

Lake Oswego had a new Kentucky Fried Chicken place down on 'A' and 1st, and their chicken tasted amazing. I realized frozen dinners wouldn't exactly impress my grandmother, and I didn't trust myself to cook one of Mrs. Fletcher's special dinners she had taught me — not for something as important as Emilee's first American meal here. "Can you pick it up? I mean, I could always send Frankie to get it."

"And what, have him break the law driving illegally? He already does enough of that with his Mustang. Seems to have forgotten the permit I issued was only to drive to school and back. I'd be happy to pick it up, and to buy."

"Not a chance. You are an invited guest. Guests don't buy, so either you come here and get some money from me first, or promise I can pay you back."

"Does anyone ever win an argument with you?"

"Not that I've ever noticed."

"Okay. What time and for how many?"

"With you, there will be six of us, so get their biggest bucket, and be sure to pick up enough of the Colonel's sides to fill it all out."

"What time?"

"I think seven. Will that work?"

"I can make it work."

"Cool, and thanks."

The doorbell rang. I opened it to see George holding a big Kentucky Fried Chicken bucket, a box, and some bags of sides.

"How'd it go?" I asked.

"The wait wasn't too bad," he said. "You know how popular that place is, especially on a Friday night. I didn't know if the bucket would be enough, so I got a box also."

I grabbed the box and one of the bags.

Beanie walked into the living room from the kitchen with a stack of plates. "Hey, I heard there's an actual bank vault in there. That's pretty weird, huh?"

"It was left over from when Oswego State Bank used the building," George said. "The manager keeps it as an office now. I always kid him that I'll close the gate and lock him up if I catch him speeding again."

"You run a tight town, Captain," I told him.

We carried everything into the dining room. Katch and Frankie joined us with napkins and silverware.

Frankie had obviously overheard our conversation. "Must have been easier to leave the vault in there than haul it out."

"More like it wasn't an option," Beanie added. "I mean, how would you even do it?"

"Good point," Frankie said.

I went over to George, reached into my back pocket and took out some bills. He tried to wave me off, but I gave him a look. "Deal's a deal." I took his hand and turned it palm up, then counted six one-dollar bills into it. "Will this cover it?"

"More than enough," he said, reluctantly pocketing the money.

Emilee came down the hall. She wore a simple pair of beige capris pants and a white blouse. Nothing as fancy as when she arrived. "Hello, George. I'm pleased you could join us."

"As am I, Mrs. Harris."

Emilee took his hand and patted it. "Please, it's Emilee. And, if you wanted to be all proper about it, the correct title would be Miss Harris, but even that is a tad too formal. I'm afraid the opportunity to marry Melanie's grandfather never quite presented itself." She paused and looked around at everyone, then walked over to me, putting her arm around me as she led me to the dining room. "But then, learning more about such things is why we have all collected here to begin with, isn't it?"

I hadn't thought of that. It just now dawned on me she would have taken his last name if they had married.

We gathered around the table and spread the food out. George and Emilee sat at the ends of the table, while Katch and Beanie were on one side, and Frankie next to me on the other. I sat next to Emilee because I didn't want to miss a thing she said. We passed the food around as we talked.

Along with the world's best secret recipe chicken, we had mashed potatoes and gravy, the Colonel's special coleslaw, and corn on the cob, or *du'ji* as Katch taught everyone to say it in her native language.

That put Emilee on a long line of questions about the Hopi Indians, their history and geography. She seemed truly interested in what Katch shared with her, and it seemed Katch took to her pretty quickly because of it.

Beanie cut in. "I've never been on an airplane. What was it like?"

"Long," Emilee answered, drawing out the word for emphasis.

Emilee told us everything about it. We peppered her with questions, as none of us had ever been on a plane before. We wanted to know every detail. I decided this had been a good way to start out. Small talk. It's not like I could have jumped right in and asked her about my grandfather. But now I was way too curious to wait any longer.

"Can you tell us about how you met my grandfather?"

She set her fork down on her plate and smiled. "I was wondering how long it would take you."

Everyone fell silent, waiting for her story. We had even stopped chewing for a moment.

"My, you are all intrigued, aren't you? Well, get on with your eating. No sense starving to death waiting for me to jibber-jabber away."

We all gave it our best efforts to commence eating again, but were really waiting for her to share her story. I spent all afternoon wondering what she was doing in Russia, and of even more importance, whether my grandfather was Russian. It obviously weighed on me, because a Russian had killed my father.

Emilee glanced at each of us, then settled in. "Well, I need to begin a little earlier than when I met your grandfather, but oh my, he was quite dashing." I could see it in her eyes, as if he were a vision standing once again in front of her. She took a

117

moment before continuing. "Let me see, I believe I had mentioned the Povolzhye Famine during the Russian Revolution. I was only twenty-one at the time. Oh, so young!"

I thought about how my relatives seemed to have a history of major events in their lives in their early twenties. First, with my mom and the crash outside Roswell. She was about twenty-four at that time, and now with my grandmother going to a country riddled with famine in the middle of a revolution and meeting my grandfather there. It made me wonder what would be waiting for me when I reached my twenties.

"When I told you earlier, I didn't want to show up here in rags, well, it was a bit in jest, because for most of the time I was in Russia, it was all I had to wear. Those of us there soon had a saying, and this was it: 'There is very little of almost nothing.'"

She pushed her coleslaw into a little pile on her plate, as if it were the whole of what she might have eaten while over there.

"You see, Russia had been devastated by one thing after another. First there were the four years of World War One, and right after that, the two years of the Bolshevik revolution. By 1921, Lenin had control of the country, though there were still pockets of resistance. But the civil war had decimated the food supplies, especially in the Volga Basin. Then a drought hit the area and most of the crops failed." She sat back in her chair and looked down at her plate. "We eat well these days, but imagine what it was like back then. There simply was no food to be had. Hundreds of thousands of children were starving and dying. There were even rumors of cannibalism."

We all moaned at hearing this. The chicken thigh I was nibbling on suddenly became less appetizing.

She looked at me. "I decided to join one of Eglantyne and Dorothy's Save the Children assemblages, which was soon to leave for Russia. They had amassed a train full of food and medical supplies to be sent to the town of Samara. We were to accompany it as the staff to dole it out. We took a ship from London down the Thames and across the English Channel to Antwerp, Belgium, and finally from there, a train into Russia. That trip was grueling enough, but nothing like what fell before my eyes as we entered the city of Samara in the heart of the Volga Basin. People packed the streets, little camps of raggedy makeshift tents everywhere. I later found out most of these people came from the countryside to the cities, hoping for work and food. Their farms were long abandoned as their crops failed due to the drought, and their animals died of starvation and were consumed.

"Mind you, this had been going on for years by the time I arrived there. A sea of terribly emaciated bodies lined up along the tracks as we pulled into the city, all staring at the train with blank looks on their faces, hope long washed from them. What little clothing they had was in rags, and some wore no clothing at all. It was such a saddening sight. I had a trunk of clothing I brought with me. It didn't last the first day. I gave away all my clothing except what I wore when we came into the city. After being there for most of a year, my clothing was in near-rags itself.

"There was an aid station already set up by those before us right outside the Camapa train station. We went to work as soon as we arrived. We would go out to find the children of the city and bring them to the aid station where we could give them a meal and first aid. My heart breaks as I think about the looks on their faces, thin little arms and legs, bellies distended. They were so grateful to have something to eat—and someone who cared."

She paused for a moment, looking around at us. "The diseases were terrible. It was like a laundry list: typhus, smallpox, influenza, typhoid fever, dysentery, cholera, even bubonic plague. It seemed a vicious circle. We would bring them in, nourish them, and then some disease would grab them up and whisk them away. I was about at the end of my rope, as you say here in America." She paused again, reliving that time, almost in a trance. "Luckily, it was then that I met your grandfather, and things changed."

She shook her head, as if to clear it and looked at me. "I think a short break would be good before I continue. I feel like I have been drudging along at the expense of all of you. It is a bit of a story to tell, and I'm only now getting to the good part. Why don't we clear the dishes? I brought some tea from England and have it unpacked. A nice cup would do me well, right now."

I could see the memories of Russia had affected her. I didn't want to stop because she was about to tell me about my grandfather, but it was easy to see a break would be good for her.

About Grandfather

We all worked together to finish the dishes, anxious to get back to her story. Katch put the left-overs in some Tupperware, and Frankie took the used chicken containers out to the garbage. The teapot sounded and Emilee moved about the kitchen setting up a service of tea for everyone. I took out a nice porcelain tea set my mother got from somewhere. I knew we had it, but I don't ever remember it being used before now.

We gathered in the living room. Emilee settled into the lounge chair while I sat on the couch with Frankie, Beanie, and Katch. George brought in a chair from the dining room and straddled it backwards, placing his large forearms on the high back, which creaked under the strain.

Emilee went about preparing the tea, asking each of us if we wanted milk and sugar, and how much. She was very formal about it all. I took a sip when she was done.

"Proper tea, don't you think?" she asked everyone.

"It's an excellent tea, Emilee," George said.

"I shall need to find a shop where I can get it here in the States. English tea has a formality not common to other teas. Don't you agree?"

We all nodded, though I had no idea what she meant. But it did taste good. Much better than the Lipton we had earlier in the day. We sat back and waited for her to start.

She picked up her cup and saucer from the table, and sat back in the lounge chair. After taking a sip, she asked, "Are any

of you familiar with the ARA—the American Relief Admin-
istration?"

We all shook our heads.

"It was an organization put together here in the States to help
ease the crisis in Russia. Of course, they have never formally
acknowledged America's help to this day, even though the
ARA brought hundreds of volunteers, and enormous amounts
of grain and food to feed millions of people every day. It made
our British efforts look puny in comparison. Though I knew it
was all needed, it was still not enough to save many young children from death." She took another sip before setting the tea
cup on the saucer again, turning the handle to face just so.
"Well, your grandfather worked for the ARA. He was an American."

I was relieved to hear he wasn't Russian. It would have been
a terrible feeling to know my grandfather came from the same
country that killed my father. I broke from my thoughts to focus
on Emilee again.

"One day while out gathering up my little street urchins, my
nickname for the children, he appeared, walking down the
street with a big box of food in his arms, handing out packages
to those huddled in the raggedy tents who were too weak to
make it to an aid station. Of all things, I suddenly became self-
conscious. Here I was dressed in rags, dirty and un-washed,
and hadn't seen a mirror in more than a month to check how
my hair looked. I hadn't even noticed or cared—until now,
when an unexpected sense of self-worth came over me. And
why? Because of your grandfather—such a sight. You see, the
Americans were a bit more equipped at their aid station than
we Brits. Their program was federally supported, where ours
was held together with string by women whose hearts were in
the right place, but bore very thin pocketbooks.

"His clothes were a touch dirty, but still in one piece, and he looked rather fresh, compared to all around us. He didn't notice me at first, not like I took notice of him. I suppose it was because I blended in with the surroundings, all dirty and such. He approached and offered me a package of food. I felt immediately embarrassed that he considered me one of the starving, perhaps even one of my urchins. I politely refused, telling him I was here for the same reason—to help those in need. He was obviously taken aback by this. Not only because I spoke the King's proper English, but more likely because it came out of such a disheveled body.

"He handed the rest of his packages to the children gathered about me. I suppose I looked like a rather bad version of Mother Goose. He offered to take me to his aid station to get cleaned up. Of course, I accepted. How could I refuse? When we arrived there, he showed me to a room where a makeshift shower had been set up. He left, and I took my time scrubbing layers of filth off my body, filth I had come so used to wearing—almost like it was a badge. When I finished, a woman arrived with a set of clothing. I was overwhelmed and cried when I saw it—something as simple as fresh clothing, not even new, and I sobbed like a child. It took me a while to collect myself. My eyes were red with tears. I knew I looked a sight, but could do little about it. I picked up a brush the woman had left and pulled at the knots in my freshly washed hair. Eventually I managed to get them out to where a brush ran freely through. My long hair once again looked blonde. I dried it as best I could on the towel provided and pulled it up, twirling it into a knot I had learned to tie that would hold onto itself, for there were no accessories available to do the job."

"What happened to him?" Beanie asked, interrupting her train of thought.

This came out of the blue, but I wanted to know too because something must have happened to him since he wasn't sitting here next to her. Then I wished Beanie hadn't asked because she got this forlorn look on her face. I knew that look, because I had found it staring back at me from a mirror twice in my life—once after Dad died, and then again with Mom.

"He disappeared."

That was it. She didn't keep going.

"Like, what kind of disappeared?" Frankie asked. "Just up and left you, or something else?"

She didn't answer right away. "Something else," she finally told us.

We all waited. She was obviously avoiding that topic. At least for now, anyway.

"We fell in love. Imagine falling in love in such a place. You would think it terrible, but it wasn't. In fact, it saved me. I didn't realize it until he came along, but I had become muddle-headed in all of this, letting myself whittle down to nothing. It was only after he brought me to my senses that I grasped the reason he handed me the food on that first day. He assumed I was one of the Volga people who hadn't eaten in months. It is hard for me to even remember, but he was probably right. I understand now that I felt too guilty at the time to eat anything myself when there were so many starving children." She looked at us, as if wondering whether we could possibly understand. "I was giving myself up to help these children, and didn't realize how close I came to dying myself. I probably would have, but he saved me."

"You haven't told us his name," Katch said. "Is there a reason?"

"I haven't? I didn't even notice. No, I'm proud of him. He went by Daniel. Daniel Grace. What a wonderful name."

I thought about how she put that. "What do you mean, went by?"

She considered my question for a while. Maybe to decide how to answer it, or not answer it.

"Because I don't know for sure if it was his name. But perhaps you are putting the cart before the horse. I will tell you why, but first I need to finish telling you about us."

I held back, though a dozen questions danced around in my head. If the others were like me, they had a ton of questions rolling around their heads as well. It all seemed like a story from a fairy tale.

"First, some more tea, I think." She started to get up. "Anyone else?"

"Oh, no you don't! You can't stop there," I told her.

Katch stood. "I'll boil some more water." She looked down at Emilee, "And you keep going with your story." She took the teapot and left the room.

"All right, then, good enough." She settled back in her chair. "I believe Daniel fell in love with me the moment I walked out of the room after a fresh shower, with a clean face and decent hair. I had somehow transformed from street urchin to romantic interest in that quick moment. I never thought to argue with his poor judgment. Why would I? There was something about him, something big. I didn't know what that might be, but it made me fall for him all the more."

We spent every moment we could together, which was hard under the circumstances. Each time we fell more in love. For me, it was as if Cupid's bow had flung a dozen arrows into my heart. And his love is what saved me. I gathered up my will and took better care of myself. I gained weight. I came to feel beautiful once again, or at least believed it for the way he looked at me with his compelling, deeply green eyes. I fell into them every time their gaze landed on mine.

"We had to steal our moments together. On the rare occasion, we were able to go for long walks. On one of them we happened upon a small, hidden valley seemingly untouched by the rest of our world. An underground stream seeped up and fed into the valley to make everything green. A small cluster of trees provided shade from the sun, with lush green moss growing under them, and white lilies all about. It became our haven. We never understood why others had not found this place. Perhaps it was for the sole reason it was meant to be our own. And it was there we first made love." She giggled. "I know. How could we? But how could we not?"

I pictured them in that valley together, resting on the cool moss under those trees. I felt as if I were one of the cupids, perched in a tree, watching their love grow.

Emilee sat back suddenly. "Then he was gone—disappeared. I asked about him at his aid station. I enquired of everyone who worked there, but no one had any idea of what happened to him, until I finally found a man who knew something. He pulled me aside and asked me, 'What exactly do you know about Daniel?' It made me wonder about how much I did know, which was really very little. It never occurred to me to ask such questions in such a place? We lived in the moment." She looked around the room at all of us. "It was, after all, fleeting, wasn't it? I told the man 'Not much.' He said, 'It is best you not ask about him anymore. It will be dangerous for you.' After that, he abruptly strode away.

"It made me wonder, had Daniel been a spy? There were still some uprisings going on—pockets of resistance. A rumor of one nearby had been going around the aid station before he disappeared. And Lenin was well on his way to control, no doubt a situation of great interest to the powers of the United States. It wasn't hard to work out the Americans could have used the ARA as a method to get their spies into Russia. But could he be one? Could that have been it? Was he killed while doing whatever he had been sent over there for? It sounds utterly ridiculous now, but I wanted to believe it. I know in my heart, he would not have left me for any other reason than he died doing whatever they had sent him there to do. It even made more sense to me after I spent some time reasoning it out. What had he been there for, anyway? He was so much bigger than simply being a worker in an aid station. I thought I must be right."

She stopped for a moment and set her cup and saucer on the table when Katch returned with a new pot of tea. She made a fresh cup, took a sip and set it down again on the table. She leaned back and put her hand on her belly. "Inside… that is not all I felt. Not more than a few weeks had passed when I realized I was pregnant. That changed everything. I needed to take care of my baby now—his baby. I arranged to leave. I had to leave. Once everyone found out about my condition, they all helped get me on the next train west, back to England. But when I arrived in Belgium, I knew I couldn't go back to my old life. Only ridicule would await me there. I wanted to find Daniel's family. I wanted them to know his child was inside me. I knew barely nothing about him. What I did know is that he grew up in a place called Lubbock—a small town somewhere in Texas."

I was shocked when I heard this. My mind spun with all the implications. My dad and mom lived there, and it was through his school he ended up at the crash site. Lubbock seemed to be the catalyst to everything happening now, and it all started with my grandmother going there to find my grandfather from a place as far away as Russia. It was too much to grasp. I shook it out of my thoughts so I wouldn't miss anything else she said.

"… made my way over the Atlantic Ocean to America. I had no idea your country was so large. It took many long months to work my way across it. All the time, I held hope that he had made his way home, unable to contact me to let me know. I arrived in Lubbock six months pregnant, hopeful to find his family. I did everything I could to locate them. I looked up the Grace family name in the phone directory, and made enquiries at the county register's office. But those with the last name Grace knew nothing about my Daniel. It was as if he had disappeared from the face of the earth. I ended up finding a little place to live, and having my daughter. There were many names I considered, but decided on Gloria because I knew although I was alone and Daniel had disappeared, he had left me with a glorious wonder…" she looked at me, "your mum."

I had so many questions for her, but she was finished. This had drained her, remembering a time in her life where she reached such tremendous highs and deep lows, all at the same time.

She got up. "I need to get some rest. I hope you don't think me rude, but I am rather drained. The time change has really befuddled me."

George jumped up first, seeming to have come out of a trance. "Please, Emilee. Get some rest. I am sure all of this has taken its toll."

She smiled. "Thank you, George." She pulled me up from the couch. "Will you be all right if I get some sleep?"

"Yes. Don't worry about me," I told her.

She leaned in, gave me a kiss on the cheek, and headed down the hall. I watched her go. It would take me a while to absorb everything she told us. It wasn't just like a fairy tale; it *was* a fairy tale.

I needed to think about it all. I wanted to know more about Lubbock and Emilee and my mom there. How did that all work, and how did my mom and dad end up being together there in 1947? There were so many questions.

There was one thought I couldn't get out of my head. It had come to me earlier because of the irony. My grandmother went to Russia to save their children in 1922. And Russia sent an agent here in 1966 to take the debris from my father, killing him in the process. I did the math. It was very possible that the Russian agent who killed Dad could have been the son of a child my grandmother saved.

Bull again

Bull leaned down with his hands against the front of his desk, pressing his palms into the sharp edge until he felt a nearly unbearable degree of pain. It had become a habit to keep himself focused in the moment. "Do you think it was Burnham?"

Miller finished pouring a cup of coffee at the credenza and walked over to sit in one of the chairs facing Bull's desk. "It had to be. He left Blue Book rather abruptly. I have feelers out and there is some indication he has hooked up with Brighton Ingram."

Bull raised his eyebrows at that. "The industrialist?"

"The same."

"That could be bad. He's not exactly Time Magazine's person of the year."

"Well, we do know he has a dark group he funds that does his dirty work. It looks like he activated them, and hired Burnham to go after the debris."

"It makes sense. If they could recover it and figure out how the technology works, it would make him millions."

Miller nodded. "It took a while, but my men in Oswego found a witness that saw Mrs. Simpson at a liquor store quickly exit a van and drive off in her car under great duress. It had to be Burnham in the van, and based on her reaction, he must have threatened her to turn over the debris."

"If he threatened to hurt the daughter, that would really explain her reaction."

"You're probably right. This all happened just before the accident. She must have been racing home to check on her. She was traveling at great speed when she careened off a truck, broke through the guardrail, and ended up at the bottom of a ravine. I understand it was pretty bad. I'm surprised she didn't die right there."

"But she did die, and that's bad luck for us." Bull walked over to the window to look down at the Potomac River and the scraggly trees on Snake Island. Even in the warm glow of the early morning sunrise, they looked decrepit. "I think we have given the Simpson girl a reasonable amount of time to mourn her loss. What, it's been a little over two weeks, right? Wasted time. We need to get back on this."

Miller walked over to gaze out the window next to Bull. "With her grandmother here now, it's a real possibility she may take the girl back to England. I'm not sure where that would put us. Maybe she would try to take the debris with her."

"I doubt it. She is as set as her father on leaving it hidden, and probably forever. At least until Burnham and his crew get to her."

"Where does that leave us?"

Bull moved back to his desk and motioned for Miller to sit down. "Working on foreign soil would make it much more difficult to get what we want, considering what we are doing is not exactly approved from above. And if MI5 found out about it, there would be real international trouble. But if it is true that Ingram has teamed up with Burnham, then he wouldn't give a hoot about foreign implications. He would send Burnham and his team out there."

"What do you want to do?" Miller asked.

Bull thought for a moment, then settled on a plan of action. "If that is the case, then we don't have much time. The whole deal with Mrs. Fletcher was a huge screw-up and set us back."

"You're right. We seem to have underestimated the power of her faith. It made her stronger than we anticipated."

"Well, hindsight doesn't help us now. Roberts blew it. That whole set-up with the professor should have worked. The Simpson girl is smarter than I thought." He turned to Miller. "Do you have any idea what strings I had to pull to get Roberts free, and what a mess it would have been if I hadn't?"

He picked up a pen and fidgeted with it while he thought, then slapped it down on the desk. "Look, I want you to handle this yourself. We need to get it right and do it quickly, before that girl ends up in England and out of reach."

Pop Tart

Emilee sipped at her morning cup of breakfast tea, her legs folded under herself in the lounge chair, reading the Sunday paper. She looked over at me. "Your country really is in a bit of turmoil, isn't it?"

I was sprawled across the couch on my stomach, still in my pajamas, reading the funny papers which were spread out on the floor below me. I nibbled at a blueberry Pop Tart. Kellogg had just come out with the frosted ones and I really liked them. I looked up from the latest antics of Snoopy and Charlie Brown. "What do you mean?"

"Well, according to your newspaper here, one of your states over on the East Coast, New Jersey, is a hotbed of Negro rioting. It has been going on for three days in a place called Newark. And what with the civil rights movement, the mess the States have made of the Vietnam War, and the protests against it—your country seems to be rather bad off right now."

"Our country has always been bad off, as far as I'm concerned."

"It's just that it comes as a bit of a shock to me. I guess I hadn't paid much attention to these problems while living across the pond."

It had been a week since Emilee arrived and she was pretty well settled in. She hadn't mentioned a thing about going back to England yet, and I was hopeful she never would.

The few times I tried to start a conversation with her about my mother had all dead-ended. I couldn't stand it any longer, and realized this may be the perfect time to get something out of her.

I stretched over to the coffee table, put my Pop Tart on a plate, and sat up. Emilee had gone back to reading the paper. She was in her pajamas too, and looked very natural as she lazily read and sipped her tea. How do I approach this? I looked outside while I thought about it, watching the morning sun spatter across the big oak tree in the yard. The leaves seemed to be dancing in a slight breeze, playing tag with the spots of sunlight.

I turned to my grandmother. "Emilee?"

She looked up from the paper. I think she could see I had something on my mind. Maybe she already knew where I was headed just from the tone of my voice. "What is it, dear?"

"You've been here for a week now, and I really like having you here. I was so worried before you arrived that you would be...well, different."

"What, like some old witch with warts?"

I laughed. *How did she know?* "Yeah, something like that."

"And..." she prodded, expecting more.

"Well, you aren't anything like that. It's just, when you first got here you didn't talk about my mom at all. Nothing about our losing her, or how she died. Not a word from the moment you arrived, and all through dinner that first day. I don't get it. And I've tried to talk to you about mom a couple of times since then, but you always seemed to change the subject or ignore my questions."

She sat up straight, set her tea cup on the table, folded the newspaper and laid it in her lap. "Fair enough. You see, that first day I wanted to be positive. And if we talked about your mum, then the subject of what happened between us would most likely have come up. I didn't think it appropriate to discuss such things in front of your friends and George. It is a very difficult subject for me. And since then, I've been in a bit of a tussle over how to discuss it with you. But I certainly don't want you to be miffed at me about it."

"Oh, I'm not. But can we talk about it now?"

"Certainly. I haven't really been able to come to terms with her death. It has been so long since we had contact. It's very surreal to me."

"Mom was an alcoholic. She had a lot of issues. One of them apparently, was not telling me you even existed. Why would she do that?"

"I can't speak to why that is. We had a rather large row many years ago, and she chose to cut me from her life. That is all I can say."

"Can you tell me how that happened?" I watched her closely, to see if she was hiding anything.

"Remember, when I told you I went to Lubbock to try and find your grandfather, but without success?"

"Yes." Her posture was formal, but comfortable. I felt I could believe whatever she was about to say.

"I decided to stay there to raise Gloria. It wouldn't do to go back to England with a child who would be born out of wedlock. Knowing my mother and relatives, they would only look at it as my putting another black mark on the family name. I didn't want to bring Gloria into the world in such a negative place. And being six months pregnant and having just traveled that distance to get here, I knew the trip to England would have been too taxing anyway."

She placed the newspaper on the table and picked up her tea, taking a sip. "I found a place to live in Lubbock; a basement flat in a house owned by a wonderful old lady, Mrs. Delbert. The day I moved in, she came downstairs with a freshly baked apple pie so we could get to know each other. It was the thing people did in those days. We sat across a small table I had managed to find in a charity shop, along with two rickety old chairs. We ate slices of warm pie while I told her my story about Russia and the loss of Daniel. She actually cried right there and then. I have always wondered if maybe something similar happened to her, but perhaps with a child."

I thought about how bad it was to lose Mom. I couldn't imagine what it would be like to lose a child. Which I suddenly remembered, was what had also happened with my mother, along with a bunch of other terrible things she had gone through.

I looked up at Emilee. "Did you ever find out?"

"No. I never asked, but as I got to know her, I noticed little hints throughout her house which led me to believe my suspicions were correct."

"How long were you there?"

"When she learned I was out of money and hadn't a clue as to how I would pay for food, let alone rent, she gave me a job. She owned an insurance company which she had inherited when her husband died, and she insisted I work there as a secretary right up until I had Gloria, and then again afterward. In those days a woman running a company would immediately bring it to suspect."

"Why?" I had to ask. "Why suspect?"

"Because they wouldn't think it could be run right. Women just didn't run companies back in 1923. It was a man's world. Even now, forty years later, you are trying to right that wrong with your Women's Liberation movement. Well, such was the case in those days, especially with an insurance company. So, she worked in the background, keeping a keen eye on it from behind the scenes. She left the day-to-day with a close chum who had worked as her husband's second. The silver lining in all of this, was she had time to watch Gloria while I worked, and offered to do so. It soon became apparent she didn't have any living children or relatives and was rather lonely, so it helped the both of us. Gloria came to see Mrs. Delbert as if she were a grandmother. We lived in that apartment the entire time we were in Lubbock. She became family."

I thought about what she said. My mom had never mentioned Mrs. Delbert, not even once, let alone tell me that I had a grandmother. *What could have happened that she would do that?*

"How long did you stay in Lubbock?" I asked.

"A long time. All through Gloria's schooling. She was a senior at Lubbock High School when—" Emilee stopped. Something changed in her look.

I knew it was time to ask. "What happened between you and my mom?"

She stood and walked over to the window, looking out. It was as if she wanted to put distance between herself and my question. She didn't say anything for a while. I knew I had to wait her out. The light filtering through the window landed on her face in soft tones. I could see the reflection of it in a tear that had worked its way down the side of her cheek.

She turned to me. "Melanie. I can't tell you. I thought I could, but it isn't the right time. I know that doesn't make sense to you, but I just don't think you are ready."

She laughed—a nervous laugh. She leaned back against the window, perhaps using it for support. "Or, maybe it's that I'm not ready. I don't know. I'm being completely chuckleheaded about this. It is so personal—between your mum and myself. But it's not, because it's about you as well. Oh, bugger, this is so hard."

She put her hands over her face and held them there, maybe to stop herself from what she might say next, until she could figure it out. She slowly lowered her hands, as if trying to wipe away her confusion. "I suppose I'm worried I might lose you, too, if I told you. Like I lost her. I have only known my grand-daughter for a short while. I can't take that chance. Not yet."

She waited for me to say something, but I didn't know what to say. What could have been so bad that she couldn't tell me, or maybe even be frightened to tell me? I don't think it was something like she abused my mother. That doesn't ring true. But I also knew it would be worthless to pursue it right now. "Will you be able to tell me someday?"

She smiled. "Yes, I think so. Just not now…not today."

"If you can't tell me what happened between the two of you, can you tell me where she went?"

"She ran away. I tried everything I could to find her. She was seventeen and very bright, just like you. I think she had some help from a school chum who gave her a lift out of town. I asked her chums, but no one would admit to knowing anything. I reported it to the police. They simply thought of her as a runaway, and couldn't really do much other than to file a report. She simply disappeared."

"Did you stay in Lubbock, in case she came back?"

"I did, but somehow I knew she wouldn't. I think that is the hardest thing I had to come to terms with."

She walked over and sat next to me. She held my hand and looked into my eyes. "I stayed for a few more months, never-theless, hoping she would. But not long after she left, I found out my mother was poorly. I hadn't been home at all since I'd had Gloria. I didn't want to disrupt her life. But I had to go back, for my mother."

She stiffened when she said this. "Well, I didn't do a very good job with that now, did I? But with Gloria gone, and even though I hadn't seen my mother in nearly twenty years, I felt I should be there to support her. I don't think I could have lived with myself if I didn't see her before she died. I was an only child, and although we had relatives, I was the only true family she had left after my father died."

"Is that when you decided to go back?"

She nodded. "It was 1940 and Britain had gone to war with Germany. The Luftwaffe was bombing England on a regular basis. I wasn't worried my mother could be in danger from the bombings, though the Germans did bomb radar stations on the Isle, and the shipyard in Newport once, killing a lot of Islanders. It's just that everyone thought it only a matter of time before the Nazis would have all of the European mainland under their control, and then set their eyes on invading Great Britain. It gave me a sense of urgency to get home.

"So, I did. I managed to find myself some transport, on an American merchant ship taking much needed supplies to England. I had convinced them I was a nurse, having learned much about the profession from the nurses in Russia. When I arrived home, I remained there taking care of my mother until she died, and then took over managing our estate."

She stopped for a moment, remembering it all with a far-off look to her eyes. "That is, until I received a call from George a fortnight ago, telling me my daughter had died." Then she looked at me, patted my hand and smiled. "And learn for the first time, I had a granddaughter."

The Industrialist

Burnham pulled up to a private hangar at Hillsboro Airport southwest of Portland, Oregon, just as a Lockheed JetStar taxied to a stop. He got out of his car and walked over as the door to the jet opened and steps were lowered to the ground. Three men in business suits walked down the steps and toward Burnham. Two of the men were young and fit, obviously bodyguards for the third. He was a diminutive man with gray, thinning hair, and well past his prime which showed in his slow walk and slight limp. The material of his suit reflected its Italian-made expense in the sunlight as he stepped up to Burnham and put out his hand. "Brighton Ingram."

Burnham shook it. He could see he was being sized up both visually and by the handshake. "Nice plane."

Ingram nodded and looked back over his shoulder to the JetStar. "Yes, just got it. I hate commercial travel, and with as much as I do, it made sense." He turned toward the hangar. "They have us set up in a private room inside. Let's go."

The four walked in a side door to be met by a young woman who ushered them into a plush meeting room. Inside, a heavy wooden table dominated the center of the room, with six black conference chairs surrounding it. A credenza against the wall was covered with food and drink, and off to one side stood a private bathroom, its door ajar.

The beautiful blonde, decked out in business attire which highlighted her shapely figure, said, "Mr. Ingram, I'm Nancy.

Everything is as you requested." She motioned to the food. "If you need anything, just pick up the phone. I'll be right outside." She pointed to a phone centered in the middle of the conference table. With that, she left the room, closing the door behind her.

The bodyguards made their way to the credenza and loaded plates with food. Ingram looked at them and then to Burnham. "It was a long flight from the east coast. And it will be even longer since I need to be in Santa Clara when we are finished here. A possible investment opportunity. I'm getting into electronics, and Santa Clara Valley seems to be the place where all the research is being done on transistors. That is where you and your little project come in. But first things first." He pointed to the food. "Feel free to make a plate. I'm going to do the same as soon as I freshen up." With that, he went into the bathroom and closed the door.

Burnham walked over to the credenza where three chafing dishes sat, along with an array of salads and three kinds of dessert. Enough food to feed twenty people, rather than four. He removed the cover to the first one to reveal Chicken Parmesan. Orzo pasta and steamed asparagus were found in the other two. He fixed a plate and took it to the table.

Ingram came out and picked up the phone. "Nancy, come in here." He set the phone back in the receiver and walked over to fix a plate of food.

Nancy came in. "Yes, Sir?"

"Oh, Nancy. I think we should have some red wine with lunch. Be a doll and go to my plane. Have my stewardess pull out a bottle of '57 Sangiovese Montanino. I think it would go well with the meal."

"Yes, Sir."

Ingram took his plate to the table and sat down. He looked over to Burnham. "So, what in the hell happened, anyway?"

Burnham was in the middle of a bite of Chicken Parmesan. He quickly swallowed before he choked on the suddenness of the question. "I had no idea how crazy that woman was. I thought if we grabbed her in the van, and threatened her and her daughter, they would turn over the debris. It was only after we got stuck in there with her, that I figured out how completely nuts she was. We weren't going to get anywhere, so I dropped her back at her car. That was it. I had no idea she would go and kill herself. Luckily no one has connected the dots to our van. We disposed of it immediately, of course, just in case."

Ingram waved Burnham off. "I don't particularly care about that. It is a setback and that is all. But we need the debris. If what you tell me is correct, and I can get this material to my people in Santa Clara, it would put us light-years ahead of what anyone else is doing in development of electrical components and other technologies. I am already rich, obviously, but this would not only make me the richest man in the world, but put me in a position of power and control. I rather like that idea."

Nancy came in with the wine and four glasses.

Ingram motioned for her to take two of the glasses away. "My men need to keep their wits about them," then turned to Burnham, "but I think you and I can indulge a little. After all, this may very well be a historic moment. The day we changed the world."

Nancy poured each of them a glass, then set the bottle on the table and left.

Ingram handed a glass to Burnham. "Try this wine, and then tell me more about the debris."

Burnham raised his glass in toast and took a sip. "This is good. I'm not a big wine drinker, but I like the taste."

"Yes, a smooth finish of red currents with a slight smoky flavor, don't you think?"

Burnham nodded, having no idea what he was talking about. He leaned over his plate toward Ingram. "When you first contacted me, I thought of how I might get material from Hangar 18 at Wright-Patterson, but there were too many layers of security—even for the number two man at Blue Book. That's when I decided we should go after the material Melanie Simpson has hidden."

"You say you have actually seen material from the spaceship?"

"Yes. I was stationed at Roswell Army Air Field when we first recovered it. I got a good look at the material Major Marcel brought back with him from the crash site. The technology is well beyond anything we have here on earth. If we could figure out how it works—"

"We would not only be billionaires, but wield the power such technology offers. And that is the important point. So how do we go about it? And what about this grandmother that showed up out of the blue?"

"I'm not sure how to put a read on that, or if she knows about the debris."

"Could you go after her, or the kids? Maybe that girl's boyfriend?"

"The Strickland boy? It's possible she might give it up if we threatened to hurt him or the grandmother. I'm just worried this Melanie Simpson is beginning to falter. She may turn the material over to the press, or do something even more stupid with it. And if that happens, we lose out completely."

"Then don't *let* it happen. Do whatever you need to get that material. I don't care what it takes." A look of evil flashed across Ingram's face and his eyes narrowed. "Am I making myself clear?"

"Very."

The expression disappeared and a smile took its place. Ingram raised his glass, but suddenly stopped when he looked at Burnham. "What is it?"

"I think I've come up with a way to get the material, that might work. But I'll need a pile of cash to do it, maybe as much as a hundred grand."

"That's a lot of money."

"Not for you."

"True. And a raindrop compared to the sea of cash we will make if this goes our way."

"Then we are set?"

"Yes. Give me a few days to put it together. But you should know, it will be a terrible waste of money if your plan doesn't work. And I *will* hold you accountable." He kept his gaze focused on Major Burnham, to make sure the point sank in.

The major shook it off. "I'm not worried. With this plan, if the donkey doesn't take the dangling carrot, then I'll still have the carrot."

Ingram laughed. "Let my men know where to deliver it." He paused, studying the major. "So, you're sure of this?"

Burnham smiled. "With that much money dangled in front of the right man, I am."

"Wonderful." Ingram finished raising his glass and nodded to Burnham to do the same. "Then a toast to your success and our great fortune."

Anniversary...kinda

I waited in my room until just before midnight, then opened the door and listened to make sure Emilee was asleep. The only sound came from the ticking clock in the living room.

Good.

When I was absolutely sure, I gathered up the bag of things I had prepared earlier and snuck out of the house. I hurried down to the easement, being careful not to make too much noise going down the steps. The bag clanked a little, so I steadied it against my side with my hand. When I reached the picnic table, I took out a white linen tablecloth and spread it across the top. I had a lot to do, so hurried. I wanted everything to be just right.

I looked out at the lake. The water had a midnight sheen to it, calm and flat. I couldn't feel a breeze at all. A full moon, low and large, sat suspended right above the treetops of the hills on the far side of the lake, its reflection dancing across the surface and right into our inlet.

Perfect.

A few minutes later the sound of footsteps came from the landing up at the bridge.

He was right on time.

The gate softly opened and closed.

A dark shape moved down the steps and approached me.

"Now I see why you were so mysterious about meeting here at midnight," Frankie said. He looked around at everything I had done. "Wow, Mel, this is friggin amazing, and very cool. So, what's up?"

I also brought a bunch of little votive candles. I placed them on either side of the walkway to create an illuminated path from the upper level of the lawn, down the steps to the lower level, and to where I stood behind the table. A single red rose lay in its center. Two big candles flickered on either end of it.

I walked over to him, put my arms around his waist, pulled him into me, and kissed him. "That's for you to figure out."

"Oh, so the mysterious Melanie Simpson strikes again."

"Yeah, something like that." I took his hand and led him to the table, where we sat next to each other, facing the water and a very romantic moon above it.

I reached for my bag and took two wine glasses out, and a bottle of Coke. Then I realized I forgot an opener. I felt a blush cross my face. "Do you have your keys?"

He laughed. "What, you want to go for a ride now?"

"No ... I don't have a way to open the Coke bottle."

"Oh, so I *do* have a purpose." He pulled his keys out of his pocket, took the bottle and worked the serrated edge of a key blade around the rim of the cap, popping it off. He handed the bottle to me.

"Thank you. After all, you are my Musketeer, so should always be ready to save a damsel in distress."

He smiled and bowed his head. "At your service, m'lady." When he looked up, the candle flames danced in his eyes. "Always at your service."

Oh, my God! He can be so romantic sometimes. I took a breath, and filled the glasses, setting one in front of each of us. I reached into my bag and pulled out a little Tupperware container. I popped the lid and took out a chocolate cupcake slathered in white frosting and topped with little red sprinkles. But it wasn't complete without a candle—a small birthday candle with swirly stripes of red and white, kind of like a barber's pole. I poked it into the top of the cupcake and held it out in front of him.

"Do you know what day it is?" I asked.

He looked at me kind of funny. "Not my birthday. I'm pretty sure of that ... unless Mom has shared some sort of shocking information with you ... that for fifteen years she has kept secret from me."

"Funny, but nope." I set the cupcake on the table. "Not that, and not your birthday. Next guess."

"Your birthday? No, wait." Frankie's brow furrowed. "That was last year, in October."

"Getting colder."

"We've done the Fourth, so that's out." I could see he was trying hard, but based on his expression, had no idea. He gave me a pleading look. "Hints?"

I kissed him again, making sure to let it linger for a while.

He kept his eyes shut for a moment, obviously savoring the kiss, then opened them. "That was a really good hint. Maybe a few dozen more and I'll figure it out."

I laughed. "I'm pretty sure my kisses muddle your mind, not make it sharper."

"Then muddle away." He pulled me into him and kissed me.

His hand caressed my back, moving along the depression of my spine, a very sensitive area by the way, but with Frankie pretty much all my areas were sensitive. I drifted into the feeling of his touch and his soft lips.

He pulled away and laughed. "Ha, got you back."

My eyes stayed closed. He had, but I didn't care. I wanted the feeling to linger.

"Now, who's the one that's muddle-headed?" he asked.

I opened my eyes, feeling a bit dreamy. "Sorry, lost my train of thought."

"See. What comes around, goes around."

"There is no defense against such logic. You have just earned your answer." I reached over and took both of his hands in mine. "It's our anniversary."

"What?" His expression turned to one of shock. "We're *going* together?"

I let go of his hands and whacked him in the chest. "*Yes*, we're going together. God, you are such a Perv."

He laughed and kissed me lightly, then smiled. "I can probably deal with that, but how do you figure it's our anniversary? I'm not sure we ever, *officially*, said we were even dating."

"Okay … *kinda* … our anniversary." I laced my fingers into his. "I had to think about it for a while, starting back with our first kiss under the raft. That was like at the very end of June last year, or maybe the beginning of July, I think."

I could see him trying to place the time. "Seems about right. So, this is July nineteenth. Why tonight?"

"Why not? It's not like we can pin it down. So, tonight seemed as good as any. Once I got the idea into my head, I figured why wait." I took out some matches and lit the candle. The sweet smell of melting wax floated into the air. I picked up the cupcake and handed it to him. "Happy anniversary."

He studied it for a moment, then looked at me. "You do know how much I love you, right?" He set the cupcake down on the table, candle still burning, and reached behind my head to pull me in for a kiss.

I looked into his eyes, dark and inviting in the candlelight. "I love you, too."

We kissed, and it felt just like the first *real* kiss we ever had together, which was completely amazing. It happened right here, in this very spot last summer. The kind of kiss you see in a movie and think, 'I want to be kissed like that someday,' only it was happening right now; to me.

When we finished, I looked down at the candle, its flame darting around as candle flames do, even without a breeze. I told him, "I never want our flame to burn out."

Then what I said hit me. *Why did I say it?* And who did I say it for—him or me? I thought about my decision to take the debris to Professor Lofton. I wouldn't be telling Frankie of my plans. I couldn't for all the reasons I had rolled through my head over and over again. I shook the thought away. I didn't want to spoil this moment.

"Mel?

I realized he was wondering what I was thinking. I picked up my wine glass and smiled. "To us."

Frankie picked his up and we tapped the rims together. He held his glass up and said, "You know, babe, I'm not sure what my boring life would have been like if you hadn't moved in next door, but I'm really stoked that you did. Even though you've been a real pain-in-the-ass, I'm still thankful."

We took a drink and put the glasses on the table.

"Well, you haven't exactly been God's gift to womanhood, but when it comes down to it, I am, too." I sat there for a minute, thinking how lucky I was to have Frankie.

An odd feeling took over. It was as if I wasn't in control of my own actions anymore. Or, maybe that's what I wanted to think. I stood and hovered over him for a moment, then leaned into him. I ran my fingers through his hair, wispy and as unkempt as always. I could see he was enjoying it. I did it a few more times, then grabbed a fist full of it to turn his head up to me. I leaned down and gave him a devious smile. "Perv, you are in such trouble tonight."

I let go of his hair and stepped over to pick up a candle from one end of the table, then walked to the other, purposefully brushing against him on my way. I picked that one up too and carried them out to the end of the dock, placing one in each of its corners. I stood between them, looking out at the lake. The moon, brighter now and mesmerizing, played across the water from the far side of the lake all the way to where I stood. I knew its reflection would place me in perfect silhouette to Frankie. Only a small amount of light from the candles on either side might reveal what I was about to do. I turned to Frankie and could barely make out his face in the light of the moon. But it wasn't hard to see he had no idea what was coming. I hadn't even a clue myself until this moment, when it came to me.

I kicked off my shoes, pulled my sweater over my head, and tossed it aside.

My pants went next … and then other, daintier things.

I stood in silhouette to Frankie, and used the best matter-of-fact voice I could muster. "You just going to sit there, or what?" and then dove into the water.

A Proper Breakfast

I lay under a pile of pillows fighting off the sunrise, which had wound its way into my room like a bright poisonous snake, slithering through the window, along the floor, climbing the footed post of my canopied bed, and slowly across the covers toward me. I thwarted its efforts by building a fortress against it with every pillow I could reach.

Everything floated within the soft edges of a dream as I remembered last night with Frankie. I didn't want the sunlight to spoil my euphoria.

It had been really late when I got home, well … more like very early this morning. I'm not sure what time it was.

The sun got outplayed by a knock at my door. "Melanie?"

It was Emilee.

I tossed the covers aside and sat up, sending a few pillows to the floor. "What … what's up?"

"Just worried about you. It's ten-thirty. You usually don't sleep so late."

"Oh. Tired, I guess. Come in."

She opened the door, but barely stuck her head in as adults tend to do when breaching a teenager's bedroom. "I thought I'd make you a traditional Full English breakfast. I'm in the mood for a fry-up, and finally have all the proper ingredients, thanks to the help of your Mr. Wizer. Are you up for it?"

Food wasn't really on my mind, but I said, "Sure. Sounds interesting. Give me a minute and I'll be out."

She walked down the hall, leaving my door open.

I fell back against the bed and pulled the covers over my head again. One more minute, just one. I dozed a moment, then the snake managed to find its way through an opening and hit my face. "Ugh." I threw the covers aside and got up. That's when the smell of bacon cooking hit my nose, and suddenly I was hungry. I went into the bathroom, took care of business, freshened myself up, and headed down the hall.

"Smells good," I said as soon as I walked into the kitchen.

"I thought this might get you moving. Excellent timing. Things will be ready momentarily." Emilee cracked four eggs into a pan, cut two bread slices in half, and placed them in another pan where I could hear them sizzle.

I leaned over the kitchen counter to look. "Are you frying the bread?"

"Of course. It's the only way to do it properly. Shallow fried in oil. Believe me, you will understand with your first bite."

She took a cup from the cupboard and picked up the tea kettle from the stove to pour. "In the meantime, here is a spot of tea I've made for you." She handed me the steaming cup.

"Thank you." I took it and sat at the breakfast table facing her as she cooked. She glanced up at me once in a while, almost pensively. I could tell something was on her mind. Maybe this wouldn't just be about sharing breakfast. "So, what is a traditional Full English breakfast, anyway?"

"I've just finished. Let me plate things up and I shall introduce you momentarily." She took two dinner plates from the cupboard. I watched as she filled them from the various pans on the stove. She walked over and placed one in front of me, and sat down across from me with the other. She had already set our places with knives, forks, spoons and napkins.

"Well, what do you think?" she asked.

I looked down at my plate heaping with food. There were things there I recognized as breakfast items, and lots I didn't. "It looks like a lot to eat."

She nodded. "In England, breakfast is thought of as the most civilized meal of the day." She picked up her napkin and placed it in her lap. "This proper breakfast was the glue that held England together during the war. It was the meal to get things suitably started, because we never knew if this would be the day our ticket might be punched during one of the German bombings."

I looked at the pile of food on my plate. "Well, I can see how this could get you going." I noticed some dark slices of something I didn't recognize. I pointed to them. "What are these?"

A knowing smile crossed her face. "Right, let me give you the royal tour." She picked up her fork and used it like a pointer at the items on her plate. "Fried eggs. Here, I believe you call them sunny side up. For the veggies we have lightly fried halved tomatoes…"

I laughed because she said this like toe-maut-ohs.

"… and Bella mushrooms. Next are the beans. Now, only Heinz beans will do. No others. Then we have a few strips of rashers. This is not bacon as you know it. Call it bacon's cousin. Then, a couple of bangers. No American breakfast sausage here, which is a completely different thing. And finally, the two rounds of black pudding, to which you had inquired. So, there we have it. The Full Monty."

"What is black pudding?"

"Taste it, and then I will tell you." She nodded to my plate.

I cut a small piece from a round, put it in my mouth and tentatively chewed at it. It did actually taste pretty good. "So?" I raised my eyebrows in question.

"It's pig's blood with fat and oatmeal added, packed into a casing, and then boiled to solidify. Frying the rounds gives it just the right amount of caramelization, don't you agree?"

I grabbed my napkin and quickly spit the piece into it, nearly gagging. "What! You've got to be kidding. How could you?"

Emilee laughed. "Well, I suppose it is an acquired taste if you don't grow up on it as I have. But you must admit, it is rather tasty."

Whatever thought I had along that line disappeared with the words *pig's blood*. "I don't care how good it tastes. I will not put pig's blood in my mouth."

Emilee broke into laughter at the look on my face. I couldn't help but join in, despite the thought of what I just had in my mouth.

Eventually we stopped, and she said, "Now try the fried bread."

I took a bite from one of the slices, with the result of a big crunch. It was very oily, but somehow the hot oil had interacted with the bread to create an amazing taste sensation. Not like toasted and buttered bread at all, but so much better. "Oh, this is good. I wonder why we don't fry it here in the States?"

"I suppose your downfall there was the invention of the pop-up toaster. Well, let's eat up before the eggs get cold."

We ate in silence for a while. I had never had beans with breakfast before, but everything tasted amazingly good, other than the two rounds of pig's blood pudding, which seemed to be staring at me from my plate.

I glanced up at Emilee to see the same expression on her face that she had worn earlier in the kitchen. "What is it?" I asked.

She set her fork down and sat back. "I'm ready to have our conversation about your mum."

This was Thursday afternoon, so it had been four days since I last asked about my mother. Nothing had been said since then. "Okay. I'm listening."

She became very serious all of a sudden. "My hope is you will keep an open mind. This is not at all what you could even come close to expecting. Will you do so?"

I nodded, not knowing what to say. A slight chill ran through me. *What could it be?*

Estranged

Emilee was quiet for a moment before she spoke. "I've spent the last few days trying to work out how to go about this, and am completely muddled by it. So, I guess I best just dive in." She slid her plate aside and put her hands on the table, wringing them while she studied them in thought. She looked up at me. "Do you remember any odd dreams—recently or from when you were younger?"

"What?" I didn't understand. "How does this have anything to do with Mom?"

She nodded, seeming to gather herself for a different approach. "Do you remember any time when your mum seemed out-of-sorts while sleeping. Perhaps sleepwalking or screaming out. Has she ever spoken in her sleep without sense?"

I remembered last spring when Mom appeared at my door naked. She was sleepwalking and talking gibberish. "Yes, I think I do. Why?"

"And you? Anything?" she asked, not giving more. Waiting.

I thought about when I had dreams where things seemed normal, but then turned darker. "Since Dad died, I've had dreams of him playing ball or standing by my bed, but then all of a sudden it wasn't him. It was someone else. I never really saw anyone as much as I sensed them there. Something would always wake me up at that point."

She nodded, like she knew. "Something that scared you, so you awoke as your shield against it?"

I wondered about this. "I'm not sure. Whenever I had one of them, I would shake it off. Try to forget it." Memories were coming back, and I didn't like them.

"Because deep inside, you didn't want to know."

I pushed my chair back and stood, some sort of defense mechanism kicking in. Maybe because she was about to reveal something I didn't want to hear. Something I had been blocking from my mind for a long time.

She looked up at me, "The question is, are you ready now?"

The slight chill I felt earlier had suddenly grown ten-fold, running through me like a heavy wave crashing against a reluctant beach. I stepped back from the table to get farther away from her. "What is it you are you trying to say, Emilee?" But as soon as that came out of my mouth, I knew I didn't want to hear her answer.

Emilee stood and walked over to me. She took my hands and gave me a reassuring smile, looking deep into my eyes, as if reading what was in them. "Melanie, I am about to open up a whole new world to you."

She pulled me into the living room and sat on the couch, drawing me down next to her. She ran her hand along the hairline of my forehead, stroking it as a mother would do with a daughter to provide reassurance. She settled and held my hands. I could feel a slight tremor in them.

"Your mum and I, well, we are what I think of as being experiencers." She rubbed my arm. "And, based on your answers, you most likely are, also."

I studied her face and how she looked at me, as if to see if I had grasped what she meant at all, which I hadn't.

Seeing she needed to explain, she went on. "Some of us—experiencers—are able to accept our situation. And others are not. I always did, but Gloria wouldn't." I could see how nervous she had become. Almost as if she didn't want to go on, but knew she had to. "I don't know that I should even be talking to you about this right now. It is just so soon. I'd hoped we could choof along and give ourselves the proper time to get to know each other. They also think it is too early. But your mum's death, and what happened between she and I, has driven the two of us to this moment." She studied me again, trying to read me. "As have your questions, relentless in their need to know, which I rightly understand. It has all made me realize I could wait no longer."

I squeezed her hands and shook my head. "I'm sorry. I don't understand. What do you mean by *experiencers*? And who are *they*?"

She looked down. I could see her shoulders slump a bit, as if to acknowledge this was not going as she had hoped. "Chums. That's what I call them. Others would say visitors. You would most likely refer to them as extraterrestrials."

I let her hands go and jumped from the couch. "What?" I backed up until I was stopped by the half wall of the dining room. I knew aliens existed, and obviously that some people, like the Hills, were abducted. *But my family?*

"What are you saying? That you and my mom were abducted by aliens?"

Emilee slowly stood and took a tentative step toward me. "Often it is thought of as abduction, and in some cases, it may very well be. But that is not what is happening to us. These beings are friends. I go willingly. I'm hoping you will come to understand the same. We have been sought out. There is something about our family, our lineage, that brought them to us. First to me, then your mum, and I believe...now to you."

I turned my head away in disbelief. My entire body shook; a trembling I couldn't control as if suddenly drifting in a frozen sea, bound by its cold grip. This can't be happening. *My God!* I never thought about it this way; that I could ever be abducted.

But my dreams, and how I always jolted out of them. I suddenly felt violated. I didn't want to face this. I slid along the wall a few steps to get farther away from Emilee. What she was saying couldn't be true. It just couldn't. I realized my grandmother must be as bat-ass-crazy as my mother.

She went on. "The first time I can remember, I think I may have been about seven. They came into my room at the Manor, floating in right through the closed window on the second floor. It was scary. It is always scary at first. And it can remain scary if you let it. But I understood them. I somehow knew right away, even at that age, something important was happening."

I slid further along the wall toward the front door of the house. I quickly glanced over and thought about bolting through it.

She took a few more steps toward me, then stopped. "After I had Gloria, when she was also about seven, they visited us in our basement flat in Lubbock. They were interested in Gloria as well. I had the feeling they wanted to know if she was special in some way. But Gloria shut out the visitations. She became scared and stayed scared. She blocked them out, but it would still come to her in nightmares."

"How long did this last?" I shook my head, understanding this was the reason my mother left. "Why didn't you stop it?"

Tears welled in Emilee's eyes and she cried. She went to the couch and fell onto it. "I couldn't stop it." Her voice adamant. "They have total control over us when they want to—or need to. But, it's not that. I didn't want to stop it. I believed in them, as family at this point, and they were helping me understand the importance of what was happening. Not just with Gloria and me, but with the world and the universe as well."

I couldn't help but remember what Mrs. Crowley said in the tarot card reading about *my* universe, or Katch's grandmother and *my* sky people. But this was too much. How could this relate to what they had meant? To be an abductee?

She looked up at me. "Gloria knew this as well. They had shared it with her, but she didn't want to accept it. She could no longer block it out. At this point she was seventeen, nearly an adult. She finally came to me one day about what she was remembering. She wanted me to make it all disappear. Even though she knew the truth herself, she wanted me to tell her it was only a series of bad dreams."

Emilee shook her head slowly. "Maybe if I had told her what she wanted to hear, things would have ended differently. But I couldn't be dishonest with her. I could no more separate her from our destiny than the moon could be separated from Earth's orbit." She wiped at her tears with her sleeve and looked at me. "I really did want her to understand, so we could share this experience together. I couldn't comprehend it would end our relationship. So, I told her they weren't dreams, they were real." She put her head in her hands and sobbed. "And she ran away. She didn't want to face the truth. I never saw her again."

I moved in slow steps toward the bedroom hallway as she told me this, not even knowing I was doing it—an escape mechanism seemingly set to automatic. I stopped at the word destiny. How could she use that word? How could this be any part of *my* destiny?

I turned to her. "The truth?" I shouted. "The truth is you're crazy! But you had to make my mother crazy, too. And all of this nonsense drove her away!" That scared me. My voice shook. "Does craziness just run in this family? Is that where I'm headed?" I tried to steady myself. I wanted control. "Wow, I am so looking forward to crazy!" I headed for the hallway again, to race down it and slam my door, to put a barrier between myself and Emilee.

"Melanie, stop! Wait a moment."

I turned back to her.

"Maybe we should talk more later, when we aren't so emotional. And when you've had time to absorb all of this. I knew it would be hard on both of us. Your mum never gave it time, to understand the importance of our being selected. I hope you will."

I looked at her and realized I was seeing a completely different person than the one who had walked in my front door a few weeks ago. The person who had totally wowed me and my friends. Who was this woman, anyway? I really don't even know her!

I backed down the hall until she was out of sight, then turned and ran to my room. I shut the door behind me and leaned against it to barricade myself from what just happened on the other side of it. How could it be true?

I quickly took the chair from my vanity and shoved the top under the doorknob, kicking at the feet until I felt it would stop her, should she try to come in.

I turned to my room. What do I do now? I can't stay in here. I would need to go out eventually and face … what? Then I had a thought. Two weeks. It had been two weeks since my grandmother arrived. But that also meant it had been over two weeks since Professor Lofton left, so he should be back home. I needed to see him. I needed to know more about my dad and the Orb. Especially now. Could any of what just happened have to do with him and the Orb.

Oh, my God! What if it did?

I ran to my closet and grabbed my book bag. It was full of old papers and textbooks still in there ever since being abandoned after school. I dumped them on the floor of the closet and walked to my dresser, taking out some clothes and shoving them in the bag. I took my brush and a few other personal items from the vanity and put them in it. As I worked, it came to me why I was doing this. I needed to get out of here. Now.

I went back to my closet for a jacket, and as I put it on, I noticed my dad's backpack tucked into the corner of the top shelf. I had to take it, too. I pulled it down and removed the old weather balloon, dumping it on the closet floor alongside the books and papers. That ruse wouldn't be needed any longer. I pulled a sweater and another top from hangers, and pushed them into the backpack.

A knock came at my door. "Melanie. Melanie?"

I turned to it, watching the knob, hoping she wouldn't try to come in. "What?"

"I'm sorry, Melanie. I know how unbelievable this must sound. I don't blame you for how you are feeling." Her voice turned to even deeper anguish. "Let's talk later tonight, or even tomorrow morning. Give it some time. Please don't be miffed at me over this."

I didn't know what to say. I hated lying. "Okay."

It stayed quiet for a while. Then her footsteps disappeared down the hall. I went to the window, released the latch and opened it to find the wind blowing hard, pushing a heavy rain sideways into the room.

I went back to my closet and took off my light jacket, shoving it into the backpack. I took out a raincoat and put it on, then reached up and grabbed a Portland Beavers baseball cap my dad bought for me at a ballgame a few years ago. I hadn't worn it in forever, but figured it would come in handy now with the weather I was about to face. I quickly put my hair into a pony-tail, put on the ball cap, and went back to the window.

A pool of water had formed on the floor below it. Oh well. I pulled the straps of the book bag over my head so it hung to my side, then dropped the backpack out the window, climbed over the sill, and lowered myself to the ground. I picked up the backpack and closed the window as best I could. But now what? The garage; my bike!

I worked my way around the back of the house, ducking under windows, then peeking in through the sliding glass door for signs of Emilee, before dashing past it. The garage was just up ahead, so I worked my way around to the side door and quietly opened it. I grabbed my bike, climbed onto it, and rode away. The rain pounded at my eyes as I headed down the street—*but to where?*

The Offer

"This is a hell of a place to meet." Major Burnham wasn't exactly happy with the location. The wind buffeted him, and he had to hold his hat in place against it. He walked a few more steps up the aisle of the bleachers, turned into a row and sat next to Captain Thornton. He set a small leather satchel on the aluminum bench next to him, and looked at the view below. He wrapped his jacket around himself against the penetrating wind. "Why here?"

"Good as any," Captain Thornton replied, "and less inhabited, what with school out for the summer and this weather going on. And, you didn't exactly give me much notice, so this is what I came up with."

The two men were sitting at the top of the bleachers facing the Lake Oswego High School football field. Rain fell heavily in buffeted sheets, but the overhanging canopy kept it from getting to them.

Major Burnham waited for the captain to speak first. It was part of his plan. The captain seemed to be focused on the football field below, where little waves were being pushed across a large pool of water by the wind. "So, what is this about anyway, and why such a clandestine meeting? I already told you I'm not interested in helping the government. Especially with anything involving the Simpsons." He turned to the major. "Particularly now that Mrs. Simpson is dead, and under very mysterious circumstances."

Major Burnham ignored the implication, turning to him. "You may not be interested in helping your government, but I do know you are vested in keeping the Simpson girl safe." He paused to let that sink in.

Captain Thornton leaned toward the major, a resolute look on his face. "If anything happens to Melanie, I know who I'm going to look to first. Do you understand?"

"Yes, of course, Captain. It is your nature. I am not interested in hurting the young Simpson girl. I only want to recover the material she has hidden. It's as simple as that. And it can be done without endangering her if you agree to help me."

Captain Thornton sat back and guffawed. "And why would I do that?"

Major Burnham smiled. Exactly the question he wanted to be asked. "Two reasons. First, you can help ensure the Simpson girl's safety, and second, I am about to make you an offer that will change your life."

Major Burnham saw a momentary look of surprise cross the captain's face, then disappear. "I doubt that very much, Major. What could the government offer me that could possibly change my life?"

"As you can see, I'm not wearing a uniform. That's because I am no longer with the Air Force. I've flown the coop, so to speak. Resigned. I may as well have had clipped wings while with the Air Force. Constrained by government red tape and slower-than-molasses decision-making. I no longer bear those chains. Now I can spread my wings."

"And what would cause a career man to leave such stability?"

"Money, lots of it, and the freedom to do what is necessary to get it. I now work for someone with the ability to get what they want. And what they want is the material the Simpson girl has hidden. To develop it—to gain riches and power from harvesting the technology. The only thing that stands between us and that goal, is her. This is where you come in. As I was saying, my benefactor," he paused, and then smiled as he re-thought the statement, "or perhaps I should say *your* benefactor, has a very generous offer." Major Burnham took the leather satchel from his side and held it out for Captain Thornton to take.

The captain gave it a tentative look.

"Go ahead. Take it. Look inside." The major nodded to the satchel.

Captain Thornton reluctantly accepted it, set it in his lap and unhooked the straps. He raised the flap, bending over the opening.

Major Burnham could see the captain's eyebrows raise at what was inside. "What do you make, Captain, huh? I'm guess-ing about what, eighty-five-hundred dollars a year? That satchel holds ninety-thousand dollars, Captain. More money than you would make in a decade, let alone what the govern-ment leaves you after having rifled your pockets for taxes. You help us get the material from the Simpson girl, and the money is yours. Tax free money, Captain," he emphasized.

Captain Thornton looked at the major. "That's a lot of money."

"Not to the man it came from. It's nothing compared to the millions he will make once he gets his hands on the alien tech-nology. But to him, it's not about the money, anyway. He has plenty of that already. It's about the power it will give him. Those are the riches he's after."

Major Burnham stood, pulled a card out of his pocket, and handed it to Captain Thornton. "This is how to reach me. Keep an eye on the Simpson girl, and figure out a way to get that ma-terial from her. That way you can help us to our goal and keep her safe in the process. I expect to hear from you very soon." He started to leave, then turned back to the captain. "Oh, if you don't come through, we expect the money back. Every cent of it."

He walked down the steps, holding his hat against the rain and wind, thinking about how this had gone. The captain just might go for it. He smiled inwardly. Even the cold wind couldn't dampen the warm feeling inside. It wasn't only that this plan could work, but he had also managed to skim a cool ten-thousand off the top for himself. Operating expenses, he told himself, laughing as he reached the football field. Not a bad day's work.

The Haven

Mrs. Crowley walked into her living room. "My, look at this place, child. I've never seen it look so good."

I fluffed the cushion one more time on Mrs. Crowley's lounge chair, and set it back in place. So much for trying to get the lumps out. It was a hard-fought battle, but a losing one against formidable odds, that being Mrs. Crowley's rather large nether regions and the lasting indentations they can make.

I looked up at Mrs. Crowley from the lumpy cushion. "I couldn't get any sleep last night and needed something to do."

The cushion was the last item in a living room all-nighter— emptying and washing ashtrays (Brillo pad required), sweeping and scrubbing the floor, wiping layers of dust from tabletops, washing linens and yellowed doilies, and clearing away piles of garbage tucked away in little nooks and crannies everywhere.

"Melanie, did you even get any sleep at all last night?"

Mrs. Crowley had offered me the use of her guest bedroom, but after about an hour of staring at the ceiling, I knew I couldn't sleep—not after the completely bizarre things my grandmother had said. I couldn't get past the idea that my whole family was crazy, which by association, included me. Better to keep busy and away from such thoughts.

"A little." I gave a weak smile. "It's just easier to deal with things if I keep busy."

All Mrs. Crowley knew was that I had a big fight with my grandmother, and it was really bad. After racing out of the house yesterday, I spent the better part of the rest of the day riding around on my bike, pretty much aimlessly, getting soaked by the rain and wind while trying to figure out where I could go. It couldn't be Frankie's or Katch's houses. Their parents would figure things out and call Emilee. I ended up at the Hunt Club, of all places, just to get out of the rain. I sat in the bleachers of the indoor arena for hours, watching riders practice their jumps.

I finally settled on going to Mrs. Crowley's. There was a big chance she would call Emilee, too. But I had nowhere else. When I got there and told her I had a fight with my grandmother, she wanted me to call so Emilee wouldn't worry. We wrangled over this for a while, at least until I told her I would leave before doing that. I still had to plead with her to let me stay. She could see I was soaked to the bone, and didn't want me out in that weather again, so she relented.

She gave a sweeping look to the room and nodded her approval. "Well, you have done such a wonderful job, I am going to reward you with a nice breakfast. How about eggs, bacon and pancakes?"

I thought about yesterday, and how things had started out that morning with Emilee's English breakfast. "Not rashers, I hope."

"What are rashers?"

I had to laugh. "Nothing, never mind. A nice American breakfast sounds wonderful to me." And safe.

While we were eating, I talked Mrs. Crowley into taking me to the bank. She wanted to know why. I said I would explain it later, but I wasn't ready yet. She seemed to go with that, for now at least.

I would need some money because I had worked out my plan overnight. I finalized it somewhere between tossing out dried flower remnants on the floor (which had to have still been there from when everyone sent Mrs. Crowley flowers after her 'abduction') and washing the front windows with ammonia and crumpled newspaper. I think the fumes did the trick. Cleared my head.

A while back my mother set up a bank account for me when we got the reward money from Major Burnham. She wanted me to have a college fund. That money would come in handy now. I needed to get to Professor Lofton in Seattle. I not only wanted to know more about my dad and the Orb, but he would also know what to do with the debris. Maybe he could use it for research and figure out how it works. It needed to be developed for all of mankind. If nothing else, at least he would be able to get it to the right people who could do that.

The next step in the plan was to make some phone calls. I needed to make sure Professor Lofton was back, and to check the train schedule for tomorrow to Seattle. I planned to be on it. And, I would call Tom. He lived up there and could help.

But I knew I couldn't make these calls from Mrs. Crowley's phone. There was too big of a risk she would to overhear me, and she still had no idea about the debris, let alone the Orb. It was taking a chance, but I needed to ride my bike to Remsen's again. I just hoped no one would see me. There was another reason to take my bike, anyway. I needed to get the debris from its hiding place.

Mrs. Crowley was in the kitchen cleaning up. "Hey, Mrs. Crowley, I need to go somewhere for a while, and no, it's not back to my place."

She turned to me, a scrub brush in one hand and a plate in the other. "Are you sure you don't want to go back home? Isn't it best?"

"I know what I'm doing." I gave her my biggest trust-me look. "I shouldn't be gone too long. When I get back, we can talk, okay? And no calling Emilee, agreed?"

She nodded, but I could see she wasn't completely convinced. "I don't know what you are up to, but be careful." She set down the brush and plate and came over to me, wiping her hands on a dish towel. "I want you back here soon. If I think you are gone too long, then I will call your grandmother." She gave me a stern look. "Do you understand me?"

"Yes, Mrs. Crowley. I do. I'll be back as soon as I can."

I walked out the side door, grabbed my bike from where I had leaned it against the house, and rode down the hill toward the bridge and across it.

❋   ❋   ❋

Captain Thornton sat in his car, parked along the side of the road on Springbrook Court facing Summit Drive. He took a drink of coffee from a thermos, and tuned the radio to a different station. The current one was getting old. He had been here ever since he got word early today that Emilee had called the police station to report Melanie missing, possibly a runaway.

While out looking for her, he had driven past Mrs. Crowley's to see her bike propped against the side of the house. He figured there weren't too many places Melanie could go from there, and most of them meant she would need to ride past him. His hunch proved to be right. Melanie whipped by the intersection in front of him, headed up Springbrook Bridge.

"Where are you headed, young lady?" He drank the last sip of his coffee, screwed the cup back onto the thermos and put his car in drive. "I guess we're going to find out."

Mel's Plan

I hung up the phone, leaned against the glass side of the phone booth and studied my notepad, my first two goals now accomplished. Professor Lofton was home again and agreed to meet with me. He lived somewhere called Mercer Island, and he gave me his address with instructions to get there from downtown Seattle.

My second call had been to Union Station to check on the train schedule. Southern Pacific's Cascade route would leave Portland at 9:45 in the morning. Luckily, a ticket wouldn't be too expensive. I planned to be on that train, but I needed to work out the details with Tom first.

I took a quick look around Remsen's parking lot to double-check. I hadn't seen anything unusual when I arrived, but wanted to make sure no one was watching me. It all looked good, so I picked up the receiver again. I dialed the operator and gave her the number from memory, since I had promised Tom never to write it down. Of course, he was going by the name Ralph, so that's who I needed to ask for. I was getting pretty good at this, and it wasn't long before I could hear the ring tone as the operator attempted the connection

"Hello?"

"This is the long-distance operator. I have a person-to-person call for Ralph Morgan from Melanie Simpson."

There was a long pause on the line. I hoped nothing was wrong. "Yes, operator. I'll take the call."

The operator told me how much it would be to add minutes. I tossed in a bunch of coins just in case. We stayed silent until a click on the line indicated the operator had disconnected from our call.

Tom spoke first. "Melanie, where are you calling from?" I could hear concern in his voice.

"A phone booth. It should be safe."

"Good. Why are you calling? Did you find something out?"

"Yes, I found someone who worked with my dad, like you said. He lives up near Seattle. A place called Mercer Island."

"Yes, I know it."

"I need to get the debris to him and find out what he knows. He can tell me what my dad was doing, and about the Orb."

"What do you need from me?"

"Help. I'll be coming on the train tomorrow. The schedule says I should arrive at King Street Station somewhere around 1:45 in the afternoon. Do you know where it is? Can you come meet me? Do you have a car? Maybe you could take me to the Professor?"

"Slow down. First, we need a plan. It is very likely you may be followed."

I waited for what he would say next but instead, there was silence. I became worried. "Will you be able to help me?" I asked again. I didn't know what I would do if he said no.

"Yes, of course I will. I promised your father to keep an eye on you. I can't very well let you come up here on your own. But I need to do some groundwork first."

"Thank you. I don't know how I could do this without you."

After another pause, he said, "Okay. This is what I need you to do. What time does the train leave Portland tomorrow?"

"Around nine o'clock." I looked up to see a car pull in and park near the entrance to the store. George got out. He wore street clothes. Maybe he wasn't working today. He looked around for a moment, and then walked into the store. I couldn't tell if he had seen me, but either way I needed to get off the phone and get out of there.

Tom said, "When you get to the train station tomorrow morning find a pay phone. Call me collect from there. Make sure it is a phone where no one can hear you. I will have a plan together by then. If someone does pick up your trail and follows you, we will need a way to ditch them."

"I'll call you then. I have to go now. Captain Thornton just walked into the store. I don't want him to see me here. If he does, he may wonder what I am doing in this phone booth."

"Will it be an issue if he has?"

George walked out of the store holding a thermos. He headed my direction when he saw me.

"I hope not. He's kind of become a friend. But I need to get off the phone. He's coming over. I'll call you tomorrow from the train station before I leave."

"I'll talk to you then. Be careful!" He hung up.

George reached the phone booth and rapped on the door.

"Bye, Emilee." I hung up and heard the sound of change falling into the dispenser, left over money that hadn't been needed for the call. I ignored it, hoping George hadn't heard. There wouldn't be extra change when it was a local call. I opened the door.

"Hi, Melanie. I saw your bike and figured it was you. Everything okay?"

I could tell he was curious as to why I would be using a phone booth.

"I'm good, George." I gave him my best smile. "I was just running an errand for Emilee. She needed a few things from Remsen's. I had a question about something she wanted."

"Oh. Sure. Well, I needed a refresher on my coffee." He held up his thermos.

I worried that Emilee may have called the police to report me missing, but he gave no indication of that at all.

I studied him. "You're not in uniform. Day off?"

"Actually, I've taken a few days off. Time to recharge the batteries. Mostly planning to do some couch surfing. Catch up on the soaps." He chuckled. If he knew anything was up, he hid it pretty well.

"I should probably get going." I held up my notebook. "Emilee needs me to get back."

George nodded and stepped aside. I walked to the store entrance. George kept pace next to me. I felt nervous—a sense that he knew something was up. I'm not sure why I got that feeling.

He stopped next to his car. "You take care of yourself, Melanie, okay?"

"Thanks, George. I will." I reached up on my tiptoes and gave him a kiss on the cheek. He smiled, got into his car, pulled out of the parking lot and drove away.

I waited until he was out of sight, and then went into the store to get a toothbrush and some other things I wasn't able to grab from home. When done, I rode my bike down Lakeview toward the railroad crossing, keeping an eye out for George's car, or anything else out of place. I needed to get the debris, but didn't want to go down Springbrook Court for obvious reasons. It would be better to take the trail from the dead-end side.

I came up to the spot where my mother had crashed through the guardrail into the ravine. I could see the new section where the guardrail had been repaired. I pulled over for a moment and looked down toward the creek. I couldn't remember much from that day. It felt like a bad dream, but the broken branches and gouge out of the tree trunk, no longer bleach white, made me even more resolved to pursue this quest.

I rode across the tracks and pulled over to a big bush where I could stash my bike without being seen. I grabbed my book bag, threw it over my shoulder, and walked down the tracks to the trail that would take me to the end of Springbrook Court. I followed the trail into the woods and around the last house on the dead-end street. It led up the hill to Summit Drive, which curved to parallel Springbrook Court not far above where Mrs. Crowley lived.

The trail turned to follow the guardrail of the road. I walked to a spot above my house, then cut down the hillside to where I had buried the debris. An old stump marked the spot. I took out a trowel I had borrowed from Mrs. Crowley (not that she knew), and dug down to the box. The top was caked with dirt, so I brushed it off as best I could and then opened the lid.

A noise from below drew my attention while I was putting the debris in my bag. I glanced down through a gap in the undergrowth to see Frankie had opened the sliding glass door at the rear of my house. He stepped outside and looked around. Emilee stuck her head out to watch him. I could tell he was worried and frustrated. He looked around and up at the woods toward me. I ducked as low as I could so he wouldn't see me. I didn't think he could, but didn't want to take any chances. What was he doing there? Emilee must have called him.

He walked along the side of the house to my bedroom window. He could see it was slightly ajar. He looked around for a moment, studying the ground and the wall below the window, then opened it, climbed over the sill and inside my room.

I quickly took the last of the debris from the box and put it in my book bag. I closed the lid of the chest and covered it with dirt and dead leaves again. I thought about Frankie and what he must be thinking right now—more like feeling right now. What I was about to do would probably end our relationship for good. Still, I had made a promise to myself I wouldn't put him in any more danger. And it was very likely I would soon be heading right into the mouth of it.

I put the straps of the bag over my shoulder and worked my way up to the trail. I looked down at my house again, now barely visible at all. I knew I wouldn't be going back there anytime soon if I could help it. Not with Emilee there. Not after what happened and what she said. I turned onto the path and headed for my bike.

Frankie and Emilee

"Frankie, Mrs. Harris is on the phone. She wants to talk to you. It sounds important."

Frankie opened the door to his bedroom. "What?" He wasn't sure he had heard her right.

"It's Mrs. Harris," his mother called down the stairs. "She's on the phone."

What could this be about? Frankie ran up the stairs two steps at a time. His mother stood at the top holding the receiver out. She raised her eyebrows when he reached for the phone, obviously wanting to know what was up. He took it from her and leaned against the wall, turning away from his mom. "Mrs. Harris?"

"Frankie?" Concern floated in that one word.

"What's going on, Mrs. Harris?" He glanced back to see his mother still standing behind him. Great, eavesdropping, something mothers seem well adapted toward.

"Have you any knowledge of where Melanie might be? Has she happened to ring you up at all?"

"No, I don't, and I haven't heard from her." He paused. He hadn't talked to Mel since the lake; playing the cool card and doing the not-calling-her-for-a-day thing. "Why?"

"I think Melanie is gone. She may have run away."

"She what?" A rush of worry overtook him. He sat down on the stool by the table near the stairwell, trying to collect himself. His forehead felt cold and damp, like the onset of a sudden flu.

His mind whirled with all sorts of things that could have happened. *Why would she do that?* He thought about their night together. Could it have something to do with their skinny-dipping party? No, they had been good—kinda … sorta. Nothing had really happened that would cause her to do something like this.

Emilee's voice brought him back to the moment. "Can you come over? I'm not doing well right now. She hasn't answered her door, and it's been blocked. I can't open it, and I'm fairly positive she isn't even in there."

"I'll be right over." He hung up and stared at the phone.

His mom's voice came from behind him. "What's wrong?"

He looked up at her. "I don't know yet. Mrs. Harris thinks Mel may have run away. I need to go over." He realized he didn't want his mom's alarm bells to go off. He gave her a reassuring smile. "I guess they had a fight, and Mel left. I'm sure it's nothing, but I should find out what's going on. Mrs. Harris is worried."

He could see his mother studying him to read between the lines. It was a trait of hers Frankie had learned over time, and probably something mothers acquire at the birth of their children; the umbilical cord never truly being severed. He did his best to keep an even face.

Her focus eased. "Okay, but you had better fill me in when you get back."

"I will," Frankie promised, holding imaginary crossed fingers behind his back.

Frankie knocked on the door and Emilee answered. He rushed inside. "What happened?"

"It was yesterday. We had rather a bad row, and she ran to her room. I thought she would come out eventually, but she never did."

She walked into the kitchen area by the breakfast table and he followed. She turned to him and he could see the heaviness of worry pulling at her features. "Then, this morning when she still hadn't come out, I tried calling at her door. She didn't answer. Eventually, I had no choice other than to try opening it, but something blocked my way. The knob turns, but I can't get the door open. I listened at her door for ages without hearing a sound from inside. I should have heard her move around, or make some sort of noise. I don't think she is in there. I'm obviously fraught at this point."

"I'll go look in her window from outside." Frankie opened the sliding glass door and stepped out. He looked around and up into the forested hillside. He stood there for a moment, thinking, then went to Mel's window.

What could have been so bad that she would run away? The window stood slightly ajar. He studied the ground below it, and then the wall under the window looking for footprints or scuffmarks. Sure enough, there was a dirt smudge against the wall where she would have put her foot as she lowered herself out. He opened the window and jumped up on the sill, pulling himself inside. A small pool of water sat on the floor below the window, with signs of evaporation. He remembered it had rained hard yesterday around noon. She must have taken off right away. She didn't even wait, like for a cool down period or something. She just bolted. Something big had to have happened for her to do that. He walked over to the door. She had jammed a chair against the knob. Why would she do that? It must have been to keep Mrs. Harris out, but why? Mel must have been really pissed off. He pulled the chair aside and opened the door.

Emilee quickly entered and looked around. He could see her taking in the scene and the messy, unmade bed. "It's hard to tell, but I don't think she even slept in her bed last night. There's a pillow still on the floor, just as it was yesterday morning when I peeked in to wake her up."

"Yeah. I think she left yesterday when it was pouring down rain. There's still a little pool of water by the window. That had to be sometime around noon when the wind was blowing and it was raining really hard."

"Right after our fight," Emilee added.

"Maybe we should call Captain Thornton."

"I already did, earlier this morning when I thought she had fled. His staff told me he is on holiday for a few days, but they took a report."

Frankie walked to the closet and opened the door. He looked down at the balloon fragments on the floor, along with text books and papers strewn about. She took the book bag and her dad's backpack with her. It was then he knew she had no intention of coming back anytime soon. *What are you up to, Mel?*

He looked to Emilee. "You need to tell me what happened."

She shook her head. It was only a slight movement, probably unnoticed by her; not realizing she had even done it. "Let's sit down in the living room." She didn't wait for Frankie to agree, but walked out the door and down the hall, seemingly buying time to answer his question.

Frankie followed her, running through all the possible things that could cause Mel to bolt like this. At least what he could come up with. But nothing made sense. It had to be something he didn't know about.

Emilee was already sitting in the lounge chair. She motioned to a spot on the couch. "Sit down, Frankie," her tone exposing her failing attempt to collect herself.

Frankie took a spot on the couch. "I don't get why she would run away like that." He waited for her to say something, but she didn't. "What happened, Mrs. Harris?"

She slumped in the chair, as if deflating a little. She focused on her hands, which had settled in her lap, holding them in a way to keep them from shaking. Frankie could see them tremble slightly. He waited her out.

She finally looked up and said, "I shared some information with Melanie yesterday. It had to do with myself and her mother. She didn't take to it well. But it's up to Melanie as to whether she shares what I told her with you or not. It's certainly not my place to do so."

"Did you tell her the reason Gloria left? Ran away, like Mel has now?"

"Yes. I'm only hoping Melanie is just taking time to absorb what we discussed. She is a very intelligent young woman. It probably doesn't help that she only recently lost her mother, and gained a grandmother she never even knew existed. I am sure these things have had some form of influence on her reaction."

Frankie sat there for a moment. She didn't know the half of it. Emilee was Melanie's guardian now. It would be a big reveal, but he knew it was her place to know about all of this, because it probably had a lot to do with how Mel acted.

"Mrs. Harris, there are a lot of things you don't know. I think it is time to share them with you."

So, he did. He told her everything that happened from the day they found out Mel's dad had been at the Roswell crash, through the discovery of the Orb, and what quest it would set out for Mel once she had it. And finally, about the mystery of Gloria's accident, and what may have caused it.

Frankie watched Emilee for any reaction, but she stayed focused on the coffee table, like needing a solid object with tight

182

lines as her safe point while considering everything he revealed. Then her look turned. It seemed she had taken what he shared and made sense of it, like a puzzle that had been missing numerous pieces until just now.

She looked up at Frankie with an expression about as dead-serious as any he had ever seen. She said, "I don't think either you, or I, have come close to understanding the importance Melanie means to our world. Or to what lays beyond it."

Realization

"Hi, Katch. Are you able to get together?"

I'm calling her from Mrs. Crowley's. We just finished dinner. I told Mrs. Crowley I wanted Katch to come over, and then I would explain everything. I realized I needed to tell her what was going on too, since I couldn't tell Frankie, and I needed one of my friends to know.

"Mel, what's the deal? Frankie called yesterday asking about you. He said you had a fight with Emilee and maybe ran away. I've been worried. What happened?"

"Yeah, we did. A bad one. I'll fill you in when we're together. Can you get away?"

"We're sitting down to eat. Can I come over after dinner? I think Mom would be okay with it."

"Sure. I'm not at home though, I'm at Mrs. Crowley's. Meet me over here."

"Mrs. Crowley's? Sure. But what's up with that?"

"Come over as soon as you can. I'll explain then." I was about to hang up, but needed to add, "And don't tell Beanie. He would tell Frankie and I don't want Frankie to know. That would be bad. Okay?"

All I heard was dead silence on the other end of the line for a moment. She finally said, "If that's what you want, but you sure have me wondering."

"It's what I want. See you soon, okay?"

When the knock came at the side door, I knew it had to be Katch. I let her in and we went into the living room.

She looked around. "I thought you said this room was a mess. It looks pretty good to me."

Mrs. Crowley walked in with a plate of cookies, and a tray of glasses filled with ice and soda pop. She set them on the coffee table and plopped down in her lounge chair. "Melanie has been a whirlwind of activity since yesterday." She did a sweep of the room with her arm. "I didn't know it could look so good."

Katch raised her eyebrows. "You've been here since yesterday?"

I sat on the couch and patted the spot next to me. "That's why I wanted you over and not the boys. A lot has happened."

She sat next to me, a very curious look on her face. She turned to Mrs. Crowley, maybe hoping to find answers there.

"Don't look at me, young lady. This is Miss Melanie's doing. I'm just as curious as you to know what this is all about."

They both turned to me.

Wow, how much do I tell them? First, there's the whole issue of Mrs. Crowley not knowing about the debris or the Orb. If I'm going to fill Katch in about seeing the professor, then Mrs. Crowley would need to know about that. What a friggin mess. And, do I even tell them what Emilee said and how crazy all that was? I guess I will have to wade in and see how deep the water gets.

They were both staring at me, waiting. I looked at Katch. "I ran away yesterday. Emilee and I had a fight. It was really bad. I grabbed some things and took off. I decided the best place to go was here, to Mrs. Crowley's."

Katch gave me her 'what about me' look, so I added quickly, "You'll understand in a minute why I couldn't go to you or Frankie."

I picked up a cookie from the tray and took a bite, chewing slowly. I followed it with a sip of pop. I needed to buy some time. But now what? I looked over at Mrs. Crowley. "This is so way out there, you will both think it sounds too crazy to be true. The only reason either of you might possibly think it could be, is because of the tarot reading ..." I turned to Katch "... and what your grandmother said."

Katch grabbed my arm. "You're freaking me out, Mel. What are you saying?"

"Okay, okay! Let me just work into this."

I decided to start with the easiest things first, as if any of this would be easy. I looked at Mrs. Crowley. "Remember last summer when we pulled our UFO hoax, and it caused the big deal about your being abducted?"

"Of course, I do, honey. Why?"

"Well, that led me to find out my dad had debris from a crashed UFO, and it was hidden somewhere. Frankie, Beanie and I found it. Now, I have it." I grabbed Katch's hand. "The four of us have been trying to figure out what to do with it ever since."

Mrs. Crowley's face took on a look of sudden understanding. "Oh, I see. I remember when reading your tarot cards, I had asked if there was something you were desperate to protect. You told me yes, but you couldn't share it with me. Was that about the debris?"

"Yes, but now I need to, because I need your help."

I told her all about the debris and the technology everyone was after, and about the Orb and apparent quest. She raised her eyebrows when I told her this, because a quest had also been revealed in the cards.

And I explained the danger it put us in: the Russian agent killing my dad, tying up my mother, and Beanie getting shot. I didn't mention Major Burnham kidnapping me. I hadn't shared that with anyone. And as I told Mrs. Crowley this, stringing it all together at one time like I was, I almost couldn't believe it myself. It really did sound like a James Bond movie.

I looked over to Katch, "Remember, when I was searching for clues about the men working with my dad, doing research on Tesla and free energy?" She nodded. "I've found one of them—a professor up in Seattle. He and my dad were studying how the Orb works, and what its purpose might be." My eyes lit up as I told her, "Professor Lofton has film of the Orb and of my dad! I need to see those films. And I want to get the debris to him. He'll probably know what to do with it. And then all of you will be safe, once everyone figures out I no longer have it."

"How are you going to get it to him?" Katch asked.

"I'm taking the train to Seattle tomorrow." I turned to Mrs. Crowley. "I'll need a ride to the station from you in the morning."

"Oh, Melanie. I don't know." Mrs. Crowley had all sorts of regret showing on her face. "I have no doubt your grandmother is already worried to death about where you are, and you've made me your co-conspirator in keeping your whereabouts from her." She waved me off with her hand. "And now you want me to take you to the train station, to let you run off to a city you know nothing about. There are all sorts of things that might happen to you."

Katch jumped in. "Yeah, Mel. Have you completely lost it or something? This is just freaking nuts. There's no way. And what about Frankie? You're going to do this to him again, after all you've put him through? How do you think he's going to feel when he finds out?"

Before I could even think about that, Mrs. Crowley piled on. "Running to my place for a few days is one thing. It is something your grandmother would eventually understand, but this?" She had obviously dropped her anchor on the whole idea. "What of her? And what could have been so terribly bad that you won't let her know where you are, let alone what you are about to do?"

I jumped up from the couch and paced the room, ending up by the picture window overlooking Summit Drive. I looked outside at what I thought had been a normal world. *What will they think when I tell them?* I turned around. "I've been doing a lot of rationalizing over the last two days about what Emilee told me. At first, I thought she was just bat-out-crazy. I mean, what she said was so bizarre, it was too much to believe. No one would believe it! But then, once the shock settled, I put it into perspective." I looked at Mrs. Crowley. "Your tarot card reading said it was *my* universe in chaos," I turned to Katch, "and your grandmother pointed to the stars and told me they were *my* sky people."

They both gave slight nods, probably not realizing they even did so, their focus so intent on me. Katch managed to get out, "What are you saying?"

I sat down on the couch next to Katch. After a moment I looked up at the ceiling and gave a big sigh. *Am I really going to tell them?* I settled, then suddenly clapped my hands together, a commitment to divulging this wigged-out story. "Remember when I said it was all too crazy to be true. Well, here it goes." I let out a big puff of air. "My grandmother said that she, and my mother, and probably me…have been alien abductees all of our lives."

I tried to read their reactions, but their faces had morphed into blank stares. Not directed at me, but as if toward insignificant space. A place where they could escape in order to absorb what I had just told them.

Katch came around first and said, "You mean, like what happened with Betty and Barney Hill? Taken aboard a spaceship and experimented on?"

I smiled. Probably a defensive reaction, more than as to what she said. "No. Actually, Emilee called them her friends, even family." I glanced over at her. "Look, I'm still trying to wrap my head around all of this. But, Katch ... your grandmother called them *my* sky people." I stopped to let that sink in for a moment. "Emilee told me our family had been sought out, that there was something special about us." I paused to think about how sur-real this all sounded. "I just don't know. How can it be true?"

She looked at me and nodded in a confirming way. "My grandmother is a great seer. I have never doubted her and never will. Her visions always come true. When we stood under the stars with you that night and she told me what she had seen, it had to be true. But this vision was about you, my best friend. So, I wondered, how it could be. Then, when she had me do the chant myself, I saw the meaning. It wasn't just a connection to the sky people, but somehow, they *were* your sky people, as if you belonged." She sat back, seeming to be taking in the won-der of it all. "Now, with what you tell us, it all makes sense. And so much more—like the connection to your father and how the Orb came to him. And how obsessive you became in studying everything about UFOs. And the hate you had for the govern-ment cover-up and how they were making out UFOs to be hos-tile, and keeping the truth from the world." She looked at me with wonder in her eyes. "It's as if you had known, deep down inside, all this time."

And it was in that moment, as she said this to me, I knew it was also Katch's vision. She truly had become a seer, just like her grandmother.

I turned to Mrs. Crowley.

She looked at me and nodded. "It is dharma, child."

I repeated it, "Dharma," as if the one word pulled it all to-gether. I thought for a moment, then said, "I remember your reading, Mrs. Crowley. It's locked in my memory. You told of a journey. You even called it a quest that I needed to pursue in order to correct a bad situation." I could tell she was remembering. "That's where I am right now, Mrs. Crowley. You were spot-on. You also said I will seek out guidance from someone new I will come to trust. And that I may need to seek other lands in order to accomplish that which I set out for myself. Do you remember?"

"Yes," she answered, almost trance-like.

"But there were things you didn't tell me. Things you kept from me, isn't that right, Mrs. Crowley?" I studied her and could see it in her eyes. "You knew my mother would die, didn't you?"

She looked down, not wanting me to see her look of betrayal. "Yes, it was in the cards. But how could I tell you such a thing?"

"I'm okay, Mrs. Crowley. I understand why you didn't. I only say it because it proves your cards are true. And they have told me what I just repeated to you. I must go to see Professor Lofton in Seattle, and he will help me." She still avoided eye contact. "Mrs. Crowley?"

She looked up, and I could see tears pooling in her eyes. "Yes, child?"

"Will you take me to the train station, so I can fulfill the quest your cards revealed?"

"Yes. I'll take you. I knew I would need to do something like this all along. I also saw it in the cards. I didn't know what it would be until now."

The Train

Mrs. Crowley turned onto the road going to Union Station where I could see it for the first time. I was awestruck by the beauty of its red tiled roof and tall clock tower, curved construction, and countless canopied windows above a long portico decorated with colorful hanging flower baskets. It could as easily have been a high-end resort on some pristine lake tucked into the base of a snow-covered mountain.

She pulled up to the main entrance and dropped me off, telling me for the hundredth time to be careful, and to listen to my inner self—whatever that meant. I made my way inside to the central atrium. The beauty of the exterior wouldn't be outdone by the interior. It was huge and had a high, ornate ceiling with a pattern of recessed squares all across it, with something like a blooming flower embossed in the middle of each square. I became dizzy just looking up at it.

The floor reflected polished marble, and all through the middle of the atrium were endless rows of heavy wooden benches, something like you might see in a church, but they were back-to-back, bigger, and more comfortable looking. They were also highly polished, probably by countless rear-ends sitting in them over many decades. An alcove set to one side of the atrium had a wooden counter with little teller openings like in a bank. I figured that must be where I would get my ticket.

I walked up to one of the clerks. "Hi, I need a ticket on the Cascade to Seattle's King Street Station for this morning." I placed a five-dollar bill on the counter.

An older woman looked up from what she was doing and studied me, as if she could know my whole life story in that short moment. I gave her my sweetest smile and kept eye contact to throw her off.

She didn't waver. "Round trip will be $6.20," she said, glancing down at my five-dollar bill, waiting.

I looked at her in surprise. "Oh, I'm going home. I just spent a couple of weeks with my grandmother. My parents drove me down." I broadened my smile. "Annual summer visit. Grams dropped me off because we've done this a million times, so she didn't bother to come in. I only need a one-way."

She focused on me even more. "We always need to keep an eye out for runaways." Her eyebrows tweaked in such a way to place me in that category. "They are big on using the train for their escape."

"Oh, yes," I wholly agreed. "I understand." I leaned in close to her. "I'll keep an eye out. Do you, like, get a reward or something if you bag one?"

She frowned at me as she took my bill. "$3.10. The Cascade leaves from track number two at 9:45." She counted out my change, slapping my ticket down with it.

"Thank you." I pocketed the money and ticket, turning to find a pay phone. A large clock above my head showed the train would leave in about twenty minutes. I needed to make that call. Off to one side I could see a bank of four pay phones. No booth, though, and I couldn't see any other phones. I was running out of time, so this would have to do. I just hoped no one else would be making a call, or pretending to, while I called Tom. I quickly walked over and chose an end phone. I dialed the operator, gave her Tom's number and asked that she connect me as a collect call. Tom was quick to answer and accept it.

"Melanie, I was getting worried."

"I know. I guess time got away from me."

"Okay, this is what I have in mind…"

A man walked up and picked up the receiver of the phone one over from me, dropping a coin in the slot and dialing. I knew I should keep what I said to a minimum, just in case. I listened to Tom's plan while taking in what the man looked like and what he wore, in case I saw him again later on the train.

Tom continued, "I'll need to be able to spot you when you get here, in case the place is busy. What are you wearing?"

I turned my back to the man next to me and hunched down to guard my voice as best I could, "I have my dad's old army backpack with me." Then I thought of something. "I'll wear a red baseball cap when I get off the train. I'll put it on backwards. You should be able to spot me that way pretty easily."

"Good," he said, "and we can use the hat to misdirect anyone trying to track you, should that happen. I'll explain more when you are up here. You'd better get going. I'll see you in a few hours."

"Okay, bye." I hung up and turned around. The man next to me had disappeared. Maybe I was over-concerned. I looked up at the clock. The train would leave in ten minutes. I needed to hurry.

I walked out the doors to the train platform and stood there a moment to get my bearings. A young couple nearby was embracing, saying goodbye to each other with a kiss. I'd seen it a thousand times in the movies, where the man and woman, deeply in love, kiss passionately before one of them boards the train, hanging from the side, looking back as distance separated their love, possibly to never to be rejoined again.

I so wished it could be Frankie and me. It would be one hugely passionate kiss—the kind where the world revolves around you and everything else is blurry. Our eyes would be closed so only the sensitivity of our lips could convey the passion of our embrace. Then our eyes would slowly open and mold into each other's to become one set of eyes, focused on our love.

Yeah. Well, that's not going to happen. I shook off the thought. This wasn't a movie, and there wouldn't be a Frankie to kiss me, because I chose not to tell him where I was going or what I would be doing. It left my heart laying there on the ground with a huge chunk out of it. I turned to the walkway and headed for platform number two so I could board my train.

George leaned against the wall inside the atrium, having watched Melanie walk out to the train platform. He had followed Mrs. Crowley and Melanie all the way from Lake Oswego. He knew it was only a matter of time before Melanie did something. She must have been putting together a plan of some sort when she was on the phone at Remsen's. He staked out Mrs. Crowley's, just as he had the day before, and it paid off again.

When they drove up to the front of Union Station, he had held back so as not to be spotted, pulling into a parking space facing the main entrance and waiting there. After a moment Melanie got out and went inside. He didn't expect she would be taking a train somewhere and wondered where she could be going. Maybe of more importance, why?

After Mrs. Crowley drove away, he got out and walked to the entrance. Inside, he spotted her at the ticket counter. He stood back, keeping out of sight while she bought her ticket and made her phone call. After Melanie had disappeared out the doors to the train platform, he headed over to the clerk who had issued Melanie her ticket.

When he got to the counter he said, "Excuse me."

The woman nodded. "What can I do for you, Sir?"

George smiled. "The girl you helped a moment ago, the young blonde one with the army-style backpack. Can you tell me where she's headed?"

The woman gave him a guarded look, like maybe he was a pervert or something. "And why would you want to know?"

George wasn't in his uniform, so he took out a wallet where he carried his badge when not on duty. He flipped it open. "I'm a police captain, and she is a person of interest."

The woman gave a confirming smile. "She's a runaway, isn't she? I thought so!"

George had seen too many people act just like this woman to give her any satisfaction. He said, in a fairly dispassionate voice, "I gave no indication to that at all. As I said, she is a person of interest. Where she is going?"

The woman's smile disappeared and she said in a huff, "Seattle. King Street Station."

"What time will the train arrive there?"

"Around 1:45 this afternoon."

"Thank you." George turned and walked away as he put his wallet back in his pocket, then looked at his watch. That would be in about four and a half hours. Plenty of time to get there before she arrives. He walked out of the station to his car.

✳   ✳   ✳

I didn't get on the first train car when I got to track two. There were quite a few people doing just that, so I walked down the tracks to the third car and got on that one. I went all the way to the back and sat in the last row by the window. The seat faced forward, kind of like on a bus, but it was a wider bench-like seat. There was another one like it on the other side of the aisle. No one was in it and I hoped it would stay that way. Some of the seats I passed faced each other, with a table between them. I wanted to be in the back though, so I could see everything in front of me.

I set my backpack and book bag next to me, and settled in. It would be a long trip. A few more people came into the car and took seats, but no one sat across from me. I didn't see the man from the phone, which was a good thing. Otherwise, I would have been worried the whole trip.

The car suddenly jerked. I watched as Portland slowly moved along my window, soon to disappear from view, and wondered what was ahead for me. I remembered my thoughts about seeing the debris for the first time and how it was like a train derailed, heading down an unknown track. It felt like that already on this train, though it sat firmly on the rails.

It may be partly due to the guilt building inside of me for not telling Frankie. I had lied to him once more, although at least this time it hadn't been directly to his face. But that didn't make it any better. It was still a lie and I knew it would be the end of us. I had no other choice. And then I thought—did I even have a choice? These things all seemed to be decided for me now. I really do believe in Mrs. Crowley's tarot card reading and how it has proven to be spot-on. It really is a matter of destiny.

I just needed to hang in and be tough through whatever was ahead. And I've had plenty of practice in that over the last two years. I thought of the song by Simon and Garfunkel, "I am a Rock," and knew that's what I needed to be—a rock, when everything else around me seemed to be crumbling apart. Hopefully, taking the debris to Professor Lofton would end it for me, at least this part of my little saga. Well, at least until I received the Orb. And then who knows what will lie ahead?

I am so excited to see the film of my dad. Hmm … what would he think about what I'm doing. I doubt he'd approve of my taking such risks, but I also doubt he had any idea of the direction things would take after he died. What would he do in my shoes? Probably what I'm doing right now.

A few drops of rain had come down when I first arrived at the station. Over the last half hour, the skies had darkened and now the rain came down in sheets. Heavy raindrops slammed against the window and slid in diagonal lines along it, desperate to find a way inside. I leaned against the glass, my cheek absorbing the penetrating cold. It seemed as if the raindrops had fallen from the sky just for this purpose, wishing themselves to wipe away all of my problems, cleansing me of them in one of Portland's famous rainouts, making me pure and innocent again.

I sat back and looked out the window through the streaks, knowing they could never make such a thing happen. Even they knew something else entirely was planned for me. I watched the tail end of Portland slip away, and as it left, it made me think of my dad slipping away so unexpectedly. I so wish he hadn't died. I could really use his guidance and a little reassurance right now. The Simon and Garfunkel song filled my head, only this winters' day was smack in the middle of the summer, but what of the walls in the song? I had definitely built them all around me to guard against the pain, and to stop the flow of tears.

I remembered my layers, always the layers … which, when you think about it, are really just walls, laid on their side, one atop another.

I needed to be a rock…and an island. I wouldn't make it any other way.

Evasive Maneuvers

The train pulled into King Street Station. I couldn't see much as we came in because it looked like the platform sat below street level. I took my red ball cap out of my bag, twirled my hair into a ponytail with a rubber band, and put the cap on my head backwards. Tom's directions were to walk into the station, then upstairs and out the front door to Jackson Street. He said to wait there for a while as if to be picked up by someone. Then he wanted me to double back downstairs, and go out the King Street entrance to the right. I was to look for a pay phone there and wait for his call.

I jumped off the train and went inside the building. I thought it would look very much like Union Station back in Portland, but it didn't. It was more like a beat-up bus terminal in a city that didn't care. Instead of a high, ornate ceiling like in Portland, it had some sort of low ceiling panels painted in offsetting shades of smoky white, like a bland checkerboard pattern. Recessed fluorescent lights were interspersed throughout the panels, reflecting a glow that gave everyone the look of the walking dead. The floor, which once must have been really something to see, was cracked in places and unpolished. It surprised me at how bad things looked here.

I walked to a side alcove with an exit sign above it to find two sets of double doors. One set going to King Street, good to know for later, and the other to Jackson Street. I went through the Jackson Street doors and up the escalator. At the top I walked to the front doors and out. The sounds of the city hit me in a huge wave. It seemed much more chaotic than the times I had been in downtown Portland. The front of the station had an area for parked cars to one side, and a pick-up area near the entrance. I stepped to the side of the doors and leaned against the brick building like I was waiting for someone.

Other people came out of the doors as well. Some waited to be picked up by cars shuffling through, and others, having been met downstairs, walked to the cars parked along the side. A man stepped out, looked around, and then stood off to the other side of the doors, going through the ritual of lighting a cigarette.

An immediate chill hit me. It was hard to tell, because businessmen all dress alike, but I was pretty sure this was the guy who used the pay phone next to me back in Portland. He seemed to be the same age and build, similar face, and had on a long gray coat and tan hat just like the man in Portland wore.

He wandered off to the far side of the building, seeming to ignore me, which made me suspect him even more. I stood for a moment longer, then decided I should go back inside before he finished his cigarette. One thing was sure, he didn't look like he was waiting for anyone. Other than probably me.

While he was turned away, I quickly darted back inside and down the escalator. At the bottom, I went out the King Street doors and looked for the pay phone. A big parking lot faced this side of the station. There were a lot of cars and people. Now I know why Tom wanted me to go upstairs. It would have been impossible to spot anyone tracking me down here.

I looked around for the phone, and found it mounted to the wall a little farther down the side of the building. A woman was using it, so I stood back to watch the doors in case the man followed me. I didn't see him. She hung up and walked away. I moved to the phone and pretended to be looking for something in my bag, coins or such to make a call. I didn't want anyone to try and use the phone. It hadn't even been a minute when it rang. It startled me; it was so loud. I guess I didn't think to expect that. I quickly picked up the receiver and looked around for anyone watching, but nothing sent up red flags.

"Hello, Ralph?" I knew I shouldn't use his real name.

"Yes, Melanie. I'm on a phone across the parking lot, but don't look over. You wouldn't be able to see me anyway. I was at the station when you arrived, and watched for anyone suspicious. I do believe someone is following you."

"I think so, too. A man in a long, grey coat and tan hat. He followed me on the train from Portland. What should I do?"

"Interesting, because that's not who I spotted. They could be a team, or there may be more than one group after you and the debris. Luckily, I anticipated this, so here is what I want you to do. Go back upstairs and out the front doors again. Take the red cap off as soon as you get outside and put it in your bag. Walk to Jackson Street and when you get to it, take a right. Head up the hill past Sixth Avenue. You will find a small Chinese dim sum restaurant on your right. It is the only one in that block. Go inside and tell them you want a baker's dozen barbeque pork buns. Now, remember, it's a baker's dozen, have you got that?"

"Take a right on Jackson, past Sixth Avenue to a Chinese restaurant and order a baker's dozen barbeque pork buns. Is the place on the left or right side of Jackson?"

"On the right. They are good friends and will take care of you."

"Okay…how do I reach you again?"

"Just follow their instructions. I'll be in touch after that." He hung up.

I stared at the receiver. What did I think earlier about this being like a James Bond movie? Well, it was getting more like one by the minute. I hung up the receiver and looked around.

The same man I had seen earlier stood off to the far side of the building, looking in my direction. Now, I knew for sure.

I slipped back inside, up the escalator and out to Jackson Street, pulling my hat off as I went out the doors and shoving it in my book bag. When I got to Jackson Street, I wanted to turn around to see if the man was following, but stopped myself. I couldn't give away we were onto him. It wouldn't be good if he got his guard up. Besides, who knows how many others were trying to do the same thing. At least one more, apparently. I tried to match the walking pace of those around me, so as not to look like I was hurrying, which could have drawn attention. Luckily, everyone in Seattle seemed to walk faster than what I was used to.

I walked to Sixth Avenue and crossed it. I didn't see a Chinese restaurant, so went further up the hill. About halfway along the block, I found it. The place was tiny on a little corner by a recessed alley that had a wooden gate across it. I walked inside to a small seating area with a smattering of customers at the tables. To the left sat a counter with a glass display case featuring all sorts of Chinese pastries and prepared foods. I got in line. There was one person in front of me, and she looked like she was almost finished. I kept an eye out the window to see if the man would show up. I didn't know what I would do if he walked in.

I stepped up to the counter. An older Chinese woman looked at me expectantly. "Can I help you?"

"Yes, I'd like to order a baker's dozen barbeque pork buns."

She studied me for a moment and then called in Chinese to the back of the room. I could see a small pass-through opening to the kitchen. I heard a reply in Chinese and a young man came out. He had on a white t-shirt and dark grey pants. A waft of black hair laid across his forehead in a very fashionable, American style. He was thin, but looked strong.

His eyes brightened when he saw me. Maybe for how young I was. "You are Ralph's friend, yes?"

I nodded.

"Come with me, quickly." He grabbed my hand and pulled me down a narrow hallway to the back of the restaurant, and out a side door to the alley.

I stopped him. "What are we doing?"

He smiled. "I'm Danny. Ralph is my friend. He asked me for help. That is what I am doing." He pulled me to the back of a van parked next to the building. It had the restaurant's name on the side. He opened the back doors. "You need to go in. I will take you somewhere."

This was moving fast. "Really?"

He said something in Chinese. The tone had a bit of an eye-rolling feel to it. Then he said in English, "Yes, really. It will make you safe."

Should I do this? I mean, this is freaking crazy. Get in the back of a van with someone I don't know, in a city I have—

I stopped myself. I had to trust Danny because Tom sent me to him, and I trusted Tom. I looked at Danny. "Sorry. This is just weird."

He gave me a look. "You're telling me?"

I smiled and then got in the back of the van. I had to work my way past a few crates they must use to pick up their produce, and make deliveries. I sat down behind the passenger seat on the floor against the side panel.

Danny jumped into the driver's seat. He handed me an envelope. "Ralph wanted me to give this to you. There is a key inside and instructions." He also handed me a paper bag. "And we want you to have this." I remembered in the rush down the hallway, someone gave it to him as we passed the kitchen. "You are probably hungry." He laughed. "Your baker's dozen."

"Thank you." Some amazing smells wafted from the bag and made my stomach growl.

"Sit tight. It is only a few blocks."

He leaned out his driver-side window and said something in Chinese. It was then I peeked between the seats to see an older Chinese man open the gate to let the van out. Danny drove through it and took a right on Jackson Street.

It didn't take long before he let me out at the Panama Hotel, which also turned out to have a tea and coffee house next door. Big glass panel windows on either side of the entry displayed a bunch of historical oriental items. I was to go in the doors next to the tea house. I opened them to a set of stairs and quickly walked up the flight to Room 304 per Tom's instructions.

I took the key and opened the door. The room was small with a double bed, a padded chair, and small table. It had an old porcelain sink angled into one corner of the room. The bed had a black cast iron frame with fluffy pillows, white linens, and an inviting puffy white comforter. All the furniture looked older, but in good condition. I felt like I had walked back in time to the early forties.

I set my pack and book bag on the bed, and placed the paper bag on the table. The wonderful smells coming from it had followed me down the hall and into the room. I opened the bag and took out a few containers of food. I also found a small thermos of hot tea inside. Man, this was great, because I was so hungry. I hadn't eaten since early this morning at Mrs. Crowley's and barely anything then, my appetite squashed by what was ahead of me.

Danny hadn't been kidding when he said it was my baker's dozen. There were all sorts of things: spring-like rolls, small custard pastries, steamed dumplings and, of course, what looked like a few barbeque pork buns. My stomach rumbled, so

I sat down and dug in. Everything tasted amazing. It was so much better than the Chinese food back in Lake Oswego.

After eating, I settled back on the bed, thinking about all that had happened in the last few days, and what was still to come. I soon fell asleep, the day finally catching up with me.

Clandestine

I'm sitting on the floor of that room again, the one where everything is in a soft white glow. I don't know if the room is tiny, or endless. I have no way to tell. There are no walls—just the soft, white glow.

Other beings seem to be moving around me. Actually, I should say "us", because my focus is on a boy sitting directly across from me. I remember the dream I had of him before. He is a teenager now. But I am sure it is him, only older. He has the same vibrant green eyes I somehow know.

I look down at my hands. They're not the hands of a four-year-old this time, but are my age, fifteen. I am holding them out, palms up, pushing at something. I look across and the boy is doing the same thing. Between us hangs a glowing, silver ball; I think reflecting light. I look harder. The light seems to come from within, snaking out like solar flares from the sun—as if it is made of energy. I think it is hanging, but that's not right. It is suspended, floating back and forth between us. We are holding it there. Him and me.

My concentration is immense, everything focused on the ball of energy. I feel him push it toward me. I push back. We do this back and forth without touching it, the force between us—caused by us—does the pushing. Sweat beads on my brow, a swish of my hair catches in it and pastes against my face. It distracts me just enough. The ball nearly hits me in the chest. I refocus and give it a final shove with my mind directed through my palms. The ball flies toward the boy, and he waves it aside at the last second before it hits him. It disappears in a flash of energy, like a miniature supernova.

He breaks into a huge grin and laughs, those vibrant green eyes lighting up, "Melanie. Good job! I think you're ready."

✳   ✳   ✳

A knock comes at the door, and I wake up.

I can feel my hair matted to my forehead and a cold dampness on my back and chest. For some reason I am standing by the window next to the bed, not laying on it, which was where I fell asleep. I am holding my arms out, bent at the elbows, my hands extended out with the palms up. I lower them and look at the bed. I don't remember getting up.

The knock at the door...*was that part of the dream?* I pull at my shirt to separate it from the moisture on my body, then go to the sink and slap my face with cold water. I need to shock away this groggy feeling.

I'm drying my face with a towel when the knock comes again. "Melanie, it's Tom."

It sounds like him, but how can I really know? I step over to the door. There isn't a peephole. I can't see out to check. I lean against it and say, "How many pork rolls?"

I hear a chuckle through the door, and his reply. "A baker's dozen."

I open it and see Tom standing there. He is such a relief. I throw my arms around him even before we go inside. Once we do, I shut the door again.

He walks over and sets a brown paper bag on the table. He sees the attacked containers of food already there. "Well, I see you managed to find something to eat. Good. I didn't know, so

I brought a few pastries, but it's not much. I do have some hot tea from downstairs, though. He took out a couple of paper cups with lids and held them up. "They make great tea." He set them on the table.

I told him, "Danny gave me a bag of food when he dropped me off."

Tom chuckled. "That is so Danny."

I sat on the bed, and Tom took the chair. He popped off the lid to his tea and took a sip. "How are you doing? I'm guessing it's probably been a little nerve-racking going through all these clandestine moves to lose whoever the hell is after you."

I thought about my dream. How surreal it was. I think that bothered me more than having to escape in the back of the van. And I didn't even want to get into what had happened with Emilee. Then it hit me. Did my dream have something to do with what she told me?

I needed to focus. "I'm okay." I grabbed my tea and took a sip. "How is it you know how to do all of this clandestine stuff, anyway?"

Tom smiled and leaned forward in a way that made me focus on what he would say.

"Back in 1950, the United States joined the war in Korea, but we weren't just fighting the North Koreans, we were fighting the Chinese, too. While in school I studied Chinese. For some reason, I had a knack for it. I mastered the language. When the government instituted the draft, right off I got a bad number. It would only be a matter of time before I'd be drafted, so I enlisted instead. When they found out about my skills with the Chinese language, they signed me up for an intelligence division of the Army. The war lasted for three years, and I learned quite a bit about clandestine operations during that time. I eventually ran the operations working our contacts in North Korea and China."

"Wow, no wonder you could plan all this out so well. But what about the restaurant, and Danny with the van? How did you get them to help out?"

He pointed with his thumb out the window. "That's the International District out there. Chinese and Japanese Americans. When I first moved to Seattle after the war, this was the obvious place to settle. It didn't take long to become entrenched in their society as a *gwailou*, a white person, because I could speak their language so well. I also had some contacts in the community from the war; Chinese who didn't favor the homeland for whatever reason, and helped in the fight against them. I lived here for quite a while before moving away.

"When I had to go underground after helping you get away from the Russian agent last year, I decided to come back here. Some of my old friends were still around, including Danny's father. I reached out to them, and that's how I could get myself set up as Ralph Morgan, along with the appropriate documentation. It's amazing what the Chinese underground can do here."

"Is Danny part of that?"

He smiled. 'Yes, and no. He is very much an American. Danny has become a good friend over the last year. When I needed a plan for you, I didn't have to think about who I could turn to in order to pull it off."

"So, what now? I need to meet with the professor. Can you help me?"

"What did you set up with him?"

"I told him what time I would get in, and we agreed to meet this evening, around six. Can you take me?"

"I don't have a car." He thought for a moment. "I will see if Danny can drive us out with the van. It means he will probably find out about the debris and Orb, if we get him involved. Are you okay with that?"

I thought about it, but Tom knew him well. "As long as you trust him, I'm good with it."

Tom stood. "All right, then. I have to make some arrangements." He looked at his watch. "It's a little after three o'clock. I'll get everything set up. If I have any issues, I'll let you know. Otherwise, be ready to go around five. We will leave sometime soon after that."

Tom turned to head for the door. I reached out to stop him. "Tom, Professor Lofton has film of my dad and how the Orb works. I want you to see it."

A look of surprise crossed his face. "I would love to. You know I helped your dad get the Orb out of the crash site, but never got a chance to see how it worked or what it did. Remember, I told you that whenever your father and I met over the years, he was very tightlipped about what he was doing with the Orb."

I did remember. I put my arm through the crook of his elbow and walked him to the door. "I'm glad you will finally get a chance." I gave him a hug and opened the door.

He kissed me on the forehead, "I'll see you soon," and left.

Chase

Miller looked over at Roberts. "How did you get duped by a fifteen-year-old girl, anyway? She even tape-recorded you."

Roberts took a sip of his coffee, keeping his eyes toward the hotel doors. "Forget her age. She had it all planned out some-how, with nothing to go on other than Mrs. Fletcher dumping out her sorrows and giving us up. But there's no way she could have known what Bull had planned."

"Well, he sent me out here to make sure we don't blow this again." He looked over to Roberts. "So, let's make sure we don't."

Roberts glanced at Miller, reading his look. "I didn't plan to the first time. I'm telling you, there's something about this Melanie Simpson."

A white restaurant van pulled up in front of the hotel and edged to the curb. Miller could make out two men in the front seats.

Roberts hastily poured his coffee back into the thermos. "We may have something here. Our local boys said a white van could have helped the Simpson girl get away." He screwed the drinking cap back onto the thermos, dropped it behind his seat, then reached for the ignition key and started the engine.

The hotel door pushed open and Melanie darted over to the passenger window of the van. There was a quick exchange and then she ran to the back, opened one of the van's doors and jumped in. The van pulled away as she closed it. It darted onto the road, accelerated, and made a quick turn at the next block.

Car tires screeched and a horn blared as Roberts cut off a car and shot into traffic to follow them. "Oh, this is getting good."

Miller held himself steady against the dashboard as they shot around the corner to follow. "There's no way we lose her this time. Keep on her tail, and call Williams in the other unit so they can track them as well in case we need help. Let's see where she's going."

✳   ✳   ✳

I pulled myself up from the floor. "What was that all about?"

Tom looked back at me. "Sorry, we didn't know if someone might have staked out the hotel, so we needed to move quickly. You okay?"

"Yeah, I guess. I didn't expect such a sudden turn." I moved up to the gap between the seats so I could see out the front.

"Hold on," Danny ordered. He took another sharp turn to the left and cut around a streetcar in front of us, then shot across an intersection, just beating a red light. When finished, he glanced back at me.

"You're crazy," I told him.

He smiled. "I always wanted to be a race car driver. So, where are we headed anyway?"

I held onto the backs of the seats to steady myself. "Mercer Island. Once you get there, I'll give you more instructions." I didn't want to give them the professor's address until I was sure we would make it without interference. Funny how I'm thinking like a spy these days.

At the next intersection Danny took a right. I could see a massive construction site on our left. I wondered what could be going on that was so big.

Danny must have read my thoughts. "That's I-5. They're extending it through Seattle. Huge project. If we are being followed, I'm hoping all of this construction material and equipment will help us lose them."

I could see Tom checking the rearview mirror on his side. "Make another turn, Danny. I think we might have a tail."

Danny shot around another corner.

I looked at Tom to see him nod. "Yep. We have a tail. Danny, any way to shake these guys?"

"These are my streets. Of course, there is." Danny quickly turned into an alley and shot out the other end, taking a right onto the street.

Miller watched as they sped up and made another quick turn. "They're onto us. Call Williams in the other unit and have them pick up the van. Once they have it, we'll drop back. We can't lose them."

Roberts pulled out his radio and made the call.

I moved to the back and looked out the window. A dark sedan careened around the corner taking the same turn we had just made. We definitely had someone following us. "They're still behind us, a few cars back."

Danny picked up his speed and darted between two cars and around a dump truck, cutting it off as he made a sharp left at the next street. He sped to the next intersection and made a right. "I'm going to cut back on our route. It might fool them."

I looked to see if they were following. I smiled. They weren't. I moved up to the gap between the seats again. "I think it worked; we lost them."

The look on Tom's face made the temporary feeling of safety drop from me. "I don't think it's going to be that easy."

Danny nodded. "We need to keep it up and make sure."

I looked out the back window to see another dark sedan swing in behind us. It wasn't the same car, but definitely following.

Danny saw it in his rearview mirror. "More company."

Tom said, "Well, it's not like we're going to pull over for them. Let's keep it up. Maybe we can shake them yet."

Danny made a quick right turn and stepped on the gas. We approached an intersection just as the green light turned yellow. Danny gunned the engine and I felt the van surge forward. He was going to run it. Danny swerved around a car and bolted across the intersection. "This should do it."

✳   ✳   ✳

Miller heard a call over the radio. "They're cutting up Maynard to Weller."

Roberts said, "That's just ahead. Look, there's Williams' car."

"And the van," Miller added. "He's running the light."

Miller watched as the van swerved around a car and across the intersection. A large cement truck driving at full steam broadsided it, tossing the van onto its side to fly along the road. It slowly spun to a stop thirty feet from the impact point.

"Damn," Roberts said.

Cars were strewn across the intersection, turned every which way to avoid the impact and each other. Roberts pulled up as close as he could, but was still quite a way from where the van had stopped. People were getting out of their cars to stare, and some were running to the van.

Miller opened his door. "Well, let's see if she's dead."

I woke to heavy throbbing through my head as if someone were banging on a drum right next to my ear. There was a beehive also in there somewhere; that kind of buzzing.

I pushed myself up and realized I was pushing up from the van wall. *How could that be?* The van was on its side. Crates had fallen on me. I tried to push them off and felt a sharp pain shoot out from my ribs. I remembered the van getting hit and my body slamming against the side as the force of the impact tried to pull me through the van wall and into whatever it was that struck us. Whatever *big* struck us. They were the same ribs I had hurt before, so it wasn't hard to reinjure them. I gingerly pushed the crates away and stood as best I could. My whole left side felt like someone had taken a sledgehammer to it. I counted my limbs. Everything seemed to be working okay, but I took a step and found out otherwise. Pain shot from my left hip when I took a step. I braced myself against the side of the van, uh, which was actually the roof.

Then it hit me. *Tom and Danny!* I limped toward the front of the van, pushing things out of my way as I went. Danny was jammed against the steering wheel, held in place between it and the crumpled seat that had forced him against it. He had taken the full impact of the collision. The steering column had skewered him. His head dangled at an odd angle; his neck broken. Blood covered his face. He was gone.

I looked down at Tom. He lay against the van door on his back. He had a big gash on his forehead with blood flowing down the side of his face. His seat belt was still attached and had twisted his body into a pretzel. I could see a stain of blood growing on his shirt near his waist.

I crawled through the seats to lean over him. "Tom, Tom!" His eyes opened for a moment. They had a glaze to them. He tried to focus on me. They lit up for a moment when he recognized me and realized what had happened. "Go. Get away. You have to go."

Tears streamed from my eyes. They landed on Tom's shirt in little damp circles around the growing blood stain. Pain shot through my body as I reached down and took his hand. "No, I won't leave you. We need to get you to a hospital."

"We can't. You're in danger. Leave. Now. You have to leave, Melanie."

I shook my head. "No, Tom. I can't. I can't!" But as I said this, the light disappeared from his eyes. I fell into shock and disbelief. How many people have to die? There is just too much death around me; too many people dying because of what I have and what I'm doing.

The sound of grinding metal brought me back to the moment. Then I heard voices. Someone had forced the back door open. A set of strong hands pulled at me, dragging me toward the back. "Come on. You need to get out of here," a man's voice said.

I turned to see him. More people reached in to help pull me out. Then I recognized the smell of gasoline. A leak, or maybe the tank had broken. They were yanking me out in case it caught fire.

I'm nearly out the back when I finally gathered my senses. I twisted free of their grip, pain shooting through me, and dropped to my knees, frantically searching for my book bag and the backpack. I found the backpack, grabbed it, and threw the straps over my shoulders as they kept trying to drag me out.

"Get away from me!"

I tossed aside crates, broken food containers, and other flotsam of the crash. A corner of my book bag appeared from under a broken crate of vegetables. I pulled it out and quickly looked to make sure the debris hadn't fallen out. It seemed to all be there.

Hands clutched at me again. Someone shouted, "Get her out. It might catch fire." More hands joined to pull me from the back of the van and onto the street.

I wrenched free of them. "Stop!" I swung my book bag at the closest of them, forcing them all to jump away. "Get back. Stop it! Get away from me."

They looked at me like I was crazy, and I was. *Yeah, so deal with that, everyone.*

I noticed some men moving quickly in my direction. Dark suits! I immediately knew who they were. I turned in the opposite direction and pushed my way through a throng of people.

Every step hurts. I'm limping, but able to walk. I try to work the pain out of my hip so I can pick up my gait. I can't let them catch me. I looked back to see the men running up to the van, one of them watching me. *Where do I go?* I hurried onto the sidewalk and down the street. Each step made it a little easier to walk.

A lot of people were still coming out of shops, drawn by the grating sound of the accident. I slid through them, hoping they would block the view until I could hide.

❋   ❋   ❋

Miller slowed as he reached the van. "Roberts, come with me. Williams, you and Benson check out the van. See if anyone's alive. And if so, keep them that way."

Williams answered, "Got it, Chief."

Miller and Roberts raced down the street in the direction Melanie had taken.

❋   ❋   ❋

I crossed by an alley, thinking for a moment of going down it. Then I saw a small Dim Sum restaurant next to it. I ducked inside and to the back. I ducked past an oriental-looking woman manning the order counter and into the kitchen. She yelled at me in some sort of high-pitched Chinese language.

I ignored her and pushed my way through a swinging door. Two men cooking at the stove jumped back at the suddenness of my appearance. I looked around and saw a delivery door to one side. I had hoped that might be the case. It must go to the alley. I limped over and opened it just a crack. Luckily, it opened in a way I could see to the side of the alley where the men would be. I watched and waited. Sure enough, they appeared and slowed, then stopped and looked down the alley. They hesitated, wondering if I could have gone that way. They talked for a moment, and then kept going.

I hurried out the door and down the alley in the opposite direction. I looked around when I got to the street. There was a small boutique shop down the road on the other side. I waited for an opening in the traffic, ran across and into the shop. Each step a reminder of how bad I must be hurt.

An oriental woman looked up from whatever she was doing at the counter and checked me out. No one else was in there.

"Can I help you?" She had a slight Japanese accent.

"Oh," I gave her a wide smile, "I was eating down the street when I saw this shop. I just love the blouse and skirt combo in the window. Funny place for a boutique shop though, isn't it, in the International District?" I was trying to make small talk.

"Many Asian women enjoy wearing western attire. We don't all go around in kimonos and sarongs, you know." She sounded pretty offended.

"Sorry. That was really a stupid question." So much for small talk. "Anyway, the blouse and skirt are great, but not quite what I'm looking for right now."

"What is it you *are* looking for?"

Of course, this being said to a young girl wearing a sleeveless t-shirt, high-top Converse sneakers, and a forced smile on her face to cover the pain she was feeling.

I didn't let her tone thwart me. "A light jacket, perhaps. And a hat." I walked over to a display of hats, trying not to limp, and picked up a nice, floppy one. I put it on. She motioned to a mirror on the wall. I stepped over and looked at myself. "It's missing something. Sunglasses?"

She stood her ground. I hadn't made a friend by what I said earlier. "You can pay for this?"

I took off my backpack, trying not to wince as I did so, and dug into the side pocket to produce a wad of bills. I waved them in the air. "Does this work?"

Money, the international language.

She smiled. "Yes, of course." She stepped over to a display and took down a pair of sunglasses with thick, white rims. "Perhaps these? They work well with the hat."

I put them on. "Perfect." And I meant it. They would be a big part of a disguise I was suddenly building. "Hair accessories? I think the hair up and under the hat would look better." And so, it went. I ended up with a mini-Mod coat in pastel green that matched the accents of the hat. I also picked out a pair of matching Go Go boots. I went into a dressing room and took off my sneakers and pants. It really hurt when I did so. I slipped on the boots and put on the Mod coat. I looked in the stall mirror to check myself out. I decided I would be properly covered, even though I only had my underwear on under the coat. I also checked my legs out to make sure there wasn't any bruising or bleeding. They looked fine, thank God. I stuffed the sneakers and pants into my book bag.

I walked out to the counter and picked up a red lipstick from a stand. I applied it using the convenient mirror on the counter. Perfect. As the final thing, I grabbed a large, oversize tote bag. I paid for everything and placed the backpack and book bag in the tote, then walked out of the store, the tote straps over my shoulder. I did my best to take on the gait of a woman whiling away her day with a shopping spree.

The two men suddenly appeared from a storefront. I practically walked right into them. A wave of nausea hit me. I wouldn't be able to get away if they recognized me. But they looked right at me and then quickly turned away to search elsewhere. No possibility I could be who they were looking for.

I strolled slowly past them and around the corner. I walked for a little while until I found a coffee shop. I went in, sat at a booth, and ordered an RC from the waitress when she appeared. It took me a moment to pull myself together. I almost thought I was getting too good at this. And then I stopped that thought as soon as it had formed. People were dead. So, I wasn't good at this at all. *Whatever this was.* Now what do I do? I can't go back to the hotel. I decided I would call a cab. I needed to move to another part of the city and find a new hotel. *And then what?*

Livingston

I limped up to room 312 at the Hotel Livingston, inserted the key and turned the knob to open the door. The hotel was at the corner of First and Virginia Street. When the cab picked me up at the coffee shop, I handed the driver a ten-dollar bill and I asked him to take me to a cheap, but decent hotel close to downtown where they wouldn't question my age. He brought me here. Maybe he got a few bucks for doing so. It's above a place called the Virginia Inn — a bar, I think — because there was a lot of noise when I got out of the cab, and no doubt a bit of drinking going on. It's late, I don't know, maybe a bit after nine or so.

I opened the door and entered the room. The sun had set a little while ago, but light still lingered at the windows, casting the room in shades of pale white.

I had stayed at that coffee shop for hours trying to figure out what to do, asking myself over and over again, *what do I do?* I kept ordering stuff so the waitress wouldn't get mad. I left her a big tip, but I still think she wondered if I was a runaway. Maybe I had that look, even with the way I was dressed. *Was I a runaway?*

I picked at my food, but wasn't hungry. There was way too much hurt happening, and not just my body, but on a lot of levels. I felt throbbing on my forehead above my left eyebrow, leftovers from that beating drum. I must have hit it against the van wall. Well, I guess more like the van wall hit my forehead. And I could only sit a certain way to keep my hip and ribs from crying out. I was pretty sure I had broken a couple of them this time. It was hard to breathe.

I decided to leave my sunglasses on in case there was a cut or bruise up there. That would surely have drawn some attention, especially if the waitress saw it. I had the feeling she didn't let anything escape her, even if it was stuff she made up in her own mind.

I needed to put on a show for her, considering how long I sat in that booth. I sipped at my RC and made small talk with her whenever she came over to check on me. My RC was in a big glass full of ice, and the waitress, Bea was her name, kept it full. I think she finally felt sorry for me, for whatever reason she decided, so no call to the police, thank God.

The whole time I sat there and tried to think of all the things I could do at this point, there was only one thing I should do, and I didn't like it. Not because it would be the wrong thing, but because of what I would have to face once I went through with it.

I stood in the doorway of my hotel room and immediately knew it had seen better days, even in the pale evening light. Well, good, we were both a little beat up, so we'll get along just fine. I threw my tote bag on the bed, along with my hat, then kicked off the Go Go boots, happy to do so. They were definitely not me. I'm Converse high-tops all the way.

The room had a small bathroom off to one side. I went in and took my sunglasses off so I could check the bump on my forehead. I set them next to the sink and looked at myself in the mirror. I studied a big lump above my eyebrow, some bruising already forming around it. I'm glad I decided to keep the sunglasses on at the coffee shop.

I stepped out of my Mod coat, tossed it onto the bedroom floor, and stood there in my underwear and sleeveless tee. Some evening light managed to filter its way through a small window in the bathroom. Enough to show bruising already forming on my hip where I had smashed against the side of the van when the truck hit us. I'm afraid to take my shirt off. I know what my side and back are going to look like underneath. Based on the way I felt, a whole lot more of that purple hue forming on my hip. I cringed as I pulled my shirt over my head, a sharp pain shooting from my ribs. No doubt this time, I'm sure they are broken. I checked myself in the mirror. My side and back looked as bad as my hip.

I let the shirt fall to the bathroom floor, stepped out of my underwear, and slid open the shower curtain. I turned the hot water tap to full, and let it run until a mound of steam rose from the shower floor. I adjusted the cold water to where I would barely be able to stand the heat, then stepped in. The hot water shocked me at first, but felt good. I settled in and let it engulf me, the spray hurting when it hit certain spots on my body—reminding me I am still alive. *But, why though?*

I should have died with Danny and Tom. I leaned forward and placed my hands against the shower wall to steady myself, then bowed my head and closed my eyes. I focused on the steady spray of hot water pounding onto all the damaged tissue of my body. Tears welled in my eyes and soon joined the hot water flowing from my shoulders to the drain below.

I couldn't get the vision of Danny and Tom out of my head, twisted up in the metal of the van. Then I thought of my mom, and how she had looked in the hospital bed—stitches and casts and those clear lines of reddish fluid gurgling from the open wound on her head. All dead because of me, and in terrible ways. Thank God I wasn't there to see my dad die as well, his body burning in his car at the bottom of a ravine where the Russian agent had left him.

I broke into uncontrollable sobs. Terrible stabs of pain raced through my body with each breath as my ribs spread and contracted. But I couldn't stop. I took in huge gasps of air, one after another, nearly fainting from the pain. My lungs filled with the torrid steam engulfing me in the shower—each breath a giant reminder of the guilt surging through me, wondering why them and not me? I decided I deserved this terrible pain; my penance for those who had died along my path.

I took in another huge breath and a sharp, stabbing pain forced the air back out of me. Something happened. Maybe a rib had somehow punctured my lung. It felt like that. I couldn't catch my breath. I started to pass out, so I dropped to my knees. I had to place my hands on the shower floor to steady myself. Water poured over my head and flowed down my hair to the drain below. I threw up, nauseated by the pain and lack of air, which caused even more pain to relentlessly shoot through my body. I watched my RC infused puke wash down the drain.

I tried to take a breath, but couldn't. My lungs wouldn't work. I couldn't breathe. I reached up and fumbled with the knobs to turn the shower off. I steadied myself on the shower floor, fighting away the oncoming faint. I focused on taking in a slow, painful breath. And then letting it out. I tried another, and could barely take in enough air to keep from fainting if I went slowly. I really must have done some damage to be like this.

I crawled out of the shower, grabbing a towel from the rack, and gingerly crawled across the room and up onto the bed. I tried to dry my hair, but it hurt too much to raise my arms. I dabbed at my body and then crawled under the sheets, laying on my back.

I should call the front desk. Get a doctor up here. But as soon as I thought of this, I knew it wasn't going to happen. I decided to wait until morning, to reassess things then. Maybe I'm wrong and the ribs are just bruised really badly. I can handle that. I've become pretty good at handling pain of all sorts.

I took long, slow breaths; trying to focus on tomorrow and what I needed to do. I always knew what it would be, all that time in the coffee shop, and ever since. There was only one thing I could do—call Frankie.

I carefully turned onto my side, and into a fetal position, wincing as one last shot of pain raced to my toes. It hurt, but reminded me that I'm still alive and there must be a reason for that. Destiny (or dharma as Mrs. Crowley called it), filled my head. I knew it was why I hadn't died. But what did destiny have planned for me?

I shook the thought, too exhausted to even deal with such things right now. I needed sleep, but knew it would be a long night of pain, loss, and anticipation. Tomorrow felt a long way off.

Pike's

I woke to a bright blue light moving through my room, float-ing along the ceiling from one side to the other. Then it disap-peared. I lay there for a while, wondering what it was. It had to come from outside my window, something shining in. It was a strange light, with firm edges, like one made by a spotlight or searchlight of some sort—bluish, bright, and stark and round. Not flat round though; more of a three-dimensional kind of round, like a blue ball of light. *But how could that be?*

I'm lying on my back in bed, naked, but perfectly laid out with my arms against my sides and my legs parallel to each other, like a mannequin right out of the box, not yet clothed in the latest styles and molded into position. There aren't any co-vers over me. I must have kicked them off during the night.

I sat up on the side of the bed and grabbed the alarm clock from the table. It was getting light enough to where the clock face showed it to be five-fourteen in the morning. Way early. I got up and walked to the window to look out and see what might have caused the strange light. There was nothing out there, no searchlights or anything that could have caused the light in my room. What did cause it, then?

Suddenly, I realized something. I had gotten up and walked over to the window without feeling a trace of pain. I reached up to my forehead. I moved my fingers around the area to be sure, but the bump was gone. I quickly went into the bathroom and turned on the light to study myself in the mirror. I looked at my hip. No bruising at all. I pressed my fingers into the area where I thought I had broken a rib or two. No shooting pain. I turned at my waist to test my ribs. Nothing. I studied my back in the mirror. No bruising there either. I leaned toward the mirror to examine the spot above my eyebrow in detail. Not a bit of the swelling and bruising I had seen the evening before. The bump was completely gone. The bruising on my hip and back now gone. The pain gone. *How could that be?*

I went back to the bed and sat down. I would think I had dreamt the whole thing about the accident, but then how do I explain being at *this* hotel and the Go Go outfit on the floor? It happened, but the physical damage from the accident seen in the mirror last night was completely gone this morning. A miracle? I've never believed in them. Well, not until now, anyway. *But, how else to explain it?*

It became just one more thing to wonder about; maybe another layer revealing itself in the Melanie Simpson drama unfolding before me. I decided there was no way I would be able to figure out my miraculous recovery, so I set it aside and wondered what to do now. It was way too early to call Frankie. I needed to wait for a while longer.

I decided to get dressed and see if I could find someplace to get coffee and breakfast. I took some clean underwear and a t-shirt out of my backpack and put them on. I thought about putting on my Go Go disguise again, just in case, but decided I would be okay in my regular clothes. I spent hours in that coffee shop yesterday with a good view out the windows, and never saw anything that indicated someone was watching me.

I put on a shirt and my pants, and pulled on my high-tops. I washed up in the bathroom, brushed my teeth and my hair, and then grabbed a light jacket from my backpack before I headed out the door. I was a little worried about leaving my book bag

226

and backpack in the room, but decided they would be safe. I was sure no one had followed me.

I stood outside the Virginia Inn at the corner of Virginia Street and 1st Ave. I looked up to see a sky with only a trace of clouds. The air smelled fresh and cool, with a slight breeze hitting me every once in a while, carrying with it the tang of seawater from the bay. I could already tell it would get warm, like yesterday, probably into the mid-seventies.

The sun had risen already, but the hills and buildings blocked it from where I stood. I looked down the hill along Virginia Street and out to a body of water. I think it was Puget Sound. Off in the distance the sun showed itself as a sliver of golden light hitting an island across the bay.

My eyes dropped to the street to see it had been paved with cobblestones long ago, now old and worn. I decided to follow them down the hill toward the bay, hoping to find something open this early. At the bottom I turned left onto Pike Place, and walked down and past Pine Street which came in on my left. A long building on my right was open to the street. People were unloading flowers and other things to set up their stands for the day, a big sign above them said Seattle Garden Center. Apparently, I had wandered onto a big open market. I noticed quite a bit of commotion at the far end where a bunch of carts and trucks were offloading things. A big truck had Pike Place Fish Company written on its side.

The activity drew me toward it. I walked along the cobbled street; little shops now on both sides of me, readying various wares for customers who would soon arrive. When I got to the end, the road turned left up the hill. On my right, and above the main opening to the market sat a big neon sign reading Public Market Center, with a big clock as part of the sign. It was still only a little after six.

Inside the building men were busy setting up the fish shop with seafood to be displayed across freshly iced stands. My thought of eating something disappeared for a moment as I became fascinated with all of the activity. I explored the area, walking in and out of the shops as they set up, going down little corridors and along narrow alleys.

I found out the market sat on a steep hillside and had lower levels. I went down a ramp and explored the next level. A Goodwill shop and the Post Office were there, along with a spice shop, malt shop, and lots of artist stalls. None were open this early. It turned out to be like a maze.

I went deeper and explored further until I got to an area that was no longer used. It was dark, but a little light seeped in from one side of the walkway, coming from the windows on the bay side of the building. The walkway was in disrepair and had many obstacles. Little rooms stood off the main walkway, like on the upper levels, but were mounded high with trash and discarded equipment. Wooden boards and beams from the damaged walls sat in mounds all over the place. Dust covered everything. It had been years since this area had been used.

Still, the tomboy came out in me and I had to explore it, crawling over things to get around. I ended up getting lost, but eventually found a door that led to a narrow, cobbled alley with tall brick buildings on either side. I walked up the alley toward the market. It jogged right and I soon came out at the corner of Pike Place and Pike Street.

I found a little coffee shop on Pike Street, just up the hill from the market, and grabbed a cup of coffee and a walnut-raisin muffin. I sat at a table and nibbled at the muffin while I thought about when to call Frankie. I should wait at least until ten to make sure he was up. I couldn't call person to person, because that would be an issue if his mom, dad, or Suzie answered the phone. I would make it a regular call and hang up if they answered. I'd lose the money, but it was the only thing I could do. My backup plan would be to call Katch if I couldn't reach Frankie. I thought about calling her first because she knew I had come up to Seattle. But that wouldn't be fair to Frankie. I had to call him first, even if it would be just so I could say I had tried.

I looked at the clock on the wall. It was still way too early to call. I went outside and walked up to the corner of 2nd Avenue. The big city had come to life. Traffic shot in every direction, and the sidewalks had filled with people. I looked down toward the market to see the stalls already full of shoppers. I walked up the hill on Pike, deciding to explore. I wondered for a moment if that would be a good idea. I didn't want to get spotted. I finally decided it would be okay. How could anyone find me in this big city after my getaway? But just in case, I stepped into a tourist shop and bought a baseball cap with the word 'Seattle' on it. I put it on, tucked my hair underneath, and put on my sunglasses so it would be even harder to spot me.

I got close to 4th Avenue and things started looking familiar. I remembered I had been to this area once before when my parents brought me here for the Seattle World's Fair in 1962. I was pretty sure the Monorail ended up around here somewhere. I decided to look for it. It would be fun to take it again.

I was right. When I reached Pike Street and 4th, I found it. A little thrill raced through me. The last time I was here it had been with my mom and dad. We had so much fun at the fair. There were some amazing things to see, and we did so as a family. Not a care in the world at the World's Fair. The thought made me smile.

The Monorail looked very modern, with arched canopies of alternating blue and white over the stairs and above the train level itself. The plaza had large mosaic circles in off-whites and rose.

I walked up to the ticket counter to find it closed and a sign that said it wouldn't open until eight. I had to wait for another twenty minutes. Bartell's Drug Store sat to one side of the plaza. Luckily it was open. I wandered through the aisles, whiling away the time.

At eight, I bought a ticket, went up the stairs and into the first Monorail car. It was where we sat when I was with my mom and dad. It made it easy to watch Seattle unfold before us as we moved along the rail.

There weren't very many tourists out yet, so I pretty much had the car to myself. The station at the other end was right at the Space Needle. I was excited to be able to see it again. It was as if I didn't have a care in the world right now; like I was still in 1962 with my mom and dad, enjoying Seattle like tourists.

✳   ✳   ✳

George slid into the last car of the Monorail train, as far away from Melanie as he could get. As big and tall as he was, it wasn't easy to tail someone, but he could pull it off.

He had followed her yesterday from the Panama Hotel, along with the two other cars. Actually, he had followed their car. They were too tied up in the chase to even notice. It didn't hurt to have a police scanner in his car; one of the perks of being a police captain. He heard the call from the chase car for the location of the accident. He was right there, so quickly parked, got out, and came upon the accident from a side street. He was about to race over to check on Melanie, but saw she had already been pulled from the back of the van.

She seemed to have survived the accident in decent shape, at least good enough to swing her book bag and make people jump out of the way. When she hurried away from the approaching men, it was in his direction. He ducked into a doorway before she could spot him, and watched her enter the restaurant. He moved to a position where he could see both the alley and the front of the restaurant, covering both escape routes.

The two men stopped at the alley and then continued down the street. When Mel came out the alley door, he followed and waited outside the clothing shop until she appeared in her new look. He had been on her tail ever since. He felt proud of himself, because Melanie had become quite good at evasion.

The Call

I'm sitting in an old-fashioned, wooden phone booth in the lobby of Hotel Livingston. Thank goodness they had a phone booth in here. It will give me some privacy for my call. The lobby isn't very big, so the clerk at the counter has an easy view of me across the room. He keeps looking over, no doubt wondering why I'm just sitting here and not on the phone. Although it's probably because he's bored, young, and I'm the only action in the room. All the same, it's making me feel uneasy.

I've been in here exactly eighteen minutes, but it's felt more like eighty because time decided to flow like molasses. I was worried someone else would hog the booth if I didn't do the same thing myself, so I grabbed it.

I eventually took a Yellow Pages phone book and placed it in my lap, thumbing through it like I was trying to find a phone number. I looked up at a wall clock for the thousandth time, which I could barely read through the mottled glass of the phone booth door. It was seven minutes before ten. I sat there, frustrated. I couldn't stand it anymore, even though my plan was to wait.

I dialed '0' for the operator and had her connect me to the long-distance operator. When she came on the line, I gave her Frankie's phone number, dropping the amount of change into the phone slot she said would be required to make the connection.

It rang only once and Frankie picked up. "Hello."

I couldn't speak. I really didn't expect this to work so easily. I opened my mouth and moved my lips. I think I would have looked like a fish sucking air if there had been a mirror in front of me.

"Hello?" he said again, fear in his voice. It prompted me to answer.

"Frankie, it's me."

"Mel. Oh, my God! Are you all right?"

"No. I'm up in Seattle, I—"

"What! Seattle. How, why?"

"Frankie, let me finish. First, can you talk?"

"Yeah, okay, sorry. Yes, I can. Dad's at work, and Mom and Suzie went shopping. It's just…you ran away. I haven't left the house, hoping you would call. I've been going nuts since you took off. You could be dead, laying in a ditch somewhere for all I know."

I didn't realize such a thought could come to him. It just now hit me how I had put him on one huge, emotional roller coaster. "I'm sorry, Frankie."

Silence on both our parts. I wondered if I should tell him about Tom and Danny. That would really freak him out. I knew he would come up to Seattle no matter what, but if someone was watching him, he needed to know how bad it was, so he could keep an eye out.

"Frankie. There's something I have to tell you and you can't flip out on me, okay? I need you to keep cool."

"Mel?" His voice took on an ominous tone. "Tell me. Don't screw around. You're scaring me."

"I figured out Professor Lofton is up here in Seattle. I came up to see him and brought the debris, hoping he would take it to study. I also wanted to see some film he has of my dad and the Orb."

"And you decided to do this all on your own, leaving me out of it again?"

"Frankie, cut me some slack, okay? Yes, I did." I stopped to gather myself. "Look, I need your help, but I'll hang up if you give me any more hassle. I can't deal with it right now."

I heard a big sigh on the other end of the line. "Sorry if the truth hurts. Okay, I'll drop it."

I ignored the criticism and continued. "I called Tom to help me out. He put a plan together. Well, it went south on us." I wavered for a moment, then knew I had to plod on. "Frankie. I need you to not wig out when I tell you this."

"What, Mel?" Frustration in his voice.

"Tom is dead. Some men were after us. He died when our van was hit by a truck."

"What?" He paused, absorbing what I told him. "Mel, were you in it? Are you hurt?"

"Yes, I was, but I'm fine." I wasn't though, because I still needed to figure out how I had healed so fast. "But I'm stuck in a hotel. Can you come up? I really need you here, for a lot of reasons."

"Are you kidding? Absolutely. I'll head out as soon as I can."

"I wasn't going to call because I knew you would lose your car privileges over this, and probably get grounded for life on top of it. I don't want your parents to take your car away. I know how much it means to you."

"You're kidding right? That doesn't matter right now, I lo—"

The operator came on the line, "Please deposit thirty-five cents for an additional five minutes."

"Hold on, Frankie." I reached into my back pocket, took out my coin purse, scrounged around in it and deposited the money. "Frankie, I haven't got much more change. We can fig-ure out what to do when you get here."

"Just give me the address, and I'm on my way."

I gave it to him. "And Frankie, I need you to call Katch and tell her what's going on. She knew I was coming up." I cringed when I said this, knowing what he would think—that I had told her and not him.

The line stayed silent for a moment, probably because he was deciding on whether to say anything about it, but he didn't. "Don't go anywhere and keep the door locked." He hung up.

No I miss you, or I love you or stay safe in any of that. I placed the receiver in the cradle of the payphone and sat there thinking about my call. Had I done the right thing to involve him again? *But what other choice did I have?*

Road Trip

Frankie stared at the phone for a moment, trying to calm his frustration and get his thoughts together. He picked up the receiver again, deciding he might as well make this call right now. It couldn't wait. He stuck his finger in the hole for the first number and spun the rotary dial until it stopped, then released it to spin back and reset. He did this for the rest of the numbers, heard a few clicks, and then the phone ringing on the other end.

Mrs. Gallo answered. "Hello."

"Hi, Mrs. Gallo. It's Frankie Strickland. Is Katch available?"

"She's in her room. Hold on, I'll get her."

Frankie heard the receiver placed on the counter.

Katch finally came to the line. "Frankie? What's going on?"

"It's Mel. She's up in Seattle and needs help. But I guess *you* already knew she was up there because she told me you did." He paused for a second. "Even though I called you the day she ran away, and you said she hadn't contacted you."

He heard her muffle the receiver with her hand and speak in a low tone, "Look, Frankie, I didn't know anything when you called. It was the next day I found out, but she made me promise not to tell you. I'm sorry, but I couldn't." She paused on the line. Frankie heard her sigh with frustration. "Just tell me, Frankie, is she in trouble?"

"Yes. And I'm going up there. She needs my help."

"Hold on, Frankie. I need to know a whole lot more than that, but not over the phone. I don't have any privacy here. Can we meet?"

"There's no time. I need to get going."

"You are not doing this without me. I'll grab some stuff. And I'm going to call Beanie, too. He needs to know. We are all in this together, whether Mel realizes it or not. Right?"

Frankie thought about it. He didn't have much money and worried it wouldn't even be enough for gas to get up there. He had planned to ask Katch for money anyway, and was sure at this point she would say no unless she could go along. "Okay. If you're coming, you guys will need to bring as much cash as you can. I don't have much, and we'll need gas and food on the trip. This will probably be an overnighter, so whatever you need for that, too. Mel has a hotel room. We can all crash there if we need to. And tell Beanie the same, that is, if he can manage to get out of the house without his mother's radar going off."

"Sure. I have money. I'll bring it. Give us half an hour and we'll meet at the easement, okay?"

"All right, but not at the easement. I don't know when Mom and Suzie will be home. I need to be gone before they get here. Meet me at the Hunt Club, in the parking lot. Just know I'm leaving as soon as possible. You get there any later than half an hour from right now, and I'll be gone without you, understand?"

"Sure. Don't worry, we'll make it. After all, we're The Four Musketeers, right? All for one...and one for all."

"Right." Frankie hung up, knowing they would be there.

Katch jumped into the front seat next to Frankie after letting Beanie in the back. She knew Frankie was probably pretty pissed off that Mel had told her and not him about going to Seattle. She figured she would need to try and smooth things over as much as possible before they got up there, so it wouldn't be super awkward.

She set her bag on the floor between her legs. "All set, let's get going."

Frankie started the engine and pulled the Mustang out of the parking lot.

Beanie leaned forward between the seats. "So, give us all the juice about what's going on."

Frankie looked right and then left before pulling onto Iron Mountain Boulevard in the direction of Lake Oswego. He didn't mince words when he answered. "Tom is dead. They were being chased by someone. Got in an accident. He died. That's all I know."

Katch was shocked by the blunt way he said this, about someone dying, someone he knew and liked. Abrupt, heartless. It only confirmed what she thought—that Frankie felt jilted over not being told, when *she* had been.

"But Mel wasn't hurt, right?" she asked.

"She says she wasn't, but I've kinda gotten to where I don't trust what she says anymore, so I have no idea."

"Well, at least she's safe." She looked over to Frankie. He didn't say anything. "She's safe, right?"

Frankie shrugged, staring straight ahead. "She's in a hotel, in Seattle, alone, hundreds of miles away, with men after her. I'm not sure how that calculates to being safe."

Katch decided to change the subject. She reached into her bag and took out a wad of bills. "Look, I brought about a hundred dollars. Hopefully that will do. It's money I've been saving, and from what I've made at work so far."

Frankie looked over at her. "A hundred bucks. Really? That's a lot."

Beanie stuck his hand out between them, holding a single, crumpled dollar bill. "Here's my contribution to add to the pot. So, I guess between Katch and me, we have a little over fifty bucks each."

"I love your math, Beanie," Katch said. "You must have excelled in algebra."

"What about all the reward money you got from Major Burnham?" Frankie asked.

"Yeah, well, my mom stuffed that cash in a bank somewhere and I can't reach it. So, I'm stuck, at least until I turn eighteen, before I can get my hands on any of that mullah."

Katch shared a quick look with Frankie to indicate that was so typical of Beanie's mom. She really was quite a piece of parental work.

"No problem, Beanie. I have you covered...again," Katch said.

"Indebted to you forever, or at least until you come to your senses and dump me."

"Don't give me any ideas."

"Good point. I should have thought about that before I opened my mouth."

"That's one of the reasons I do keep you around, because you always say things before you think them out. It lets me know there are no hidden agendas with you. Funny how that works, huh?"

"I am constantly awed by your womanly powers of insight."

"Don't push it, Beanie."

They rode along in silence for a while. Katch watched out the window, glimpses of the Willamette River appeared between the trees as they drove down Macadam Avenue toward the connection to I-5 North. She hoped Mel would be safe until they got there, wondering what happened so that Tom was now dead? And who was after her? Although she had the *why* figured out already. It wasn't until they had crossed into Washington State before anyone said anything.

"It should take about three hours from here," Frankie said. "I'm going to have to stop and get gas along the way, and we need to check to see if they have a map of the Seattle area." He looked over at Katch. "You'll need to be my navigator because I have no idea of how to get around Seattle."

Katch smiled. "I'm huge with maps, so no problem."

Beanie said, "Yeah, better Katch, than me. If I were giving directions, we'd probably end up in China somehow. I get lost going to the bathroom in the middle of the night."

Katch and Frankie laughed.

"Don't worry, Beanie," Frankie said. "We are well aware of your limitations, which by the way, pretty much on their own, seem limitless."

They were at a gas station in Olympia: needing a bathroom break, gas, and snacks. It would still take about another hour to get to the hotel in Seattle.

Katch jumped back in the car and opened the map to study it. Luckily, the gas station had one with pretty good detail of the Seattle area. "I think this will work. I'll figure out a route for when we get there."

"Sounds good." Frankie pulled out to the road and worked his way back to the freeway heading north. He had been quiet about Mel the whole way, but broke that silence now. He gave Katch a quick glance. "So, why is it, do you think, that Mel told you about Seattle and not me?"

Katch studied him for a moment, trying to get a read. She was hoping he'd break the ice on this subject. It would work out better this way. "Hmm, maybe it had something to do with your breaking up with her. You were the one who walked away, remember? So, why should she?"

"I guess that's a good point. But it's such a huge decision. You think she would have discussed it with all of us, to help her make the right choice."

Katch gave him a look like he didn't know Mel at all. "What? Mel? Are you kidding? When has she *ever* kept us in the loop for any decision she's made?"

Beanie shot his thoughts through the gap between the seats, his mouth full of Lay's potato chips, "Yeah, Frankie. She's always been in her own world. You, if anyone, should know that."

"Frankie," Katch added, "I'm glad you brought this up. There are things you need to know before we get up there."

Frankie kept his eyes on the road while he passed an old Rambler that had seen better days. "Like what?"

"Like she had a big fight with Emilee, and that's why she ran away that day."

"I know that much. Emilee called me. I went over there. She told me about the fight, but wouldn't tell me what it was about. Something to do with her mother." He glanced over to Katch. "Do you know?"

Katch did, but couldn't tell him. It wasn't her place. She decided to sidestep the question for now. "Mel called me and had me come over to Mrs. Crowley's. That's where she stayed those first two nights."

Frankie nodded. "Of course. I should have known."

"It was while there, with the three of us talking, that Mrs. Crowley and I came to realize how this was all meant to play out."

Frankie stayed silent for a moment, before asking, "How did you come to that conclusion?"

"Think of it. Mrs. Crowley has her special talents with fore-seeing things, like she did with the tarot reading. And I have been studying under my grandmother as a Hopi seer for years, and I'm getting pretty good at it. So, Mel was with two people who could foresee her destiny through our individual gifts. It just took all three of us getting together to finally understand."

"Okay. Go on," Frankie said.

"Mel knew the professor was up in Seattle, and that she had to see him."

"She told me about the professor when she called, and why she *thought* she needed to go see him," Frankie replied.

"Well, I can see that you're definately not on board," she said in frustration, "so let me explain. Do you remember in the tarot reading, Mrs. Crowley called it *Mel's* universe? And then my grandmother pointed to the stars and called them *her* sky people."

Frankie nodded, "Sure. How do you forget that?"

Beanie said, "Yeah, pretty weird stuff."

"Well, then you should also remember Mrs. Crowley's reading told of a journey, a quest she must undertake. She also said Mel must seek other lands, and guidance from someone new who she will come to trust. Do you remember all of that, too?"

"There isn't much I don't remember about that reading," Frankie said.

"Well, Mel feels that's what drove her to Seattle and the professor. Because the tarot reading foretold it."

"But, how can we really come to that solid of a conclusion?" Frankie asked.

Katch knew the missing piece was what he didn't know: the abductions. But it wasn't her place to tell him.

"Frankie, there's more. It's also what Mel and Emilee fought about. But like Emilee said, it's up to Mel to share that with you or not. Just know this—as Mrs. Crowley and I came to understand that day—whatever is happening with Mel, is way bigger than any of us."

Katch thought for a moment, then looked over at Frankie and Beanie, putting an unbendable tone to her voice, "I think we all need to understand one thing; we are simply three passengers riding along on the meteoric tail of a comet called Melanie."

Together Again

A knock came at the door. Three taps, a pause, and then two more. It was the code I had set up with Frankie over the phone so I could make sure it was him. There wasn't a peephole for such purposes.

I opened the door to be surprised by Katch jumping into my arms. "Oh, thank God! You're safe."

"Katch! Beanie! I didn't know you were coming too."

Katch said, "Frankie called and when he said he was coming up, I wouldn't let him come without us."

Then she stepped back, maybe thinking she should have let Frankie come in first. He was still standing in the hall, looking in at me.

Beanie shoved him from behind and into the room. "Geez, you sure can make things awkward sometimes."

I closed the distance and wrapped my arms around Frankie, holding him tight. "I know we have gone through a lot; too much really. But none of that matters right now. I'm just glad you came." I stood back and looked into his eyes.

"Mel, how could I not? It seems it doesn't really matter what you do, or even how you treat me sometimes. I don't think I'll ever stop loving you."

I threw my arms around him again. "I love you, too." I gave him a big kiss.

"Ugh, all right," Beanie cut in, "are we done with the melodramatic soap opera crap now?"

Katch hit him in the side. "Quit ruining the moment."

Beanie feigned pain. "Ouch." He strutted around the room, running his fingers over the frayed arm of the worn couch. "Wow, Mel. You really went all out with the accommodations. After we came all this way to save your ass. Couldn't you get a suite or something? Wasn't the penthouse available?" He then plopped down, throwing his legs up and over the arm of the couch.

"What I did, was to find a place where the desk clerk wouldn't ask what a fifteen-year-old runaway was doing getting a hotel room."

Frankie said, "So, we're safe then? No cops to worry about?"

"No police, but that would be the least of our problems."

"Yeah, Mel," Beanie asked, "bring us up to speed. How did Tom die, and what kind of danger have you managed to get us all into *this* time?"

I gave Beanie my cursory 'shove it' look, which I use whenever he said something stupid directed at me.

Katch said, "Look Mel, if you don't want to talk about it, we understand."

"No, I do. I need to tell you, and I will soon, but I've spent the last day wallowing in the pain of it all. I don't want to think about it right now. I just want some Mel time hanging out with her friends."

Katch came over and gave me a hug.

I returned it, then walked over to the phone on the small desk by the window. "Well, I bet you're all starved." I looked at Beanie. "Oh, by the way, I also managed to find a place where the bar downstairs makes a mean pizza and will deliver. And they don't ask for ID when beer is ordered with it because they never have to leave the building. I slipped the desk clerk a five for that rich information. So how does that sound?"

Beanie quickly sat up on the couch, his stomach already rumbling. "Sorry, Mel. I was way wrong, Now that I think about it, this *is* the penthouse suite."

I picked up the phone and dialed the Virginia Inn downstairs. While it rang I said, "It's two-thirty. We'll need to get some rest. It's going to be a long night. I set up a meeting with Professor Lofton at his place, but he can't see us until nine o'clock." Someone came on the line. "Yes, I'm a guest at the Hotel Livingston, and I'd like to order some pizzas."

Psycho

I watched as Katch tried to read the map by the light from the car window, which seemed to be disappearing quickly. She was in the front passenger seat playing navigator. Beanie and I sat in the back. It was already after nine and we had yet to find Professor Lofton's place.

"I think we're lost," Frankie said. Frustration in his voice. "We've been on this windy road for a while. Maybe we missed it."

It didn't help that a late evening thunderstorm had found its way to the area and decided to hang right over our heads. Thunder, lightning, and rain were in unlimited supply right now.

"No, this has to be right," Katch said. "But I'm having a hard time reading the map. It's getting too dark. We need to pull over so I can use the dome light."

Frankie pulled over to the first spot he could find, and then turned on the dome light.

Katch studied the map. "Okay, we're still on East Mercer Way—"

"And have been for way too long," Frankie cut in.

"No. I think we're okay. Didn't we just pass Fernridge Lane?"

I answered. "Yeah. I saw it. The last road we went by, on the right."

"Then Appleton should be ahead on the left, and East Mercer Highlands Drive after that on the right. We should be fine. Let's just keep it slow, so we don't miss the streets."

I looked out the window at the darkening sky as another lightning bolt lit up the car interior. "I hope you're right. It wouldn't be hard to miss a side street in this mess."

Frankie drove along the twisting route. The whole way tall trees had lined the road, leaning over it, weighed down by the heavy rain falling from the very dark and ominous clouds above. I hoped this wasn't an omen for what lay ahead.

"There it is," Katch said. "Take a right here."

Frankie turned onto an even narrower, one-lane road. It immediately climbed a steep hill, winding along its contours. We passed an occasional house, but most of the way deep underbrush lined the road, while tall trees overhung the road and shrouded us in darkness.

"He lives up at the end," I said, "so I guess we keep going until the road stops."

We worked our way along, following a ridgeline cut into the side of a steep hill. A flash of lightning appeared overhead. A Gothic-looking three-story house appeared above us on the hill, silhouetted against the lightning-filled sky.

Beanie said, "Hey, guys? Remember in the movie Psycho, when the girl first sees the house up on the hill? Does this remind anyone else of that scene?"

None of us said a word, because we were all thinking the same thing.

We got closer as the road ran below the house. It looked like a portion of the house sat on stilts, straddling the side of a cliff.

This is just, plain, spooky.

The road eventually curved up to the top and ended at a driveway leading to the house. We looked at each other like: *Are we really doing this?*

We finally got out and hurried up to the front door, rain pounding down on us. Everyone stood aside for me. The entry had intricately designed double front doors made from some sort of dark wood, with matching heavy brass door knockers; something only seen in movies—horror movies. I tried to remember if the Psycho house had door knockers?

I glanced back at the gang and gave them an 'okay, here we go' look, grabbed one of the knockers and rapped it three times. The sound reverberated through the house. We waited. A little foot shuffling on our part could be heard.

After a moment I sensed some movement on the other side. The door opened and a middle-aged man in an old, frumpy sweater stood there. His hair was all tousled and his dark-rimmed glasses sat skewed on his nose. He had a rutty, mottled appearance to his face, like someone who avoided sunlight at all possible cost.

He looked me over, and then to my friends. "Well, isn't this a little party?"

"Hi, Professor Lofton. These are my friends, pointing them out—Frankie, Katch, and Beanie."

"Melanie Simpson, I presume then?"

"Yes. I hope you don't mind my having brought my friends. Well, actually, the truth is, they brought me. But it's a long story."

"Then I suggest you come inside, get out of this inclement weather, and into a more hospitable environment in which we can discuss such things. I've made some hot tea. Seems like the right thing to do on such a night." He waved us in.

We walked into the house, and into what also appeared to be a museum. The foyer opened into a huge, main room. Tall cabinets lined every wall: full of artifacts, statues, parchments, and all sorts of oddities. The tables throughout the room were also adorned with little statues and relics of different sorts.

"So, what kind of professor are you?" I asked.

"I'm a physical anthropologist. A rather complicated study. Where an archeologist, such as your father, studies humans through their material remains at particular moment in time, physical anthropology is concerned with the origin, evolution, and diversity of people."

"Oh, okay." As if I understood.

I looked up. The ceiling was at least two stories high, with an intricate wood pattern holding tile accents all across it. At one end of the room stood a large, stone fireplace. A warm fire snapped and crackled in it, tossing out flicks of blue flame every now and then.

There was an array of comfortable seating in front of the fireplace. He motioned us toward it. "Have a seat. I'll fetch the tea and be right back. I am so excited to finally meet Roger's daughter." He hesitated. "I had thought your mother would be here also."

"More of the long story," I told him.

"Oh." He paused, thinking for a moment. "Well, then we probably shouldn't delay. I'll be right back."

When he returned, he had a big pot of tea and five cups already filled. Nothing like the porcelain tea set we had used when Emilee first arrived. Just a typical tea pot and some coffee mugs. "I'm not into formalities, so help yourself. Cream and sugar, if you like." He grabbed his own cup and sat down in a lounge chair. "Okay, shoot."

I wasn't sure what he meant at first. "Oh, my story, right?

He settled in and nodded.

"Okay..."

So, I told him everything: from how we found the debris and figured out the Orb existed, to how my dad was killed by a Russian agent, and my mom's questionable death. I also told him about my grandmother coming. But not what she told me. I couldn't share that here. Not now. I finished up with how Tom and Danny died, and who I thought had been after us. He needed to know, since he could very well be in danger, too.

He seemed focused on every word and had only a few questions. When I was finished, he said, "First, I am so sorry that you have lost both your parents. Thank goodness your grandmother stepped in, and that you have such good friends."

I let the grandmother part pass without comment.

He continued. "It appears your father has kicked a hornet's nest; and now *you* have been dragged into it."

"It's okay. I need to finish what he started. I know it's some sort of quest. That's why I came. And, because I want to give you this." I reached into my book bag and took out all of the alien debris, placing it on the coffee table between us.

"Wow!" Katch said, "I've so been looking forward to seeing this stuff." She got down on her knees and picked up one of the struts, turning it in her hands to study it. "This is the alien writing you told me about, right?"

"Yes. That's what we think, anyway," I answered.

"As did your father and I," the professor added.

Frankie and Beanie jumped down next to Katch, picking up pieces and studying them. It had been nearly a year since they'd last seen the debris, and after all, this was alien stuff from another world. Beanie showed Katch different pieces, explaining what we thought they were. He held out a piece of the foil, crumpled it in his hand, and dropped it on the table where it flowed back into its original shape, not a fold in it. An audible "wow" came from her lips.

The professor sat forward in his chair. "I haven't seen this material for years. It still amazes me, the advanced technology shown just in these few items."

I looked over to him. "Would you like it, you know, to do research and figure out how it works?"

"Oh, Melanie. That is a wonderful offer, but also a big responsibility, and a commitment to years of study. Thank you, but it's just not my discipline. I haven't a clue on how to conduct such technological research."

"Do you know who would? Someone you can trust?" I stayed hopeful.

"No, I'm afraid not. My circle of peers is small, and similarly focused. None of them works in this realm. I know your father had been developing contacts, but he kept things compartmentalized. No doubt because of the danger involved—which proved itself out. So, I never knew whoever they might be. You will need to find another way to get this material to the appropriate scientists." I could see he was trying to stay positive. "I'm just not your guy for this, but I'm sure you will find someone."

"That's okay, Mel," Frankie cut in. "We'll figure it out."

"Yeah, Mel. And that wasn't the main reason you came here anyway, right?" Katch added.

I nodded. "Professor, you said you have film of my father and the Orb. Can we see it?"

"Of course. I have it set up in my research lab. Along with something else I want to show you." He stood and motioned for us to do the same. "Come with me."

Theatrum Orbis Terrarum

Professor Lofton led us through a labyrinth of narrow hall-
ways. There were rooms tucked away everywhere. When we
passed any with an open door, they were filled with cabinets
and tables full of his discoveries and research. He guided us up
an ornate stairwell, which at one point came to a landing overlooking the great hall below where we had tea. He talked the
whole time about how my father had approached him, and
their slow discovery of the intricacies of the Orb and what they
might mean.

We went past a window on the cliff side. Rain drove against
it, a sheet of water washing down the outside. I couldn't make
out the ground below. It must be very far down. I shut my eyes
as a bolt of lightning flashed through the window, thunder following. I couldn't help but feel the ominous nature of it all.

The professor continued, "… we eventually settled on the
fact that somehow the Orb is tied into Earth's energy, with centered points throughout the world marked by notable, mysterious structures. You certainly know of the great pyramids of
Egypt, and perhaps similar grand edifices. We feel they are connected through what we have decided to call ley lines. Now, ley
lines, as a concept, already existed in pseudoscience. They are a
little different than those of our discovery, but still have simi-
larities in that they are believed to be lines of focused energy
connecting physical points around the earth.

"It is a concept fairly new to scientists of our time, and still very much on the taboo side of things when it comes to *true* scientific research. In other words, no scientist in his right mind would touch such ideas, lest they be laughed out of the scientific community." He stopped in his ascent and turned to look at us. "Not unlike the concept of studying the possibility of visitations by extraterrestrial beings." He gave me a wink, then turned and continued up the stairs. "Well, obviously, with the discovery of the Orb, that was not a concern to either your father or myself." He laughed. "Do I look like a mainstream scientist, anyway?"

He turned right and continued up another level of stairs. "Your father and I had no such qualms. We conducted our research as the scientists we were, damn the rest of them."

We reached a landing and came to a large, attic-like room with a vaulted ceiling. He stepped aside for us to enter. "Welcome to my study."

We walked in. It covered the entire top floor of the house. Large wooden support beams crossed above us. The walls were covered in some sort of white plaster, looking like it had been hand applied. At one side of the room sat steel tables with a bunch of things a scientist would use: glass flasks of various shapes, Bunsen burners, an area along the wall with a long steel sink, and cabinets full of—who knows what.

The middle of one wall had a big picture window overlooking the cliff side of the house. I imagined the view it must have on a clear day. Through it, a flash of lightning lit up the sky. Thunder followed a short time later. The storm seemed to be moving away from us.

Books were stacked high on tables, some precariously balanced and ready to tip over. Discarded dishes and drinking cups covered the few spots his study materials didn't. It was obvious a woman had never set foot in this room, or hadn't been in his life for a long time, if ever.

Then I saw it. A projector set up to the far side of the room. I turned to him. "Professor Lofton, do you really have footage of my father?"

He was showing the others around. I hadn't even noticed, I'd been so caught up in my own world, well, his world.

"Yes, of course. But first I must show you something very special. Your father and I managed to get a copy at auction, at a hefty price, I might add. But how could we not, when the Orb revealed itself to be the channel by which wonderful discoveries could be made."

"What do you mean?" Beanie asked.

"You will understand momentarily. Come." He moved over to a large, wooden table covered with all forms of charts and graphs stacked inches thick on top of it. He leafed through them to pull out a large map and laid it over the table.

He beamed when he looked at us. "This is Theatrum Orbis Terrarum." He looked at me. "Do you remember what I told you over the phone that first time you called?"

I looked down at the map. "Yes, it's the map that comes up when you open the Orb."

"Correct!" He slapped his hands together in glee. "Now, this is only a replica of the actual map. Your father and I wanted a larger version to study. But you all need to see this." He put on a pair of white gloves and hurried over to a cabinet against the far wall; one with glass doors and a lock. He took a key from his pocket and opened the cabinet, delicately removing an old, leather-bound book. He carried it over and set it on the table.

"This is an original production of Theatrum Orbis Terrarum, first created by Abraham Ortelius in 1570. By 1612 there were over 7,300 of these books produced, but only 900 are known to still exist today. This is one of three hundred made in the1606 printing."

He opened the book and turned a few pages to where it showed the same map as the one covering the table. "This is believed to be the first atlas of the world, or at least what civilization knew of it at the time. You can see how North America is mostly Terra Incognita, which is a term used by cartographers for lands yet to be mapped or documented."

He slowly ran his hand across the pages, almost caressing them. "I am still in awe every time I take this book out and look at it." He paused, I think to cherish the feeling again. "It is interesting to note, that at the bottom of the map, as you can see," he moved the book off to the side and pointed to the bottom of the larger map, "is a phrase written in Latin, *Quid Ei Potest Videri Magnum In Rebus Humanis, Cui Aeternitas Omnis, Toti-usque Mundi Nota Sit Magnitudo.* I have studied many variations of the phrase, but the one that reads most true to me is, 'For what human affairs can seem important to man, who keeps all eternity for his eyes, and knows the vastness of the universe.'"

I stood there awestruck by those words—mainly the last ones, 'knows the vastness of the universe.' I reached out to the book.

He held his hand out to stop me. "Gloves first. And for the rest of you also, if you wish to handle it." He pointed to a box of gloves on a side table.

We all put them on, because we all wanted to check it out. I mean, how often do you get a chance to touch a book over four-hundred years old? *And one that appears as a hologram when the Orb is opened.*

I looked to the professor.

"Go ahead. It won't bite."

I picked up the book and felt the weight of its old, thick pages. I turned them carefully, one by one, studying the typesetting of the descriptive pages, though I couldn't read them because they were in Latin. I turned the page to see an individual map of what looked like Europe, but it was in Latin and spelled, *Evropa*.

The professor explained. "There are fifty-three maps in the volume. Each of a different area of the world. It is from these individual maps that Abraham Ortelius created the atlas."

I leafed through a few more pages to see other maps. All beautifully done and delicately colored. I looked over the images and they made me feel as if I had somehow traveled back in time. Frankie, Katch, and Beanie all stood at my shoulders, each with gloves on. I turned to Frankie and handed him the book, so they could study it in detail.

I looked over to the professor. "Thank you for sharing this. But how does it work with the Orb? You said you had film of it, and of my father, right?"

"Yes, I have film of him, the Orb and the expeditions we undertook. We wanted to record our findings and needed visual documentation."

I waited for him to continue. I didn't want to interrupt.

"Your father working with the Orb is quite an amazing sight." He paused, maybe for effect. "Would you like to see? I already have it threaded up on the projector."

The Orb

He led us over to where he had the projector set up. It pointed to a section of bare white wall. No need for a screen. He looked around, "I hadn't expected so many of you. We'll need a few more chairs."

Frankie and Beanie grabbed a couple of chairs and brought them over. They all sat down. I was too nervous to sit.

The professor turned off the lights and moved to the projector where he threw the switch to start it. The wall lit up with an image of my father. He held a small object in his hand. The professor must have been the cameraman, and he wasn't the best at shooting film footage, so the camera jittered around a bit. He moved closer to my father and pointed the camera at the object in his hand. There wasn't any sound, but it was in color. The object had an oval, almost egg-like shape. It was wider at one end than the other. The surface had a shimmer to it, and a dark blue, satin-like finish. My dad turned it over in his hand to show it was symmetrical on all sides.

The image drew me toward it. I had to get closer. I made sure not to block the view of the others. The camera panned up to my dad's face, a big smile spread across it. I could see the excitement in his eyes, which were blue, though it was hard to see the color of them on the grainy film. I remember though, how vibrant they were, almost aqua in color. I could see them every time I looked in the mirror, for we shared the color. Dad eyes, that always shined with his love for me.

I got closer and stayed to the side, reaching out to touch his image, as if I were reaching out to touch him. It had been two years since he died. I missed him so much, but it felt good to see him again.

Then the camera moved back to take in a full shot of my dad, and that's when I realized they were filming right here, in Professor Lofton's study. I backed up and looked to my right. I recognized the very spot where he was standing in the film. It made me feel close to him.

My dad held the Orb outstretched in his open palm and said something to it. He lowered his hand and stepped back, but the Orb remained there, floating in the air. Then the top appeared to open, or light up in some way, and all of a sudden the map appeared. It unfolded and laid itself out horizontally, about a foot above the Orb.

"Your father was reciting the Latin phrase 'Theatrum Orbis Terrarum.' It activates the Orb. Pretty amazing, huh?"

"Really amazing," I told him.

"Since it translates in English to Theater of the Orb of the World, he nicknamed it the Orb, for short."

The camera moved closer again, and rose at an angle above the hologram to point down at it. We could see it had subdued colors, similar to those painted on the original map, but it also had an overall veil of blue. Parts of the map were raised, where the terrain might be raised. Everything had a three-dimensional feel to it. The ships and sea creatures we had seen on the printed map earlier were now animated on the hologram. The sea creatures swam and dove in and under the water, sometimes jumping out and making large splashes. The sailing ships moved about, often in an attempt to avoid the sea creatures. It was overwhelming just watching this demonstration.

"You can see whoever created this map had a bit of a sense of humor. I never lost my enjoyment in watching the animations whenever we opened the Orb and the map appeared. I conducted some research to find out why the creatures were there. It turns out that mythical sea creatures and monsters were used by cartographers during that time to note unexplored territories, often referring to such locations as Here be Dragons, because the waters could be dangerous."

The film suddenly ended and the image on the wall went white. I stood there, speechless. I turned to see Frankie, Katch, and Beanie all with expressions of awe on their faces.

"I'm afraid that is all I have of the Orb. I would have shot more, had I known how things would go. Your father learned to manipulate the map. For instance, he could convert it to a globe surrounding the Orb. It was in that configuration we discovered the ley lines and energy points. But I never had the opportunity to film it." He removed the reel of film we had just seen from the projector. "I do, however, have another film. It is a compilation of our expeditions together. Would you like to see it?"

"Yes, please," I told him.

He set the Orb film reel on the table, and took out another, larger reel from a box. He threaded it through the gears of the projector and said, "Your father and I went on two expeditions together. One to Central and South America, and a second to Brittany, France."

"Why those places?" Beanie asked.

"Because the Orb directed us to them. Your father learned how to control the Orb and work with it. Those sites appeared as focused points of energy on the hologram. There were other locations we planned to visit as well, but," he said sadly, "we never had the opportunity."

"Where are these places?" Katch asked.

"I'll explain as we go." He finished loading the film and then threaded it onto the take-up reel. "Okay. Showtime." He switched on the projector.

The space on the wall filled with an image of large, standing stones.

"These are the stones of Carnac. It's really quite an amazing site."

There were various shots of the stones, some with either the professor or my dad standing next to them to show how big they were. Long shots of the stones, running off into the distance. Hundreds of stones in long lines, row after row. Some shots showed my dad writing in his notebook. It looked like the same one I found in the storage box; the notebook which eventually directed me here.

"It is believed there are over 3,000 of these stones at Carnac, in three arrangements extending over four miles. Dating takes some of them as far back as 4,500 B.C. Mind you, that was over 2,000 years before the Egyptian pyramids were built. Long before the Romans, or Greeks, or even the Celts arrived in the area. No one has been able to figure out what people placed them here, or how they could move so many large stones into such specific alignments. Only now are we discovering the intricacies of the formations, such as summer and winter solstice placement, and positioning in ways that show mathematical precision. There are similar stone systems throughout Europe, but Carnac is the largest in the world."

The next scene showed my dad holding the Orb as he entered a structure of stones.

"This is the Mané Kerioned dolmen at Carnac. Dolmens are thought to be tombs, though there is no evidence to this fact. We believe they were built with another purpose. Your father sensed focused energy here, and it became stronger inside the dolmen. He said he could feel it through the Orb. He believed the dolmen may be a portal of some sort. But he said the Orb would not reveal anything more to him."

The film switched to another site, with an image of the professor standing next to a rock wall, but the stones were giant and fit tightly together. The camera, I'm guessing being held by my dad, moved to a close-up where four stones came together to show how tightly they had been fitted. But these weren't square stones set one on top of another, like bricks, but stones with all sorts of odd angles and sizes, that needed to be cut just so in order to fit that tightly together.

"This is Sacsayhuaman, outside of Cusco in Peru; an extensive site covered with eleven square miles of these massive and intricately fitted stone walls and buildings. It sits at over 12,000 feet in altitude. One wonders how these stones could have been so intricately carved to fit like puzzle pieces when they are so large, some weighing tens of tons, and thousands of them. Here, as opposed to the Stones of Carnac, we know the Incan people built this site back in the fifteenth century. At the time, Cusco was the Inca capital. But the question remains, how did they do it? How were they able to move these massive stones from quarries as far away as twenty-two miles, through this rugged and hilly terrain? Our studies concentrated on this site as a primary focal point of energy revealed by the Orb. We believe there are hidden secrets yet to be exposed here. It would take much research and a greater understanding of the Orb's processes to gain this kind of information. We planned to come back, but never had the chance."

We watched as the film showed them moving about the site, the walls were enormous and intricate. I couldn't understand how such a massive complex could be built.

Then the film switched to an image of a large, stepped pyramid. It was huge, and had a long, wide stairway going to a temple of some sort at the top. Tropical trees and vines surrounded it like a cape over someone's shoulders. I could tell the forest had owned the pyramid at one time, and once enveloped it in its swath. Then man intervened, cutting it back. The forest though, like the rust on the railing of the bridge overlooking Oswego Lake, had time on its side. One day, it would reclaim its realm.

I had no idea why such thoughts came to me, just watching the film. I could tell the pyramid had power, and whoever harnessed its energy, be it plant or human, would master that power. My skin came alive with the thought. I rubbed my arms to calm myself.

The camera panned the area to show a large plaza in front of the pyramid with other structures surrounding it, all very old and some in very bad shape.

"This is the Temple of Inscriptions in the Yucatan Peninsula of Mexico, a Maya site. The Orb showed this as one of the more prominent points of energy. We were excited about this location. While at the site in Peru, Roger indicated we needed to come here. But I am afraid, not long after we arrived, we had to stop our studies. Our trip was cut short because Roger had to return to the States. I wanted to stay. We both agreed there was something big here. But only Roger could use the Orb. He thought it could show a way to enter the temple, and to reveal … well, we never found out."

"Why was it cut short?" Beanie asked.

The professor turned to me. "You, Melanie. Roger received a telegram from your mother that you were very sick. Do you remember?"

I tried to think. Then I did. "I had meningitis. I ended up in the hospital for a week. I know my mom was scared. And my dad showed up a few days after I got there. I remembered he had been on a trip. I had no idea it was with you."

Professor Lofton turned off the film and stood there for a moment in the darkness. I could see a reflection from the window in his glasses. A distant flash of lightning lit them up and then disappeared, like some sort of exclamation point. I could tell he was thinking, maybe trying to reach some sort of a decision.

He walked over to me and said, "You need to know something. Your father wasn't able to get any further with the Orb when exploring these sites. He realized it had never been his to finish. He came to the understanding he was only the delivery boy. The Orb was meant for someone else."

He guided me to a chair, sat me down and plopped down on a stool opposite me. He reached out, took my hands and looked me in the eyes. "He believed it is you."

I sat back. "Me? How me?"

The professor studied me for a moment, as if wondering how I might take what he was about to reveal. "I have no idea how your father came to that notion. In hindsight, I believe he first realized it while at the dolmen in France." I could tell he was reflecting back to that time, as if making sure.

"After you recovered, he came to see me again. We talked. It is then he said he figured out that even though the extraterrestrial being gave the Orb to him at the crash site, it wasn't intended for him. He said he had a vision at the dolmen. He told me the Orb was meant for you. He couldn't share this back then at the site because, well, he wasn't quite sure he believed it himself. But after seeing you in the hospital, he said he knew."

The professor scoffed. "I truly doubted this line of thought. Even with the Orb and its wonders, I thought perhaps he must have just been overly upset by your illness. I know how much he loved you. I didn't see where such thinking could come from."

A flash of lightning lit the room, and a roll of thunder sounded from outside. *What kind of timing is that?*

He walked over and flipped on the lights. "I set the whole nonsense aside, and hadn't considered it since." He turned to us. "But then you called a few weeks ago, and now you are sitting here, right in front of me." He walked over, pulled me to my feet and held my chin up to look into my eyes. "That's when I also knew. It *is* you. Roger told me that if you figured things out enough to make it here—to me—then he was right."

"But how would he know that?" I asked.

"There is only one way—the Orb."

I couldn't think of anything to say. I looked at Frankie, then Beanie. They were just as dumbfounded as I was. Then I looked to Katch. She locked eyes with me, not because she questioned what just happened, but because she knew it was true.

"Katch?"

She shook her head, to tell me we would discuss it later.

"Well, it's getting late. I hope this has helped, though I am sure it has only created more questions." Professor Lofton motioned to the stairwell, about to direct us down it, then stopped. "Oh, I can't believe I almost forgot. Maybe too much excitement for this hermit scientist, and it has been nearly two years."

He walked to his desk, opened a drawer, and pulled something out. He came over and held out a small bag made of crushed velvet, deep purple in color, with a gold draw string tightly cinched. He laughed. "A Crown Royal bag. Our favorite drink after a long day in the salt mines." He motioned to me. "Here, take it. Your father left it for you."

"What?" I didn't understand. "He left it for me? How could he be sure I would even make it here?"

"Like I said. Somehow, he knew. He told me that if you did manage to make it this far, then I should give you this. The rest you will need to figure out." He handed it to me.

I opened the draw string, turned the bag over, and a small key fell into my hand. I looked at the professor with confusion.

"Roger left it with me. To keep it safe." He paused. "It was as if he knew something might happen to him."

I studied the brass key: small, but not too small, with a rounded blade, and a key cut much different than any used to open a regular door. "What does it fit?"

"I really don't know. He never said. But it looks like a key to a safety deposit box. That's my guess, anyway."

Frankie took the key from me and studied it. "My dad has a safety deposit box. He keeps important family papers in there. This key looks a whole lot like that one." He handed it back to me. I was going to put it back in the bag, but decided to put it in my pocket instead.

"But how am I supposed to figure out where the safety deposit box is?"

The professor put his arm around my shoulder as he walked us to the stairwell. "Remember, he said if you found your way here, then you would be able to figure out the rest."

The Music Box

We stood outside the Virginia Inn, having checked out of the hotel, ready to head home. It was almost eleven o'clock. We were exhausted from the night before, so slept in as late as we could. Frankie had parked his car in a garage a couple of blocks down. We headed that direction.

Beanie turned to me. "Mel, you are an enigma sitting on top of giant question mark."

"Wow, Beanie, you *are* using big boy words these days," I bumped him with my shoulder. "I'm proud of you. Or maybe I should be proud of Katch. It looks like she's doing a good job with you."

"Stop avoiding the topic," he replied. "So, what gives with the key and you being the cosmically anointed one to receive the Orb?"

On the trip back to the hotel last night we didn't talk about it, all of us in our own thoughts, trying to absorb everything that happened at Professor Lofton's. By the time we did get back to our room, we were too exhausted to even think about it.

"If I had a clue, I would tell you. But I haven't," I said.

Katch jumped in. "We have plenty of time to figure it out, including on the drive home."

"Speaking of which," Beanie said, "I see a restaurant ahead. I'm starving and the drive home will take hours. Let's get something to eat first."

"Sounds like a good idea to me," Frankie agreed.

We were just passing a toy shop. I glanced at the window display and stopped, a little idea popping into my head. The rest of them had made it to the restaurant before noticing I wasn't with them.

Frankie stood with his hand on the door handle, about to open it, then looked back at me. "You coming?"

"What's up, Mel?" Katch asked, wondering what I was doing.

"Just want to check something out. I'll be right there. Order me a burger and fries, and an RC." I walked into the toy store as they continued into the restaurant.

HQ

The phone rang in Director Bull Patton's office at CIA Langley. He picked it up. "Yes?"

The secretary said, "Sir, I have Agent Miller on the phone, per your request. He's on line two."

"Have him hold for a moment."

Bull hung up the receiver and stared at the blinking button for line two. He wasn't very happy with Miller to have lost the Simpson girl again. Luckily, she hadn't died in the accident. If that had happened, they would never recover the material. Without knowing where it was hidden or how well, there would always be the shadow hanging over his head of someone discovering it. Still, they might have gotten something positive out of the accident. This call would hopefully fill him in on exactly what.

He hit the blinking button and put the line on speaker. "Miller, what have you got?"

"Still no sign of the Simpson girl, but we have men all over Seattle, so it shouldn't be long until we find her."

"Good. How about those men who were with her? What have you found out?"

"One died on impact. His name was Yǔxuān Liú. Went by the name of Danny. His family owns a Dim Sum restaurant in Chinatown. His father is a known member of the Chinese underground in the area. Not much else on him."

"And the other one? Is he still alive?"

"Yes, but in intensive care at Swedish Medical. Docs don't know if he will make it or not. Got quite a shot to the head when the van crashed on its side, and his spinal cord is severed. If he does make it, he'll never walk again. We have a man there to keep tabs on his status."

"Good. Let me know of any updates." Bull leaned into his desk. "Have you figured out who he is yet?"

"We think so. Based on his prints, his name is Tom Richardson. He was going under an alias, though. Had ID on him under the name of Ralph Morgan."

"Sounds a bit clandestine to me. Why? Do you know?"

"He had a career in the Army in Korea. Worked with intelligence and was fluent in Chinese. So, that would mean he had training in the art of staying covert. And, based on what we found in his apartment, including some Lake Oswego newspapers, it looks like he had been keeping in touch with Melanie Simpson and her mother."

Bull stood and looked out the window. Snake Island seemed to be in particularly beautiful display this midday afternoon, the sun highlighting it as never before. He liked where this conversation was going. If, in fact, it was going where he thought. "The reason for that would be?"

"I think he's the man who helped Roger Simpson get the material out of the crash site back in '47. We learned he had lived in the Roswell area during that time. Not long after the crash, he abruptly left. It has to be him."

Bull gave out a big sigh. "We finally found him."

"We did."

"Do everything you can to keep him alive." Bull paced behind his desk. "Get whatever specialists you need from wherever they may be; you understand? I want him to recover. We need to know what he knows."

"I'm on it, Sir."

Bull leaned against his desk, pressing his palms into the edge to where he could feel it cutting deep into his flesh. "And the Simpson girl?"

"We're close. I have a lead. One of my men spotted a red Mustang with Oregon plates pull into a parking garage late last night. On a hunch, I ran the plates. They're registered to Frankie Strickland's father. He's the Simpson girl's boyfriend. We have the garage staked out. She's either with him, or he will lead us to her. They won't get away this time. I have too many men on the street for that to happen."

"Find her. We need that material! I'm tired of dealing with this Simpson girl. Get it and get rid of her. She's been too much trouble, and I have no doubt we'll just get more of it if she stays alive."

"We'll make it happen."

"Good, and if you find Burnham, put a tail on him, too. He may lead us right to her."

On the Run

Frankie pulled up to the exit to leave the parking garage at Virginia Street. "Katch, which way?"

I looked back at Katch in the seat behind me. She was studying the map. "Okay, turn right. Then take another right on 3rd. Stay on it for a while. I think we can catch I-5 down around University Street."

We had driven for a few blocks when Beanie spoke up from the back. "Hey, guys. I've been kinda checking out our backs, you know, just in case."

I turned to him with a hint of alarm. "And?"

"Being pretty good at spotting spy cars, like I did back in Portland, I thought I should keep an eye out. Well, I think we're being followed. We just went through another intersection and the same car has been back there for a while."

I looked at Frankie.

He said, "Maybe riding in a bright red Mustang isn't exactly the best way to stay incognito."

"Yeah," Beanie added, "especially when every bad guy out there and his brother knows this car."

I could see Pike Street coming up. "Let's make sure. Turn left on Pike."

I watched out the back, along with Katch and Beanie. "Which car?" I asked.

"That black sedan." He looked at me. "I mean, like, do they drive anything else?"

Frankie made the turn. The car did the same. I glanced out Frankie's window to see we were passing the Monorail Plaza on our left.

A plan popped into my head. "Okay, let's be sure. Take a left up ahead on 6th Avenue."

We did, and the car made the same turn.

"Yep, they are definitely following us," Beanie said.

Frankie glanced over to me. "I can outrun them. This thing has got some serious torque."

I grabbed his arm. "No! No, don't do that. Tom and Danny died that way. I don't know what I'd do if the same thing happened to all of you."

"Okay. Okay. I won't. But let go of my arm or you will cause an accident. What are we going to do then?"

I could see the Space Needle over the buildings ahead. The plan was coming together. "What time is it?" I asked.

Beanie answered from the back seat. "My watch says one-twenty-four. Why?"

I reached into a pouch on my backpack where I kept some change and took out three quarters, then turned to Frankie. "See the Space Needle up there?"

Frankie leaned forward to glance up through the windshield. "Yeah."

"Head for it. Get to the Space Needle. I know what to do."

"Uh, Frankie," Beanie said, and in a way to make me look back at him.

He stared at me as he continued, "Her eyes are doing that twitching thing again. You remember what happens when they do that, right?"

Frankie glanced over and studied my eyes for a second before turning back to the road. "Usually, disaster."

"Stop it, you guys. This will work. Just get there."

"The car is still behind us," Katch said. "Go with her plan. What else are we going to do?"

Frankie made a few more turns, using the Space Needle as his guide. We made a final turn onto Broad Street and the base of the Space Needle appeared up ahead on our left.

I looked over at Frankie. "Stop when you get to it. I can lose them here. We need to split up. I know they'll follow me when they see I have the backpack." I grabbed it and my book bag to get ready.

Frankie looked over at me in disbelief. "What do you mean, split up? No way!"

"Just do it. Pull over or I'll jump out while the car is still moving." I grabbed the door handle to prove my point.

Frankie gave me a pissed-off look and screeched to a stop. I threw open the door and leapt out. "Meet me at the Virginia Inn: one hour. Find somewhere safe to hide 'til then. And make sure you aren't followed!"

I slammed the door and raced across the grass toward the Space Needle. I heard the Mustang's tires squeal as Frankie quickly pulled out, probably because he was mad. I glanced back to see the following car stop and two men jump out.

Good.

I ran as fast as I could past the Space Needle to the Monorail station and up the ramp, dodging people as I went. It was tourist season and the place was packed. I had seventy-five cents in my hand, ready to go. I knew how much it would cost from riding it yesterday. I jumped past the line and dumped the change on the ticket counter, grabbed a ticket, then raced to the train and into one of the cars. It was already full, but I squeezed in.

I looked back through the window to see the two men trying to work their way to the ticket counter. People weren't too helpful in letting them by. When they finally made it, one of them pulled out his wallet and hurriedly slapped a couple of dollar bills on the counter. They raced for the train, but the doors shut just as they got to it. I couldn't believe my luck. I knew the train ran every few minutes, and my timing had been perfect. They gave me hard stares as it pulled out. I smiled and flipped them the bird. I couldn't help it.

I worked my way through the passengers to the other side of the car so I could see the road below. The Monorail followed 5th Avenue. The sedan was down there, following along on 5th. Which meant it wasn't following the Mustang. Knowing that gave me a sense of relief.

I knew they would have to contend with the lights and traffic, where the train wouldn't, so they couldn't possibly keep up. And at the end, the Monorail cuts over to 4th Avenue, when they would have to stay on 5th. I knew I should be able to keep ahead of them, but the ride would still feel excruciatingly long, even though it only took a couple of minutes. Yesterday, I had enjoyed it. Today, I just wanted to get to the other end.

I lost track of the sedan. They must have gotten hung up in traffic. The train approached the station and pulled in. I grabbed my Seattle tourist hat out of my book bag, put it on, and tucked my hair up underneath. A different look, just in case.

I worked my way to the doors and jumped off as soon as they opened. I dove ahead of the mass of people coming out of the cars and ran down the stairs to the plaza. My plan was to head to Pike Place Market. If anyone managed to follow me to this point, I could lose them there. I had the layout and I knew the place would be packed.

I headed down Pike Street. I looked back to see the sedan again. Somehow, they had managed to get here quicker than I thought. They may have spotted me. The Army backpack was a dead giveaway.

I ran down Pike and ducked into the Ben Paris Restaurant at the corner of 2nd Avenue. I looked around the interior. A fancy place: tables covered in white linen cloth, crystal wine glasses, and silver silverware. I sat at an empty table near the window, facing it.

A waiter wandered up and checked me out—a young girl in a sleeveless tee, high-top Converse, and carrying an Army backpack—apparently not his idea of a potentially big tipper. And definitely someone who shouldn't be in here. Attitude oozed from him. "May I help you?"

I glanced up, taking my hat off to let my hair cascade down my shoulders. I looked at him like he was distracting me from more important matters. "Oh. Ice water, please." I put a five-dollar bill on the table. "Daddy wants me to find a nice restaurant for this evening. Boring, right? But he is much too busy tending to business at the top of some tall building downtown and can't be bothered. Visitors; Orange County." I waited for some form of understanding. When it didn't come, I let him see I felt so very sorry he was poorly educated in such important geography. "Near Los Angeles, if you didn't know. Daddy asked that I take care of the dinner arrangements. For six of us." I gave him a sweet smile. "So, a dinner menu as well, if you don't mind."

He smiled back. "Yes, Yes. I am sure your father will love our offerings. I'll be right back."

I watched out the window. Nothing at first, but then there they were. It's not hard to spot someone looking frantically for something, even though you don't recognize them. They only appeared for a moment. Two men. Dark suits, of course. Not the same two, though. But they had that look on their faces as if they had lost something important and wanted it back. Me.

They walked out of view, but not before I took note of what they wore and looked like. I decided to wait here for a while. A cold glass of water sounded good right now, anyway.

Fool Me Twice

I stepped out of the Ben Paris restaurant and stood on the sidewalk looking in both directions along the street. I had been in there for about twenty minutes and hadn't seen anyone go by who looked suspicious. Same for the people, mostly tourists, passing by in both directions.

I tucked my hat back into my book bag and put my hair into a ponytail as I headed down to Pike Place Market. I knew I could easily get lost in there for the next half hour, then walk the interior of the market to where I would come out at the far end of the flower center. From there it would pretty much be a straight shot up the street to the Virginia Inn.

I walked into the main entrance for the market, right under the big sign with the clock I had seen yesterday. A bunch of people stood around the fish counter, anxious to get the freshest catch. Men in fishermen bibs called out their orders. I looked at all the fish, crab and clams on display, reading the names on the little hand-drawn signs sprouting out of the ice all over the place: Halibut, Wild King Salmon, Dungeness Crab, Rock Fish, Live Pacific Oysters, and on and on. I turned to my right, planning to take the nearby stairs down to the next level where I could disappear.

"Hello, Melanie." I froze at the voice.

Major Burnham blocked my way. One of his henchmen stood off to his side. Both wore sweet-looking, very dangerous, very you-are-screwed kind of smiles. I took two steps back.

Major Burnham stepped toward me. "It's over Melanie. Give me the backpack."

I had to think fast. *What do I do?* There were three ways I could go. Well, there *were* three ways, but only one now. Major Burnham had placed himself in a way to block the best route, in the direction of the stairs. There were all sorts of escapes that way, but I wouldn't make it past him. I couldn't run back out to the street either, because his man had stepped over to block that direction. So really, there was only one way to go. I looked in that direction to see a stairwell and a small hallway next to it. I think the stairs led down to Post Alley. I could get away there. I bolted for them.

"Melanie, must you?" I heard the major call, disappointment in his voice.

I reached the stairs and skidded to a stop. A man stood on them, staring up at me. One of the major's men. I altered my course from the stairs to the hallway and flew down it, dodging tourists and darting past shops. I quickly glanced back to see Major Burnham following me, but not particularly in a hurry.

I came to a kind of dead end, double steel doors closed and locked, blocking my way forward. But there was a small hallway to my left. I ran down it to see it connected to another building. I looked out a window along the way to see it was suspended over a street, Post Alley, where I would have come out if I could have taken the stairs.

This part of the market wasn't used much and there weren't any tourists around at all. I came out of the hallway to a mezzanine overlooking an open area one level below. To my left, another hallway went out toward the street. I ran in that direction just as one of the major's men turned into it and headed toward me. I was getting boxed in.

✳   ✳   ✳

Major Burnham followed the Simpson girl as she ran from him. He smiled. She was playing right into his hands. Thank God he had turned Captain Thornton to his side. At the time, the major had no idea how valuable an asset the captain would be, but it didn't take long to find out. The captain had followed Melanie up here and been tracking her ever since. Seattle was quite the maze for locating someone, but the captain somehow had the nose to find the cheese at the end.

When Melanie jumped on the Monorail to escape the CIA at the Space Needle, Captain Thornton was there, and immediately called Major Burnham on his radio to let him know she was probably headed to the market. That gave the major enough time to formulate a plan and lay a little trap.

He had watched her run from him, and abruptly stop when she saw his man on the stairwell. She thought she would get away by running down the hallway next to it. Perfect. Just what he wanted. He followed, taking his time. No hurry. With that last move, there was no longer an escape. He was a spider, watching as a fly unknowingly work its way down his funnel web.

He came to the entrance onto the mezzanine. Melanie stood trapped between his men; one in the hallway going outside, and another at the far end of the mezzanine walkway. The mezzanine overlook was angled in an 'L' shape. The major entered the room. As soon as Melanie saw him, she backed as far as she could down the other side of the mezzanine away from him and his men.

The major smiled. There was no escape in that direction. "Give me the backpack, Melanie. It's over. You have nowhere to go."

He could see her eyes dart back and forth, as if thinking of what she could do. Nothing, was the answer. He laughed. "No options, eh?"

Melanie looked at him. "If I give you the backpack, you will leave me alone, right?" She set her tote bag on the floor and took off the backpack.

The major took a few steps toward her. "I have no interest in you, once I have the pack."

"Then step back so I can leave the way I came."

The major stepped back to expose the hallway for her. "Okay." He motioned with a sweep of his hand. "Your escape route. Now, the backpack."

Melanie took a step closer to the wooden railing and held the pack over it. "Here it is." She dropped it to the floor below, grabbed her book bag and bolted for the hallway.

Major Burnham stepped toward the railing to look down at the pack as it landed. He shouted to his man near the stairway. "Get that pack and bring it to me!" He hardly noticed Melanie race by him, down the hall crossing Post Alley and back toward the heart of the market.

Burnham's man grabbed the pack, brought it up and handed it to the major. He undid the straps and looked inside to see nothing but clothing. He pulled out a wad of clothes and dropped them on the floor. His brows furrowed. He reached in and took out what looked like a music box—a Popeye music box. With little scenes of Popeye, Olive Oyl, and Wimpy on the sides. He handed it to his man and looked into the pack, pulling out a few clothes from the bottom. Other than that, the pack was empty.

He set the backpack on the ground and grabbed the music box. He tried to pry the top open. Maybe the material was inside, although that didn't seem sensible. He couldn't get it open. He noticed a little handle on the side, like on all music boxes.

He cranked it, hoping for the best. The theme to Popeye's music played. The top suddenly flew open and a can of spinach popped out and from the top of that, jumped Popeye, making a noise like air escaping through a kazoo.

His closest man laughed, but quickly shut up when the major stared him down. Major Burnham stood there dumbfounded, focused on the music box. He couldn't believe it. She had pulled a bait and switch again, just like she did with the old weather balloon fragments. He grabbed the backpack, shoved the music box into it, and threw it on the ground. He fumed. This was not over. He looked to his men. "Go get her!"

Face Off

I ran down the hallway and across Post Alley to the fish stand and past it, coming to the stairwell I originally wanted to take. Just as I headed down it, I looked back to see two of the major's men race out of the hallway and another appeared in the street. I shot down the stairs. I didn't know if they had seen me or not, but I wasn't about to wait and find out.

Now I was super glad I had explored this place yesterday. It was a maze of stairs, ramps, and walkways going in all directions. I came out on the second floor, but kept going, deeper into the lower levels. I wanted to get down to the rubbish and hide there for a little while, where it would be dark and hard to find me.

I had seen an exterior stairwell yesterday on the bay side of the building which led down to Western Avenue, seven levels below. I couldn't go back up to the market now. Major Burnham and his men would probably have all of the exits staked out by now. But if I found that stairwell, I could get down to Western Avenue and walk up it to where it met Virginia Street, and then up the hill to the Inn. I just needed to hide out for a little while.

I made it down to the level where garbage and old building materials were scattered everywhere. It was dark, but I could still see by the light coming in through dingy windows scattered along the bay side of the level. The light turned a murky brown as it cascaded into the rooms and out to the hallway. Some floor boards were broken and missing, so I had to be careful with my step, and skirt around beams and stacks of rubble laying in my path. Rooms and alcoves full of debris, old equipment, and rubbish appeared in the dark on both sides of the hallway. Dust covered everything, giving it all the same gray pallor. The whole place smelled musty.

I ducked into a side room, which turned out to be pretty big. It must have been some sort of a meeting room from the days before this whole level got trashed. The walls had places where they were smashed through, as if some sort of demolition and remodeling had started and then suddenly been abandoned.

A high pile of timbers sat at the far end. I thought it would be a good place to hide. I walked over to it, but stopped in my tracks. A voice quietly called out to me.

"Melanie."

I turned toward the hallway, but didn't see anyone. Had I imagined it? I must have, because I recognized the voice, but there was no way he could be here.

Movement drew my attention. Someone stepped out of the shadows and into a glint of light coming from one of the windows.

It was him. "George? What are you doing here?"

"Melanie. Don't be afraid." He walked over to me. "The bigger question is, what are you doing here?"

I grabbed him and gave him a hug. "Thank God, you're here. Some men are after me."

"I know. And if you keep this up, you're going to get yourself killed. These men aren't playing games, Melanie. People have already died. I don't want that to be you."

I stepped back. "Wait." This didn't make sense. "How did you find me?"

"I followed you yesterday. I've actually been following you ever since you left Portland. Earlier today, when you were running from those men and took the Monorail at the Space Needle, I knew this is where you would end up."

"But, why George? Why follow me?"

Major Burnham stepped into the room, his men in tow. "Because he's helping me, Melanie ... to recover the material."

I quickly stepped back to get away from the major, and from George. I glanced around the room. It was big, but didn't have any way to escape that was near me. All the demolition was over on the major's side of the room, and his men had spread out to cover those exits. I looked to the bay window on my right, but knew it was stories above Western Avenue. I backed up until I felt the wall behind me. George hadn't moved from where he stood next to the pile of timbers.

I looked over at him. "Why?"

"It was the only way I could get you to stop; to keep you from getting yourself killed."

Then it came to me. "You set me up?"

Major Burnham and his goons stepped closer to keep me contained. "Give me the material, Melanie. I know it's in your book bag. There's no way you would have left it with the other kids. And definitely not what you'd do if you're living up to your father's wishes." He nodded toward my book bag. "It's in there, isn't it?"

George walked over to me with a determined look. "This needs to stop." He held out his hand.

I looked down at the book bag and the debris inside. I had been guarding it for almost a year now, but I knew it was over. I handed him the book bag. What else could I do? If George had turned on me, what use would there be to keep going?

George took a few steps toward the major and tossed the bag to him.

He looked inside. A wide smile filled his face. "Now, it's over."

I looked at George. "But why?

He stepped toward me as he answered. "Because I don't want you to die over that material, and the best way to make sure that doesn't happen, is to get rid of it."

Burnham turned to me. "Yes, there's that. And maybe a nice, big cash payoff."

I looked at George. "You sold me out?"

He shook his head. "Melanie, no! Let me explain. It wasn't the money, it—"

"What do you say we save the sob story for later?" A man stepped into the doorway of the meeting room. Three other men were with him. I recognized one of them as the man George had released from jail. The two other men stood at openings in the wall. All of them had guns pointed at the major and his men.

Major Burnham recognized him. "Agent Miller. I'm surprised to see you here. I thought you preferred riding a desk."

The man smiled. "No. Actually I've always enjoyed the field, especially when there is going to be a little action. I can't let Roberts here," pointing to the man I recognized, "have all the fun. Oh, and thank you, Major. Without your help, we may never have found Miss Simpson. You don't check your back very often, do you?" He smiled and pointed toward the book bag with his gun. "So, we win. Hand over the material."

Major Burnham's face went red hot with anger. "Never!" He jumped to the side, pulled out a gun and fired at Agent Miller.

Everything went crazy from there. George grabbed me and yanked me down behind the timbers, sheltering me with his arms. The deafening sound of gunfire filled my ears, heightened by the echoes bouncing off the meeting room walls. Cries of anger rang out, and grunts of pain when someone got shot. The pungent smell of burnt gunpowder filled my nose.

I peeked through a small opening between two wooden beams to see men shooting it out only yards away from each other. Some hidden by stacks of rubbish on the floor, others through holes in the wall. None of it looked like good protection. Not like the pile of timbers George and I hid behind.

George pulled a gun from behind his back and held it ready. Two of the major's men and one from Miller's side were on the ground already, laying still, maybe dead.

I looked at George. No, he had morphed into Captain Thornton now, all business. He put his arm on me to force me down and said, "Stay low. Let's see how this plays out."

I couldn't help it though, I raised my head just enough to watch. I saw Major Burnham get hit. He dropped the book bag from the impact. Blood blossomed from a wound on his side. He reached for the book bag, but Miller's men were advancing, firing. He would die if he tried to get it.

I looked around. All of the major's men were on the ground. He knew he was defeated. He held his gun up in the air as a sign of surrender, his other hand pressed against his wound, and slowly backed away from the book bag. Suddenly he jumped through an opening in the wall and disappeared. Miller's men fired at him, but were too late. I'm sure they missed.

Miller picked up the book bag. He looked inside and then closed it, handing it to Roberts. He nodded in our direction. "You and Williams get rid of those two. No loose ends. I'm going after the major." He hurried from the room.

George didn't wait. He opened fire on Williams, knocking him to the ground. Roberts dropped the book bag and fired back. I ducked down while they kept firing at each other. My eyes were shut tight. Things were way too scary. I heard a grunt at my side. I open my eyes to see George had been hit. Blood oozed from a hole in his shirt below his left shoulder, near his heart. He slumped to the ground, his back against the timbers. He put his hand to the hole in his chest and I could tell he knew it was bad. Blood was pouring out of it. The bullet must have hit an artery.

He looked at me. "I'm sorry Mel. I screwed up. The money didn't mean anything to me. I used it as an excuse to keep track of Major Burnham. I knew he'd find you eventually. I didn't want you dead." He grabbed my hand and squeezed it, showing me how much I meant to him, and also to stave off the pain. "I thought if I kept control of the situation, he'd get his material and then you'd be safe. You are much more important than what's in that book bag. But, I sure blew it, didn't I?"

I jumped to George's side. I let go of his hand and pressed mine against his wound to stop the bleeding. "George, George! Please. It's okay. I know. I know you would never want to hurt me."

His eyes turned glassy. It made me think of Tom—that look I had seen before. I fell onto him and cried. "George. George?" I looked into his eyes again to see the life in them gone. Something deep inside me boiled and built up. It rolled through my body. A power of some sort. Nothing I had ever felt before. And then I remembered, I had. In a dream, and a ball of energy.

I stood and held my hands out toward Roberts. Heat rushed from deep within me, through my arms and into my palms. I heard a gunshot and looked down at my waist. It had hit me, but I couldn't feel it. I stared at Roberts while focusing on the energy flow to my palms. I had practiced this somewhere, I knew, and now it came back to me.

Roberts fired again and again. I watched the bullets come in, not like slow motion or anything. I could just see them as they advanced somehow. With the energy came an acute sight that could capture such speed. I moved my hands to intercept the bullets, and when they reached me, they stopped in mid-air, inches from my palms, and dropped to the ground.

I glanced up to see Roberts' look of surprise. It matched my own. *How could I do this?*

He quickly picked up the book bag and ran from the room.

I dropped to my knees and looked at George slumped against the timbers, dead. Tears flowed down my cheeks. I put my hand to the place I had been shot and pulled my fingers away to see them covered in blood. I looked down and my front had blood everywhere, but I still couldn't feel a thing. Adrenaline, no doubt. Lots of blood, though. Probably not a good thing. I felt a little wobbly. The room tried to spin.

I looked up to someone standing over me. I worried it might be one of the men from the fight, but it wasn't. I recognized him somehow. *What is he doing here?* I blinked, but he didn't go away. I tried to keep my focus. "I know you."

"Yes, we know each other."

I sat back on my knees, holding my stomach. "It must have been you who stopped those bullets?"

He gave me a funny look. "I didn't do it. You did."

"Me?"

He kneeled down next to me and studied my wound with a look more of curiosity than concern. "Yes, but you seemed to have missed one. I guess we have more work to do."

I looked at him. "The debris. It's gone. I lost it."

He laughed. "Let them have it. There are more important things."

I felt like I was about to black out. He helped me lay down on my back.

"Am I about to die? Are you my guardian angel?"

He covered my wound with his hand. An immediate warmth emanated from his touch. "Now, that would be something, wouldn't it?" He laughed again. "No, I'm just your brother."

"My brother? I don't have ..." My eyes wavered and were closing. I felt time going backwards. Not outside of me, but inside.

"Don't worry," he said. "I only told you because you won't remember when you wake up."

He leaned over me. I looked into his familiar green eyes, shining like beacons on a dark night. Instant comfort in them. Trusting eyes.

He gave me a warm smile that matched his touch. "Mel, don't be worried. Go to sleep, now. You're going to be fine."

"Mel, do you hear me? Mel?"

I look up to see Frankie standing over me. I glance around. I'm sitting in a booth at the Virginia Inn. Katch and Beanie are across from me. I have no idea how I got here. A half-eaten piece of apple pie sits in front of me. A coffee cup, also half empty.

Frankie nudges me over so he can share the booth. I move and then immediately look down at my stomach to where I had been shot. Or had I? I reached down to the spot only to feel smooth skin, and I didn't see any blood on my clothes. *Another dream?*

Frankie settled in next to me. "Are you okay? We couldn't get you to respond for a moment.

"Yeah," Beanie said. "We thought you had found zombieland or something. You were completely out of it."

Katch reached across the table. "Are you okay? I'm worried."

I blinked a couple of times. I couldn't remember what happened. I know I had been chased and got away, but everything after that went fuzzy. "Yeah, I guess I'm just overwhelmed right now. I think all of this has finally gotten to me. I don't even remember ordering the pie and coffee."

"Okay," Frankie said, "no more splitting up. Got that?" He looked around the seat and under the table. "Where's the backpack and book bag?"

I quickly looked around. I remembered losing the backpack to Major Burnham, but had no idea where the book bag went. "Things are kind of jumbled in my head right now. I can remember some things. I know I lost the backpack. I wish I still had it, because it was Dad's, but it didn't have the debris in it. That was in the book bag and I don't know what happened to it. I must have lost it, too."

"You lost the debris?" Beanie squawked. "Really? I mean lost it, like set it down? What, were you Ferdinand the bull or something, smelling some lovely flowers, and just forgot to pick it up again, overly mesmerized by their delightful scent?"

"Lay off, Beanie," Katch kicked in. "She's having a hard enough time as it is."

Beanie gave a sheepish smile. "Sorry, Mel. I guess I got a little carried away. It's just that now our evidence is gone."

Frankie said, "Well, at least they won't be after you anymore. No reason to be now."

"Hey," Beanie said, "there's something big going down at Pike's Market. We saw it on the way here. Tons of police cars and the whole place is roped off. It must be something pretty badass for that to happen. Do you know anything?"

I looked at him. "I was there, at the market. I lost the men chasing me in it. I used the backpack as a decoy. Somehow, I must have lost the book bag there, too. I can't remember anything more, or how I got here. I really don't know why the police would be there."

Beanie beamed with an idea. "I know! They found the book bag and discovered the debris. Those guys after you knew it was alien material, and now they have the whole place closed off so they can cover it up." He puffed out his chest and looked at each of us. "I mean, it's not exactly rocket science to come to that conclusion. So, I'm right, aren't I?"

"You could be," Frankie said. "That would explain a lot."

Katch asked, "So, if we don't have to worry about the debris any longer, then the question remains, is there any way they could know about the Orb?"

I thought about it. "Very few. Us. Professor Lofton, but he should be okay. And Tom and Danny, but they're ..." I stopped, not wanting to finish the sentence.

Frankie cut in, thankfully ending my thought. "I told Emilee too. She had to know. She needed to understand all of this stuff, especially because of how you bolted."

"What did she say when you told her?"

"She seemed to all of a sudden realize something. I could see it in her face. And she said a kind of cryptic thing, about your importance to our world and what lays beyond it. But I really didn't understand what she meant."

A lot of things fell into place for me just then. I looked over to Frankie, took his hand and squeezed it. "Thanks for letting me know."

"Sure. And she won't say anything, so that means you're safe." He slid out of the booth and held his hand out to help me up. "Come on. Let's go home."

We walked out the door and down 1st Avenue, headed to Frankie's car. When we passed Pike Street, we could see the cop cars down below at the market, the place roped off, and some news trucks arriving.

We continued on our way. I couldn't remember what happened down there, but wasn't worried about being followed. I had no reason to be, anymore.

Heading Home

We were halfway home and had spent the whole time talking about my lost time at the market, trying to jog my memory.

"Maybe it's like what you hear about, you know, a shock kind of thing?" Katch said. "When something horrific happens and a person blocks it from their memory."

I looked over at her. She was sitting behind Frankie so we could talk easier on the way home. "What do you mean, horrific? Do you think something terrible happened?" I could feel my throat tighten as I said this, as if somewhere deep down, there was a truth to it.

"No, no. That's an example," Katch explained. "It wouldn't have to be bad. Just something that makes your subconscious want to block the memory. I mean, how else do we explain it?"

"You didn't kill anyone while at the market, did you?" Beanie asked. "I mean, I don't want to be tried as an accessory to murder for helping you escape."

He was sitting behind me. I turned so I could give him the look. "Right, Beanie, and I'm getting a taste for it now, so watch out what you say next."

He drew his fingers along his lips, to show he was zipping them up, then made the motion of locking them and tossing away the key.

"Good idea." I turned back around. A sign appeared ahead saying we were approaching Chehalis. I suddenly thought of something. "Hey, guys. This is Chehalis. You know how everyone started calling spaceships flying saucers. That began with Kenneth Arnold. He took off from here, flying his small plane near Mount Adams when he spotted a bunch of UFOs. That was back in 1947 too, right before the Roswell Crash. I read about it in *The Investigator*. When asked to describe them, he said they looked like saucers skipping across the water. Some newspaper guy picked up on it and called them flying saucers. I think it's pretty awesome to be driving through the place where it all started."

"That is way cool," Beanie said, apparently having decided to unlock his lips.

We all looked out our windows toward the sky, hoping to see skipping flying saucers. No luck.

I added, "That was a big time for sightings. I read there was a flurry of sightings right around that same time all over the country."

"It makes me wonder about the Orb," Katch said. "How your father somehow directed his group to be at that exact site where the spaceship crashed."

"Yeah, how does that all get planned out?" Frankie added.

I thought about it. "I don't know that they would *plan* to crash their spaceship there. It had to be more fortuitous than that."

"That's where destiny stepped in," Katch said.

Beanie piled on. "Yeah, dharma, just like Mrs. Crowley foretold."

Katch continued, "It doesn't seem these things are planned out as much as they are destined. Like what has happened to you over the last few days. Weren't you simply following destiny's path?"

I couldn't believe I was hearing this. "What are you guys saying, that Tom and Danny died because it was destined? And what about my mom and dad? Did they die too, just so I could get the Orb for whatever effing reason? Think about what you are saying. Their deaths are on my hands! Don't you all realize that?" I turned to the window so I didn't have to face them, and so they wouldn't see the tears running down my cheeks.

No one said anything for a while.

Frankie finally broke the silence. "Mel, we know you're hurting, but don't take it out on us, okay? We never thought of it that way." He paused. "But obviously you do."

Katch touched my shoulder. "Mel, none of this is your fault. You didn't put this into motion. We still don't know why, or what, this is all about." Her voice took on a firmness. "You have no right to blame yourself."

I turned to her. "Katch, they're all dead."

She took my hand through the gap between the seats. "You remember back at Professor Lofton's? I gave you a look. It was when Professor Lofton said the Orb was destined for you. I gave you that look because through the abilities gifted to me by my grandmother, I knew it to be true. So how could their deaths be your fault?"

I cried, "But I don't want this. Whether it's some big universal plan or not, they are all still dead."

Katch squeezed my hand and made sure to capture my eyes. "None of us have a choice in this. It's the whole, wide-open universe out there that has it all planned out. And you, and Frankie, and Beanie, and I, and really everyone else on this planet or any other, are only pawns on the big chessboard of life, being directed by whatever God-like hand is moving the pieces."

I nodded. Could she be right? Everyone stayed silent for a while, probably because we were all thinking about it. *How could such a thing be?* Is everything I'm doing destined because I am driven to it? It made me feel like I didn't have a choice in anything that happens to me.

I shook my head to lose those thoughts. I hated it when my mind went down this path. I needed to change the subject. "Well, I'm actually glad the debris is gone."

Frankie glanced over. "I'm glad you won't have a bunch of dangerous men after you anymore."

"I want to get back to normal again, at least for a little while," I told them. "It would feel good to actually not have the weight of the world on my shoulders for once."

"Well, at least until you find out what's in the safety deposit box," Katch pointed out.

"You know that destiny thing?" Beanie said. "Maybe it was time to lose the debris, because it happened right after you were given the key. Like the game Clue. You just turned over the next card and found the candlestick; one step closer to solving the mystery."

Katch added to that. "Yeah, I've been thinking about it. Why did you put the key in your pocket instead of in the bag? It seems pretty normal to slip it back into that nice little crushed velvet bag of your dad's, and drop it into your book bag. Why put it in your pocket?"

"I don't know. I didn't really even think about it. I just did it."

Frankie finished Katch's thought, "If you *had* put it in your book bag, the key would be gone, along with the book bag and the debris. Maybe everything *is* set out on a path."

"Yeah, that's what I said. The candlestick," Beanie added.

I shivered at the thought, wondering what might be on that path forward.

"What I find interesting," Katch said, "is how according to Professor Lofton, all of these discoveries made by your father with the Orb at those sites, are now yours to finish."

"All those points of energy," Beanie added. "I wonder what they mean. Or maybe I should say, what they do."

I didn't want to think about this anymore. My mind was scrambled enough. "Look, you guys, it will be a long time before I can do anything. Remember my dad's letter. He said I would need to be much older and wiser before I could continue his quest."

"All the same," Beanie tossed in, "do you think the safety deposit box could hold the Orb?"

"I don't know. I have no idea what could be in there," I said.

"Do you remember your father ever having a safety deposit box?" Frankie asked.

"No, I don't think so. Not that I remember, anyway."

"Another mystery to solve, I guess," Katch said.

"Yeah, the next card in the game of Clue to turn over," Beanie added.

"Right now," I cut in, "we have a more pending issue we need to talk about, like how to deal with a bunch of pissed-off parents when we get home. I for one, need to apologize to Emilee. I overreacted. It wasn't fair to her. I know she must be worried to death."

Beanie moaned from the back. "Why did you have to bring that up? I don't even want to think about what my mom is going to do. If you never see me again, find some sticks and start poking the ground for loose soil behind my house, because I'm pretty sure I'll be in a shallow grave back there somewhere."

"I just hope Frankie doesn't lose his car." I looked over to him. "I would feel so bad if you did."

"Mel, I told you that wasn't a big deal when you called me from Seattle and asked for my help. It was worth it. The car means nothing compared to you being safe."

I leaned over and kissed him on the cheek. "Thank you."

Beanie said, "How about you Katch? What do you think your parents will do, ground you for life?"

Katch looked at him and laughed. "Nothing. I told my mom what I was doing. She trusts me. The Hopi handle things a little differently than white people. In our culture we are set on our own paths at this age. How else do you learn and mature? She supported my going."

I looked back at Beanie and then to Frankie. We all had the same look on our faces, that we wished our families followed Hopi tradition.

Beanie said, "I think this country would have been a whole lot better off if it's original inhabitants still ran it."

The Locket

I heard a knock on my door. Emilee called through it. "Melanie, can I come in?"

"Sure."

I'm in my PJs and putting my hair up, about ready to go to bed. I still couldn't cut through the fog in my head to remember anything that happened after I pulled the switch on Major Burnham.

I had already apologized earlier to Emilee for running away. I didn't tell her everything, well, of what I knew anyway. But I didn't need to. The main thing was to let her know I acted badly.

She came in wearing her night clothes and a Terry bathrobe. She sat on the edge of my bed, patting the spot next to her. I went over and sat down.

Emilee took my hand and held it in hers. "I know you apologized, but this is not your fault. You had a right to be miffed. I shouldn't have thrown our whole family history at you the way I did."

I leaned my head on her shoulder. "Emilee, I scared you when I took off. You had no idea where I was. It wasn't fair."

She turned to me so she could look into my eyes. "Melanie, I lost your mum because of what I told her. I couldn't bear losing you as well." She paused. "I do want you to know, I did try to find her. But how do you locate a seventeen-year-old girl in a country as big as the United States when she doesn't want to be found. I even hired a private investigator to look into it. I had hopes. But time eventually dashed them. I never did find her."

"I'm glad you told me. It's important to know you looked for her."

"Melanie, things are a bit muddled right now. I understand that. So, I want you to think about what I say next. No need to answer right away."

I could see a touch of doubt turn to resolve as she pushed forward. "I would like you to consider going to England with me. There is still enough time before your education starts up again for us to make the trip."

I jumped in. "England? But I thought we were staying here."

"Just to visit. I want you to see what life is like over there, and see our family home—which will be yours one day." She patted my hand. "And, I think things might become clearer if you did."

What could she mean by that? I studied her, and something in how she looked told me she was right.

She patted my hand. "I found a passport of yours, so there would be no issue there."

"Yeah. A few years ago, Dad took us on a trip. He was visiting an archeology site, so decided to make it a family vacation as well. But if you are trying to get me to think about moving to England, I won't. I don't want to lose my friends."

She smiled. "I understand. Let's just take little steps for now. What about if you bring your chums with you on the trip? I'll cover their expenses. Will that suffice?"

I brightened. "Really? You'd do that?"

"Certainly."

I thought for a moment. Even if I liked England I still wouldn't want to live there, so what was the sense of going. "Emilee, that's really nice of you to offer. But I don't want to go. There really isn't a reason to. I hope that's okay with you?"

She gave me a hug. "All I ask is for you to think about it. Will you?"

I hugged her back. "Sure."

Emilee sat back and stroked my arm. "Good. Now, I have something for you."

"For me?"

"Yes. I found it when going through Gloria's things while you were gone." She took something from her pocket and set it in my hand, holding hers over it. Whatever it was, felt heavy.

She looked at me. "I know your mum would want you to have it." She gave me a kiss on the cheek and left the room, closing the door behind her.

I looked down to see a silver locket on a chain in my hand. I took the chain and raised the locket so it dangled in front of my eyes. It felt kind of heavy; more than I would imagine lockets to weigh. And it seemed bigger than the few lockets I'd seen. My eyes went wide when I noticed the shape. Most lockets are round. This one was oval, but tapered at the bottom, just like the shape of the Orb.

The locket slowly spun on the chain to reveal both sides. It looked like one side had some sort of space scene on it, little stars all over, with three bigger stars angled in a diagonal line across that side.

The other side had what looked like tall stones lined up in rows. I jumped up from the bed in shock. These were the stones of Carnac! They had to be. They looked like the ones in the film we saw at Professor Lofton's.

I took the locket to my desk and turned on a small lamp so I could study it better. I looked at the side with the stars again. The three stars looked familiar. I tried to remember from where, and suddenly my body radiated with excitement. They had been pointed out in the night sky to me by Katch's grandmother outside their home earlier this summer. They were the three stars making the belt in the constellation Orion. The stars she pointed out while telling me they were *my* sky people.

I turned the locket over again, to the stones. They were definitely the stones of Carnac. Had I not seen the film of my dad, I never would have known what these stones were. It really did seem a path had been laid out for me and I was on it, even right now, sitting here. Destiny. Dharma.

I studied the rest of the locket and found a small latch pin on the side. It took a moment to figure out how to open it, but I finally did. I cried at what it revealed—a picture of my mother on one side, and my father on the other. The pictures were of them when they were younger, not much older than me—probably before I was even born; maybe just after getting married.

I took a handkerchief out of my drawer and wiped at the tears on my cheeks, and then had to hold it against my eyes for a while to capture the free-flowing tears until I could pull myself together. I didn't hurry, though. The crying was a release I really needed.

I finally settled myself enough to continue. I looked over at a music box on my dresser. I got it and sat in the chair again, placing it on my desk.

I remembered the day my dad gave it to me. It was my fifth birthday. He got down on his knees, his eyes bright with excitement as he put it in my tiny hand and said, "You will always be my Mel Belle. My little ballerina." He told me he gave me that nickname because it came from the French fairy tale, *La Belle et la Bête.* Beauty and the Beast.

He nodded to the lid and said, "Open it." I did. A little ballerina jumped up and danced a beautiful dance of pirouettes. *Swan Lake* played across the room. "Now look at this," he told me, reaching into the small compartment in the music box and pressing a tiny latch along the side wall. A hidden drawer popped out of the back. I remembered my eyes going wide with surprise. I looked up at my dad. He told me, "This is where I will always keep my love for you. A secret place no one can find, so no one can ever take it." He made the motion of kissing the air, grabbing it and placing it in the drawer before closing it. "Love for my Mel Belle, anytime you need it. Our little secret forever."

Hidden Truths

I opened the music box to watch the ballerina dance to Swan Lake. I had done this so many times since Dad died, I was surprised it hadn't broken from wear and tear. I watched and listened until it wound down, the song finally clicking its last notes and ending. The little ballerina stopped mid-pirouette, which seemed very sad to me every time it happened.

I reached into the box and clicked the little latch. The hidden compartment popped out and I took something out of it. I balled it up in my fist and then dropped it on the desk. The piece of memory metal remained crumpled up for a moment before flowing back into its original, seamless shape. I smiled. Not all of the evidence from the Roswell crash had been lost.

I decided to put it in the locket. I planned to wear that locket every day for the rest of my life and wanted to keep the metal with it, with my dad. I took a nail file from my dresser and studied the picture of my father in the locket. It was held in place by little stays in four corners. I slipped the tip behind one edge of the picture and popped it out. The memory metal was thinner than the foil from a cigarette pack, so it easily folded small enough to fit in the space. I took my dad's picture and fitted it back into the locket to cover the foil.

I looked at the picture of my mother, then picked up a small hand mirror and studied myself. It was amazing how much we looked alike. I touched the picture, just to feel close to her again, running my finger across it. But I accidentally knocked it out while doing so. It fluttered to the floor. I picked it up to replace it, when I noticed something behind the picture.

It looked like an odd shaped coin or token of some sort. I took the nail file and popped it out of the locket to fall on the desk. I picked it up. It was about the size and thickness of a quarter, but only half of one, looking like it was missing the other half. The edge where it would connect was jagged, like a piece of a jigsaw puzzle, where only its counterpart could fit. I turned around it in the lamplight for a better look. It was made of shimmering silverish metal, brighter than even platinum. The metal was very smooth, as if there were a film of some sort covering the surface, giving it a slick feel. I had never seen anything like it before.

I studied the first side; a pattern of circles and lines. I ran my finger across it and could feel they stood out in relief. The circles were of various sizes. The lines ran between them, connecting some of the bigger circles with thicker lines. Other lines, smaller, ran to smaller dots. Many of them ran off the edge of the token to where the connecting piece would fit.

I rolled the token over in my hand to see the other side. It was also in relief. It had what looked like a pyramid on it—a stepped pyramid, very much like the one we saw on the film. I sat back in my chair. Could it be the same pyramid? What did the professor call it? Oh, yeah. The Temple of Inscriptions. I studied the token again. It had the same stairs going up the front to a small temple on top, only on the coin this was all cut in half. I could see tropical trees around it, like in the film. But I suddenly stopped because I saw something that wasn't in the film. An oval shape next to the top of the pyramid, floating in the sky. That's funny, it sure looks a lot like a UFO. A chill hit me. It was a UFO!

I turned the coin back over to look at the other side again. Those lines and circles—something about them felt familiar.

But from where? I thought for a moment. And then I knew. I jumped up from my chair and ran to my closet to where I kept some books. I took one down and went back to my desk. It was *The Interrupted Journey*, about Betty and Barney Hill's abduction. I turned to the page of the map Betty Hill drew. I compared it to the circles and lines on the token. They matched! The circles were the planets on Betty's map, and the lines were the travel routes.

I was stunned. How could this be? What could it all mean? I had to think. How did my mother get it? Maybe of more importance was, *who* made it and why? I only now began to absorb the significance of what it meant. What did Beanie say? "The Candlestick." I knew I had just turned over another card. And if this were a tarot card, Mrs. Crowley would definitely call it a Major Arcana card. Especially after returning from Professor Lofton's and what he shared with us. Somehow all of this fit together. Spooky.

But then I thought of the most important question of all; where was the other half of the token *and who has it?*

A thought hit me. I went to my closet again, got on my knees, and dug through all the school stuff I had dumped out of my book bag in my haste to run away. I found a thick geography book and carried it to the desk.

I flipped through it until I found the map I was looking for; a map of Europe. The professor said the Carnac stones were in Brittany, France. It took me a moment to locate the area, and even longer to find the town of Carnac. But there it was. I looked at the spot on the map as if I were standing right there in the middle of the stones. I drew a line from there to the Isle of Wight, just across the channel from France. Not close, but not that far, either.

I thought for a moment, looking at the small amount of water separating England from France. I tried to remember; it was only about twenty miles across at one point in the channel. And here I was in Lake Oswego, Oregon, more like 5,000 miles away, with a great big ocean in-between. It may as well have been on the other side the world.

I closed the book and walked out to the living room. Emilee sat comfortably propped in a chair, reading a book. She glanced up when she heard me coming. I stood there for a moment.

She sat up and closed her book. "Melanie, what is it?" I must have had some sort of look on my face.

"I want to go to England."

Look for the other
Melanie Simpson Mystery Series books
The prequel,

The Roswell Quest

and Book One in the series,

The Tale of the Tarot

Find them at
your favorite online publisher.
Or ask for them at your local
independent bookstore and library.

Shoot me an email at **DJSchneider1947@gmail.com**
and I will send you release notifications on future
Melanie Simpson novels, special content and articles,
updates, signing events, and presentations. I will also
send you a bonus short story not available anywhere
else.

Acknowledgements

First, I want to thank my sons for their inspiration, both talented in their own right: Nathan as a scriptwriter, producer and director (you will know his name one day dancing across in the subtitles of a film, or perhaps at the Independent Spirit Awards, or even the Oscars). And Tyler, who I know in my heart will someday design the most popular 3-D immersive gaming platform in the videogaming world. There are so many others throughout my life I would like to thank for nurturing my writing career—from my Lake Oswego High School English teacher, Mrs. Lee, who prodded me on, to the Magnificent Seven at The Cabin in Boise, Idaho where I spent many very precious years with those talented writers. For *The Tale of the Tarot*, I wish to thank the Gresham Writer's Group: Tiffany Martin, Nannette Taylor, Dave Baker, Doug Hartley, Jennifer Helgerson, and Marshall Welch for their many hours spent editing this work, chapter by chapter. I need to extend a special thanks to Suzi Wiser, who through her natural talents has become my editor. Thank you, Suzi, for the relentless time you have spent making this novel so much better than it would have been without you. Also, a shout-out to the SCBWI and ALLi for their endless resources on writing, marketing, and publishing. And my new friends at NIWA.

I also, and always, am indebted to the pioneer investigators who uncovered the greatest government cover-up in UFO history in the crash outside Roswell, New Mexico (Yes, I know, Corona, Mr. Friedman). Without their work, we may have never known what happened. They are: Stanton T. Friedman,

Kevin Randle, Donald Schmitt, Charles Berlitz, William Moore, and Col. Philip J. Corso (Ret.). Without their great investigative work and dedication, I wouldn't have known about Roswell, and the seed for this novel series would never have been planted, sprouted, and grown into the wonderful tree it is, branches stretching toward the universe.

About the Author

DJ developed his creative writing skills at the San Francisco Art Institute, and then at the Log Cabin Literary Center in Boise, Idaho with a writing group called the Magnificent Seven. DJ also spent many years in the advertising and marketing fields writing and producing creative content for radio, print, and television. When DJ isn't out traveling the stars following Melanie Simpson around and documenting her great adventures, he is buried deep in an Oregon burrow he calls The Writing Cave, honing his craft and building his novels. It is there under the light of a gooseneck lamp he can be found diligently working on Melanie's next story, and on an upmarket novel titled *River of Dreams.*

Call to Action!

Post a review and get an exclusive, unpublished short story!

If you really enjoyed *The Tale of the Tarot*, please go back to the site where you purchased the novel and write a review. You can also post a review at Goodreads.com by searching for the book's title. Then email me at **DjSchneider1947@gmail.com** to let me know where your review is posted and **I will send you an exclusive, unpublished short story related to The Tale of the Tarot.** Whether you do a review or not, send me an email and I will keep you up to date on when the next book is due out, along with early release information and sample chapters for you to read. Please help me get the word out about the Melanie Simpson Series!

Lightning Source UK Ltd.
Milton Keynes UK
UKHW012133111022
410331UK00002B/26